Negative Images

Rebecca Schier-Akamelu

This book is a work of fiction. Any references to historical events, real people, or real places are used fictitiously. Other names, characters, places, and events are products of the author's imagination, and any resemblance to actual events, places, names, or persons, is entirely coincidental.

Text copyright © 2025 by Rebecca Schier-Akamelu

All rights reserved. For information regarding reproduction in total or in part, contact Rising Action Publishing Co. at http://www.risingactionpublishingco.com

Cover Illustration © Nat Mack
Distributed by Simon & Schuster

ISBN: 978-1-998076-21-5
Ebook: 978-1-998076-56-7

FIC015000 – Horror
FIC012000 – Ghost
FIC031070 - Thrillers/Supernatural

#NegativeImages

Follow Rising Action on our socials!
Twitter: @RAPubCollective
Instagram: @risingactionpublishingco
Tiktok: @risingactionpublishingco

For my parents, Jim and Nancy

Negative Images

CHAPTER ONE

My phone pinged. Monica.

How's the event going???

I shoved my phone in my pocket. This event—a charity auction to raise money for St. Anthony's High School—was one of our biggest yet. Not only in scale but also in terms of potential repeat business. The woman in charge, Carrie, was well-connected and served on several boards throughout Omaha, all of which hosted fundraisers. We needed this.

The thought of how much this night meant made my hands sweat and stomach clench. And the little "check-in" text from Monica wasn't helping.

She had her own event to handle tonight, or I was sure she would've been here. Thankfully, I had help.

"Where do you want the last auction item?" my husband, Dan, asked.

He and Tricia, our assistant, each held the edge of a large painting.

"In the middle."

Tricia stumbled, and it took all my self-control not to yell out to be careful.

Once placed, everything looked perfect. Nearly.

Dan came up to me and rubbed the back of my neck. "Try to relax, Anita. Take a deep breath and enjoy what you've created."

"Oh! I almost forgot. Tricia? Can you please take some photos of the space before people arrive? Monica will want them for Instagram."

"Sure thing." Tricia gave a small smile as she started photographing the centerpieces.

Dan rubbed my neck and shoulders, but I shrugged him off. "That's making me more nervous."

He gave a throaty chuckle. "Hey, I almost forgot ... how are you paying me this evening? What currency?" His brown eyes glinted with mischief.

"Maybe pizza? Plus, something extra."

"How about Chinese with extra fortune cookies?" He raised his eyebrows suggestively.

"Sure." I couldn't help but laugh as he walked away.

I slipped my phone out of my pocket and took a picture that captured the whole room. Then I sent it to Monica.

Don't worry. It's fabulous.

I added a sparkle emoji for emphasis.

Now, I just had to hope that it really was.

As I rejoined Tricia and Dan up front, I wasn't so sure.

"I can't bid on anything without the app?" an older woman asked.

"Yes, everyone who wants to bid has to use the app," Tricia explained. I could tell from her tone of voice that she'd already gone through this at least once.

"I have too many apps on my phone. There must be another way."

I flinched.

"Anita can probably explain it better than I can." Tricia clearly wanted to pass off this problem to a more authoritative person. In this case, me. Now I *was* wishing Monica was here.

I plastered a smile on my face and stepped forward. "It's actually quite easy to use," I started, but then I felt Dan's hand on the small of my back.

"If I may, I'd be happy to help you download it and delete it once the auction is over."

The woman smiled, and a dimple that had previously been hidden under her wrinkles appeared.

"Would you, really? Thank you."

I mouthed a quick thanks to Dan as he stepped aside with the woman.

Other guests entered, and my nerves finally calmed as I got into a rhythm of answering questions and helping guests find their tables. As the room began to fill, Carrie practically glided to the microphone up front and welcomed the guests to the auction. She looked impeccable in a long black gown and diamond necklace. She was so poised, so elegant. I wished I could speak as easily.

The dinner and auction went by swiftly. Soon, the noise of talking and dining faded into a soft, unobtrusive music that filled the room. As the evening began to wind down, someone tapped my shoulder, and I turned to see Carrie.

"Anita, I just wanted to thank you for a perfect evening."

"I'm so glad you're happy with how it went."

"You did a spectacular job. I'd like to come by tomorrow and discuss a benefit I'm in charge of this spring."

I had to hold my muscles still; my legs wanted to jump like a kid who'd just been surprised by a long-wanted puppy.

"That sounds wonderful; I'd love to hear more about it. My morning is fairly open."

"Perfect. I'll have one of my assistants call and set something up."

As Carrie went back to say goodbye to her guests, Dan came over and gave my hand a squeeze.

"Best event yet, babe," Dan whispered as we gathered our things.

"It was!" I squealed as Dan opened the door to the parking garage stairwell.

He popped the trunk, and I maneuvered one of my large, plastic emergency bins, filled with worst-case-scenario event supplies, inside. Dan slid his things in next to mine when an abrupt whining made me freeze. Dan craned his neck to look around the garage, then gave me a shrug.

At first, I thought one of the bins had scraped the car, but then the whining went up in pitch. A staticky sound mixed with it, like someone was trying to find a radio station. I clapped my hands over my ears and was about to close the trunk when I saw a hint of sparkle to my right, something out of place in a parking garage.

I paused and took a step towards it. Despite the incessant feedback that overwhelmed the space, I could just make out the sound of crying. I took a few more steps, going past two other cars, then I saw a woman.

She was crouched on the ground with her back against a driver's side door, her purple dress and sparkling heels on the oil-stained concrete. Mascara ran down her face and she had her hands clasped over her ears. She didn't notice me—she had drawn her knees up to her chest and rested her forehead there.

Someone else stood on the passenger side of the car, looking over the top of it and shouting at her. At least, that's what it looked like, but I couldn't hear a word he said. He was definitely harassing her. He stood eerily still, and when his mouth moved, it seemed fast or somehow disjointed, like a bad dubbing on mute.

"Dan!" I turned around to get his attention. "This lady needs help, Dan, come on!"

At that, Dan jumped into action, racing to my side and then getting ahead of me as we walked between the cars and approached the woman. He walked past her, so she was just between us.

"What's wrong?" I asked as I knelt and placed a hand on her arm. I wished I had a tissue to offer her.

When she looked at me, it was like she'd never seen a person before. Her wide eyes kept scanning my face, and her jaw was slack. It took her several minutes to come back to herself. She gulped, her throat bobbing up and down.

"Ma'am? Where did he go? The man who was yelling at you?"

She didn't answer right away. I felt Dan's eyes boring into me, and when I looked up, he motioned for me to stand. He led me to the rear of the car and whispered, "There's no one else here. Seriously. I don't see a soul."

"What?" I turned in a circle, hoping to catch a glimpse of movement.

Dan shrugged and took a few steps down the line, looking between the cars or under them as he went.

"You saw him too?" the woman asked from the ground.

I turned back to face her. "Well, yes, of course. He was just on the other side of the car, and it looked like he was yelling at you, but I couldn't hear anything over that noise."

"Noise?" Her voice squeaked a little, and her eyebrows rose.

"Yeah, that shrieking, staticky sound." Could she have been so upset that she'd managed to tune it out?

"The person you saw," she whispered. "What did he look like?"

It seemed like such an odd question, so I froze for a moment. "Well, he had on a dark shirt. He was Black, maybe a little taller than my husband, but he had grey hair."

The woman's mouth went slack, and she stumbled against the car as she tried to stand up.

"No," she said, little more than a breath. "No."

"Ma'am?"

With some effort, she straightened herself up. Her purple dress was dark where she'd sat on the ground.

Her eyes darted to the passenger side, then to me, the exit, then the car.

"I have to go."

She opened the door and slid inside. Her dress caught in the door, and her hands shook as she took the wheel.

"Wait, are you okay? Is there someone I can call for you?"

She didn't respond except for a slight raise of her hand after she'd backed out of the spot. I watched her drive away, grateful to see her make it to the exit in a straight line. From the way she was dressed, I thought she must have been one of the guests from the auction, although I couldn't place her.

"What was all that about?" Dan asked.

I looked back at him. He wasn't staring at the woman's car but at me.

"What do you mean?"

"Why did you call me over here like that? You said she needed help."

NEGATIVE IMAGES

"Well, she did." I peered around him as if the man I'd seen were just out of my view, still here and waiting to be found.

"I can see all the way to that door over there." Dan pointed to his left. "Now that the whine has stopped, it's quiet." He had a point—his voice echoed. "We've both got a clear line of sight to the exit. There's no one here."

He wasn't angry, but he seemed upset that I didn't agree with him.

I crossed my arms in front of my chest. "There was! Even the lady saw him. She wanted me to describe him."

Dan stared. "That's ... odd. Wouldn't she know who she was with if there was really someone here?"

"What do you mean 'really'?"

Dan let out a loud sigh. "I just mean ... I don't know, Anita. She could have been upset about anything. Then someone she doesn't know comes up and asks her about a man—wouldn't that be upsetting? No wonder she wanted him described. She didn't know he was there. I mean, he *wasn't* there."

"He was. I saw him."

"Look, Anita, I don't know. Let's just go home."

He walked back to the car and got in, leaving me fuming.

I hated being questioned like that. Didn't Dan trust me to know what I saw? Worse, it hurt to know that he didn't believe me. In my emergency bin I had Kleenex, and I thought I might need them.

I surprised myself by getting to work early the next morning. Usually, I was exhausted after such a big event and blocked off part of the morning so I could sleep in a little. But I hadn't slept well, and at 6:30, I forced myself out of bed.

When I got to work, Monica was practically giddy with excitement.

"I had Tricia call over this morning, and Carrie's coming at 10:00! Dan told me everything went absolutely perfectly."

"Wait, when did you talk to Dan?"

Monica rolled her eyes and tucked a strand of blonde hair behind her ear. "Well, you weren't responding, and I had to get the news somehow."

I laughed. "That's fair. But you know how I feel about using phones at an event. And, yes, it did. I literally could not have planned it better."

Tricia rapped on the door of Monica's office. "She's here," she whispered.

Carrie sat with her hands clasped loosely on the table in front of her and gave a wide smile as we walked in.

"It's good to see you this morning, Carrie," Monica said. "It sounds like—from what I heard—it was a successful event?" She said this last part as a question, with an eager smile on her face since she already knew the answer.

"We were thrilled!" Carrie's voice was loud and clear as if she was addressing the crowd from last night instead of just the two of us. "Honestly, it was one of our most successful auctions in years. And, as I mentioned to Anita yesterday, I have something coming up in the spring, and I'm hoping to work with you again."

I could barely keep my smile at an acceptable, professional level. We spent several minutes discussing Carrie's next event. We'd gotten as far as color schemes when the energy in the room shifted.

NEGATIVE IMAGES

I was taking notes, my head bowed, when a slight tingle went through the room as if it had just gotten a small shock of static electricity.

I was sure Carrie and Monica had felt it, too, because they stopped talking. When I looked up, an older woman stood just behind Carrie, her white hair pouring out from her head like a misshapen halo. She leaned over Carrie, most of her face obscured in shadow.

"Excuse me, ma'am? Can we help you?" I asked, not knowing what else to say. At this point, I was mulling over how she'd gotten in without anyone noticing and wondering why we hadn't heard her in the hallway.

The older woman opened her mouth, and noise filled the room. No words, even though it was clear she was talking. All I heard was a static, white noise—more dissonant than what you'd get from a sound machine. It wasn't quite the same as the noise from the parking garage, but looking at this woman sent me back there in my mind.

Monica and I exchanged a look. Carrie's eyes grew large.

"What ... what is that?" I asked no one in particular.

Carrie turned around and saw the woman for the first time.

She let out a shrill scream, and her face went pale white. Her head fell back, and she slumped against the chair.

"Shit, shit, shit!" I whisper-yelled.

"What do we do?" Monica grabbed my hand. The being bent over Carrie, its movements like flipbook-style animation. I pushed my chair back from the table and stumbled over it.

"Fuck this, let's go." I grabbed Monica's hand and hauled her out the door.

"What about—"

"It'll probably follow us."

But it didn't.

It—she?—crouched next to Carrie and reached for her face. Then she looked up at me. I'd avoided staring at her face before, or I'm sure I would have already noticed it.

Opaque black holes had replaced her eye sockets. It was impossible to tell if she had eyes at all. She smiled, showing crooked, yellow teeth.

"Holy crap." Dan handed me a drink. Not wine. After a scare like that, I needed something a little stronger. Whiskey and Coke suited nicely. "What happened afterward?"

I shuddered. "It vanished after staring me down. And then Monica and I went back in. Carrie had only fainted, thankfully. She wouldn't let us call an ambulance or even her husband to come help her. She just took off. Honestly, she looked like she'd seen a ghost."

I laughed and clapped a hand over my mouth, hearing what I was saying. Wasn't a ghost the most likely explanation?

"The way she reacted when she turned around and actually saw it, though …" I shuddered and took a long sip of my drink. "I just feel like maybe she knew this woman. But a ghost?"

"I'm sorry you went through all that. If you and Monica hadn't both experienced it, I'd say it was unbelievable."

I shot him a look, unsure what he was trying to imply about my credibility.

"I just wish that she hadn't rushed off." After a few hours, I'd sent her a text, just asking if she was okay, but she hadn't responded.

Dan grabbed the remote and plopped down on the couch.

"Come. Sit." He patted the spot next to him. "Let's just take a break from it for a little while."

He held his arm out to me, a warm smile on his face as though this was a minor problem with an obvious solution.

I grabbed a coaster and sat down next to him. I had no idea what I'd seen, but I could at least avoid a nasty white ring on our new coffee table.

Dan flipped through channels. My mind wandered, but it kept coming back to the last moment with the old lady—her flat, black eyes. And sometimes, the man in the parking garage popped into my head.

And, when those thoughts weren't occupying my brain, I was thinking about what this meant for our business. Carrie left before finalizing any plans with us—when would she be in a place where she might want to get back to that discussion?

Of course, I scolded myself right after that thought—she'd basically been horrifically haunted, and here I was, wondering when we'd get our next check. *Stupid.*

Then I thought of those eyes again.

The thoughts played in a loop in my head. I was barely aware of what was on the TV until Dan nudged me.

"Hey, this is like what happened to Carrie, right?"

Glancing up at Dan's face, the pallor of his already pale skin was enough to pull me out of my spiraling thoughts.

"On tonight's 'True or False,' a woman in Argentina claims her dead husband has been appearing to her. Elaborate hoax or something more concerning?" The anchor, Kim Brandt, gave a relaxed smile that showed she clearly didn't find the news alarming.

"What?" My voice came out as a whisper. My mind was already reeling and working overtime to piece everything together.

The show cut to footage of an older Latina woman speaking very fast. She waved an arm behind her wildly, and I thought I saw her fingers trembling. She couldn't focus on the man interviewing her; her eyes darted around every few seconds as though she were looking for someone else. The banner at the bottom of the screen identified her as Maria Vasquez.

"I don't know how it happened," a translator narrated over her rapid speech. The translator's voice was almost robotically calm as if nothing could rattle her perfectly enunciated English. "I was preparing food, and he just appeared to me. I thought, at first, he was an angel out of heaven. But when he opened his mouth—" Maria Vasquez stopped and gasped in pain. She put a shaking fist up to her mouth as if it would keep the words in. Tears streamed out of her eyes, and she shut them against the memory. "He does not speak like my husband. He knew. He knew terrible things about me. He asked me why I was bothering to cook such awful food for our grandchildren. He told me how disappointed he was, and he accused me of harming ..." She couldn't finish her thought and stopped, covering her face with her hands. The camera pulled back to include a younger man in the room, who put his hand on her shoulder. The man's brow was furrowed, though he wasn't as frazzled as she was.

The reporter conducting the interview came into view. "What do you think of this?" he asked the man. "Have you seen this apparition?"

Eduardo Vasquez, son of the victim, according to the footer, began to speak. He gave his mother's shoulder a reassuring squeeze as he did so. He was soft-spoken and articulate. "I've seen him, but I cannot accept that this vision is truly my father. My father always treated her with love and respect."

"Did your father speak to you?" the interviewer asked.

"No. He doesn't speak to anyone except my mother. I can hear him, but ..." Eduardo paused and looked to his mother for guidance. Finally, with a shrug, he said, "I can't understand him when he speaks. He makes noises, but it's unintelligible to me. Like a bad radio signal."

"Oh my God." I squeezed Dan's hand. Eduardo's description was close to what I would have said about the noises I heard, and for several seconds, I couldn't breathe.

"Whatever this thing is, it's not my father," Eduardo continued. "I beg whoever is responsible, please, stop and give my mother some peace."

I thought the woman would have been content to let her son conclude the interview. Her whole body shook, and when she took her hands away from her eyes, her face was wet with tears.

"It *is* my husband. I don't think anyone can make him stop."

The reporter and her son looked at her, both a little surprised.

"What makes you so sure?" the reporter pressed.

Maria Vasquez looked at him, her big eyes still wet but determined. I didn't understand what she said until I heard the translation, but she spoke with conviction. Her voice was steady and sure instead of frenzied like before. Her lips curled back in a snarl of anguish. "I know."

A shiver went up my back. At the same moment, Dan said, "What do you think it is?"

I shook my head and blinked several times to clear the tears that had welled up.

"As tempting as it may be to write this one off as a joke or a prank, there hasn't been a satisfactory explanation for these events," Kim Brandt said. She gave a wry smile and folded her hands on her desk. "It appears there may be more to this story than we originally thought, as we've just gotten word of a similar event in the United Kingdom, and we'll update you as more information becomes available. In the meantime, head to our Facebook page and vote: Is this True? Or False?"

Kim Brandt changed her focus to another camera in the studio, ready to move on to the next story of the day. But I couldn't put it behind me.

"Turn it off. Please, now."

Dan grabbed the remote too slowly, but finally, the TV was off, and the anchor's perky, incessant chatter was gone with it.

I felt like I'd been glued to the sofa.

"Anita? Babe?"

I held up a hand.

"That was it, wasn't it? That's what happened to Carrie today?"

I nodded, and Dan grabbed me, crushing me to his chest and forcing me to move.

It seemed real and unreal at the same time, and weirdly, all I wanted to tell myself was that I didn't need comfort because it wasn't happening to me. It was happening to Carrie.

CHAPTER TWO

Hi Carrie,

I hope you're doing okay. I was hoping to talk to you about the other day. I had no idea what was happening at the time, and that you were one of the first people in the world to have a Negative Image. I'm very sorry for the way I reacted.

Please let me know if there's anything I can do to help.

Best,

Anita

I called yesterday. Monica had, too. But Carrie hadn't responded at all.

What I really wanted to say, but hadn't, was that I was sorry I'd run out of the room and left her alone with it. I'd thought only of myself, and at night, I still saw Carrie slumped over in her conference room chair with that woman bending over her.

It wasn't the sort of thing to say in an email. *Sorry I left you for dead. When can we discuss your upcoming benefit?*

"I think it's good. Just hit send."

I'd been so lost in thought that I hadn't heard Monica come up behind me. She sounded resigned, and I couldn't blame her.

With a sigh, I hit send.

An automatic reply came back a moment later.

Thank you for your email. I'm taking some time off to handle a personal matter. I'll respond as soon as I can.

"Well." Monica sighed.

"Well," I answered.

I sat still, absorbing all the implications. We'd probably be low on her list of people to respond to. The likelihood of the repeat business we'd been hoping for was almost nonexistent.

Even our other clients seemed slower to respond than usual. Their upcoming work conferences, anniversary celebrations, and birthdays seemed less important now than before. It had been less than a week since coverage of Negative Images had begun, but the problem seemed to be cropping across most states. Omaha didn't have many people with an NI that I knew of, but people were still worried.

I started noticing small things, mostly suspicions. No one knew why some people had an NI and others didn't, and without knowing how they had come about, the chances of getting one were also unknown.

My phone chimed with a new text, and I pounced on it.

My go-to florist, Nicole, had been slow to respond lately, only reaching out via email and text. I was supposed to get a delivery from her today, but she hadn't confirmed the time.

"Oh no," I blurted out. "We've got a problem."

"What?"

"Nicole was supposed to drop off the floral arrangements. She always does. Now, all of a sudden, she can't."

"What? Why?"

"She didn't say." I stood up and started to pace the small room. "Just that something came up. But we can't have the shower without these flowers—it's unacceptable. So, either I'll have to go get them, or we have a crappy event."

"I can't believe this is coming from Nicole." Monica's eyebrows rose in confusion, and she looked around at the stacks of papers as though she would find a solution somewhere in the files. Nicole always had a plan B.

"She offered to let me use her van to transport the flowers."

Monica motioned for me to sit back down.

"I mean, that's weird, right?" I asked.

Monica nodded. "Even if she couldn't drop it off, she could ask someone else to do it."

We regarded each other for a minute. I couldn't be sure what Monica was thinking, but from her pursed lips, I thought it was the same thing I was.

"She probably has a Negative Image," I said after a few moments.

Monica nodded and massaged her temples. "Yeah. This could get tricky. She's scheduled to do a lot for us over the next three weeks."

"I guess we'll just have to ask her about it so that we can be better prepared next time." I stood up and checked the time. "I'll come with you to help."

"Do you think I should see if Dan could meet us there?"

Monica shrugged and put her coat on. "You'd know better than I would."

I could already imagine us stumbling and unable to see as we shuffled through the doorway with large arrangements. Flowers were so deceptive—all color and so small until they were grouped together in vases.

"I'll call him."

We were almost at the florist's—it was only a ten-minute drive from our office—when I heard sirens. We pulled over to the right to let a police car, fire engine, and ambulance pass.

Flashing lights met us at Nicole's shop. I couldn't see what had happened, but I knew in my gut that it concerned me.

Later, I would remember the cool plastic of the car door handle as I opened it, the quick shock of cold air that hit me in the face. At the time, all the noise seemed distant, and I scanned everyone, looking for Dan. His car was parked just a couple of spots down from Monica's.

He wasn't in it.

"Oh my God," I whispered. "Dan? Dan!" My voice grew louder, and my heart beat wildly. I rushed up to the nearest person I could find. "Please, I'm looking for my husband—"

"Ma'am, please step aside."

"What happened? I was supposed to meet him here. Please."

The paramedic put his hand up to brush me off again when I saw Dan in the back of another ambulance.

My vision was blurry with tears, but I ran forward anyway, reaching for him, only to be blocked again.

"Please, you have to let me through. He's my husband."

Even as I pleaded, the back doors shut, and the ambulance pulled away.

I think I screamed, but I'm not sure. Monica came up beside me and put her arms around me. She managed to find out where they were taking him, and before I knew it, we were back in her car, speeding to the hospital.

We lost the ambulance as it zigzagged through traffic. When we arrived at the hospital, Dan was being prepped for surgery, and I couldn't see him. At the front desk, I was an incoherent, blubbering mess. So much so that Monica had to repeat everything for me. I still didn't have a grasp on what was happening.

Eventually, a nurse shunted us off to a waiting room with a promise that a doctor would come out to see me soon. Blue and white tiles patterned the floor, with chairs arranged along the room's perimeter. A man leaned against a vending machine in the corner, sipping coffee and staring at his phone. Across from him, a middle-aged woman flipped through a magazine with dozens more spread out on the table in front of her.

It felt like a small room to wait in without knowing what was going on. I didn't quite know where to sit, but I ended up in a chair two seats from Magazine Lady.

"Anita, I'll be right back. Just have to make a few phone calls."

I nodded but couldn't meet Monica's gaze.

"Hey." Monica rubbed my shoulders. "Hang in there, okay?" When I looked at her, it was impossible not to tear up again. She gave me a small smile before quickly walking out of the room.

I remembered the bridal shower we had booked and looked at my phone. 1:25 p.m. It was supposed to start at 1:00. No doubt Monica was calling the client. Would she make up an excuse or go into grisly details about the truth?

I closed my eyes and leaned my head back against the wall. I was starting to feel a little nauseous. What *were* the grisly details?

Instead of letting my mind get the best of me by concocting its own story about what happened, I thought about the bride. Someone else's tragedy was going to impact what should have been a perfectly planned moment to celebrate her upcoming nuptials.

My own bridal shower had been a little extravagant—I remembered how Dan had hinted at the details. Monica had planned it, and I'd done my best not to overhear anything—putting on music, going for lots of coffees, and covering my ears whenever they spoke of it.

Dan had told me to expect lots of Kelly green and carnations. The thought made me smile just a little. He'd done his best to keep a straight face, but we'd both burst into fits of giggles, knowing that it wasn't true because Monica knew those were some of my least favorite things.

Dan had always helped us with the business on top of his regular job. He was a saint. We'd relied on him so much—too much.

Why couldn't I have planned better today? We should have hired a second assistant. I shouldn't have let Tricia have today off. Everything would've been fine if I'd just planned better.

"Who are you waiting for?" I opened my eyes and sat up a little straighter. Magazine Lady was staring at me.

"You look very tired," she continued.

"My husband." I wanted that to be the end of the conversation, but I also couldn't stand to be rude. "What about you?"

NEGATIVE IMAGES

"My sister." She grimaced. "She's having some complications after her knee surgery. I told her to come in yesterday—I hope she didn't wait too long."

She looked at me like she expected sympathy or at least some sort of agreement, but my heart felt like wood. I swallowed and dropped my eyes to the table.

I couldn't bear to ask her for more details or to share anything about Dan. I hoped she'd go back to her magazine.

What I needed was something warm. Vending Machine Guy wasn't just blocking the vending machine, though—he was also in the way of the Keurig. If I wanted tea, I'd have to ask him to move.

Not willing to have that interaction, I picked up an issue of *HGTV Magazine* and started flipping through it, but I was drawn to the sound of the videos that Vending Machine Guy was watching. He hadn't even bothered to put on headphones.

A man's voice with a British accent came through the phone. "At first, when Sarah said she'd seen Chad, I thought she was a bit ... that she was just really grieving, you know? Then she called me one day and asked me to stop by. She said Chad was saying terrible things to her. I was quite shocked. I thought she must be really daft. But the whole thing was starting to feel off because my brother was always the peacemaker type. He hardly spoke a bad word of anyone in his life. So, I went over. I was really concerned for Sarah. She sounded like she was in pain, you know? When I got there, she was in a right state, just sobbing, and she said she had something to show me. So, I walk in, and right by the staircase is Chad. And I about lost my mind. Only it wasn't quite Chad. His eyes were just completely black. It was some creepy"—*bleep*—"and I said to him, 'Chad? How are you here?' He just really gave me the creeps, you know? And he didn't answer me. He cocked his head, gave me a smile that turned me cold all over and pointed at Sarah.

"And Sarah just sobbed harder. She was completely distraught. And she said, 'Ethan, I can't make him leave!'"

Vending Machine Guy shook his head and let out a groan. Magazine Lady and I looked up at him.

He seemed surprised to see us, and I wondered if he somehow hadn't realized we were there. "I'm just sick of hearing about all that." He shrugged and let out a humorless laugh.

I stretched and dropped the magazine back on the table. "You know, the nice thing about having a phone is getting to choose what you watch."

My cattiness surprised even me, and he let out an awkward laugh.

"Yeah, I know. I can't help it. I just really want to know what these things are. This guy—Greg Patisis—has been uploading all these announcements and footage whenever he hears about someone new with a Negative Image. I clicked on one, and now they're all over my feed. I can't get rid of them, you know?"

I nodded. Maria Vasquez's story had gotten the most coverage at first, but Carrie had been in the news yesterday. Someone had caught her walking into a medical center with her husband, who'd decided to confront the rumors head-on by making a statement. With so many NIs cropping up, it was almost impossible to avoid hearing about them.

"I just turn it off whenever I can," I said.

Again, I saw a flash of Carrie slumped at the conference table, the menacing woman curving over her as if she were laying claim to something. I shivered.

"Don't you want to know what's happening, though? Just to understand why this is going on?" Vending Machine Guy asked, his brow furrowed.

Magazine Lady tossed the copy of *Star* she'd been browsing onto the table with a thunk. "I think it might be beyond explanation. No one's come up with any reasonable theories yet."

"Everything has an explanation." Vending Machine Guy crossed his arms in front of his chest.

"Even if it does, I don't think it's one we're capable of understanding." Magazine Lady raised an eyebrow as if she were challenging him.

"You know, I don't really care *why* they're here. I think we all just want to figure out how to get rid of them." He dragged a hand across his face. He looked like he needed several more cups of coffee.

Magazine Lady shook her head slowly. "I think everyone feels that way, but I don't think we'll be rid of them until we understand what they want. I suppose what I mean is that I don't think we'll understand what they *are* or what caused them to start appearing," she explained thoughtfully. "But they must have their reasons for being here. I mean, they must want something, right? It's not as though everyone who dies comes back as one of these ... what do they call them? Negative Images? Only some."

"That's what scares me." I crossed my legs.

"I'm not convinced that these things appear all by themselves. I think there's something messed up with the people who have them," Vending Machine Guy said with a tone of finality.

"I don't think anyone would want this," I challenged.

"Maybe some small part of them *does*. Maybe they all have some mental issues or something." I glanced at Magazine Lady to see if she was going to debate Vending Machine Guy. Magazine Lady picked her magazine up and shot me a look that said she wasn't going to argue anymore, but then she paused with the magazine open in her hands. "There could be something wrong with the people who have them. Sure. But there could also be something off about the people who died. Maybe it's a mixture of both. After all, we all have our messy histories and secrets. No one's perfect."

I covered my mouth with my hand to keep from laughing. She was reading a tabloid—of course, she thought everyone had a hidden scandal.

The three of us lapsed into an awkward silence, Magazine Lady essentially shutting down the conversation as she refocused on the celebrity gossip du jour.

"Who are you waiting for?" I asked the man. His videos had been annoying, but the silence was worse.

"My fiancé." He didn't look at me. "Car accident." His fingers danced over the vending machine buttons. After a moment, he continued. "They're not sure how severe her injuries are."

His eyes dropped to the floor.

"These people, though," he said to neither of us in particular. "There's just gotta be something wrong with their heads, right?"

Footsteps squeaked down the hallway, coming toward the waiting room. It sounded like a nurse's shoes with non-slip soles. The three of us looked up as the nurse approached, wondering who she'd summon.

"Mrs. Matthews?"

I startled a little. It felt like I'd been waiting forever and also like I'd just arrived—and where was Monica?

"I wanted to give you an update on your husband. He's still in surgery."

I nodded. "Please. What for? I haven't been able to find out from anyone."

The nurse led me to a corner. "I'm so sorry. Well ... your husband was shot in the upper abdomen. He'll probably be in surgery for a while—he had some internal bleeding. We'll update you more as soon as we can."

I nodded and blinked away the tears in my eyes. "Thank you."

The nurse went back down the hall, shoe squeaks getting softer.

For a few minutes, I sat with the words *shot* and *internal bleeding* in my head. Monica came back in. She stared at the chair where I'd been sitting with a frown on her face until she did a quick scan and realized I had moved.

"How are you doing, Anita? Any updates?" She took the seat next to me.

He's still in surgery." I left *shot* and *internal bleeding* out of it for now. It was too unreal.

Monica nodded, lips drawn into a thin line and her brows drawn together. "I had to call that bride. And Tricia. Between the two of us, we should have tomorrow covered."

"Oh, wow." I let out a sigh—tomorrow had completely gone out of my mind. "Thank you."

"Of course." Monica snuck a look at the clock on the wall, then looked back at me like she didn't know whether she should stay or go.

"You can head out if you want," I said after a moment.

"Are you sure?" It was a question, but she'd already stood up.

"Yeah, I'll be okay."

"Call me if you need anything, okay? I'm here for you."

I nodded and watched Monica as she walked away. She seemed to relax as she left, her shoulders falling back down from where they hunched.

Time lost meaning.

Squeaky Shoes came down the hall to collect Magazine Lady. A while later, someone else with shoes that didn't squeak came for Vending Machine Guy, who'd been standing the whole time and drumming his fingers on the table by the Keurig. I hoped his fiancée was okay.

Finally, a nurse came for me.

"He's in recovery, but he'll be in the ICU for a few days."

"He's going to be okay, though, right?"

"Unfortunately, I can't make any promises. He'll have a long recovery."

I nodded even though I still wasn't sure what that meant.

In the ICU, Dan lay in bed, asleep, with an oxygen tube in his nose. Various machines were hooked up to him, cords and wires snaking down off the bed.

"You can sit near him if you want. He should wake up soon. He was stirring earlier, and it sounded like he was calling for you."

I took a seat next to Dan and threaded my fingers through his. Seeing him like this was so weird, so wrong. I didn't even try to stop the tears from coming. I just sat with him, listening to the rhythmic beep of his heart monitor.

As doctors and nurses stopped by to check on him, they reminded me that there was a bed I could use. But I just wanted him to know I was there.

At some point, the heart monitor lulled me to sleep. A persistent *beeeeeep* woke me. My back was stiff, and pins and needles shot down my right arm. My fingers were still interlocked with Dan's.

NEGATIVE IMAGES

At first, I couldn't remember why I was in this room and what the noise was. Then I placed the sound, one I knew from so many movies and TV shows.

I looked at Dan's face.

It had changed.

It was still his face, but it also wasn't. I could tell, somehow, that he wasn't in his body anymore. I froze—part of me knew what this meant, but I couldn't accept what was happening.

"Dan?" My voice came out hoarse and small.

Then, nurses and doctors flooded the room, shuffling me aside. They started moving him down the hall, back to the operating room. I stood there, not knowing what to do.

CHAPTER THREE

M any people want to avoid Calla Lillies at their events because they're synonymous with death. They bring to mind coffins and cold churches where you shiver in a black cardigan as you say goodbye to loved ones.

They weren't something I recommended. Ever. But here I was, sitting next to an arrangement of them in the lobby of Watts Funeral Home.

I stared at them, thinking they must be fake.

"Calla Lillies are a beautiful flower, aren't they?"

I started and looked up to see a bald man with glasses standing in front of me. He looked older than 60, and I wondered how he felt about getting older when he knew all too well what was waiting for him. Had he planned his own funeral in advance? What about his retirement?

"You must be Anita. I'm Leon Watts."

I rose and shook his hand. He led me back to his office, our footfalls silent on the thick, seafoam-green carpet. We passed empty sitting rooms filled with muted shades of mauve and gray, the colors blending into a soothing, yet eerie, harmony.

His office featured hues of green and gray, as well as landscape paintings—blue skies with a scattering of white clouds. Peaceful.

"I heard about your husband on the news," Leon said. "I'm very sorry for your loss."

I'd heard Dan's tragic story on the news too often. The coverage almost felt like an attack, triggering a wave of emotions ranging from grief to anger to surprise. I just couldn't bear the idea of coming across his smiling face from an Instagram photo during happy times without any warning. I'd let it happen twice before I stopped looking at my newsfeed.

"Thank you," I said to Leon and then immediately had to clear my throat. Anytime someone mentioned Dan, a lump formed in my throat. I wasn't sure how I was going to get through the appointment.

"When we lose someone suddenly and well before their time, it can be difficult to plan their services. I'd be happy to do all of this for you if you wish. We have several packages available."

He offered me a binder filled with photos. Small rooms, medium rooms, a variety of hearses … I closed it. Calla Lillies appeared on almost every page.

"My husband—" I paused, swallowing around the word, "… didn't like white flowers. They reminded him too much of funerals."

Mr. Watts pursed his lips slightly.

"He didn't even want me to use any white in my wedding bouquet," I added, as if this bit of knowledge would make a difference to the man who was burying Dan.

"Of course," Mr. Watts said smoothly. It was no surprise he was amenable to my suggestions and my wishes and that he was kind about it. I was paying him. "What would you prefer? We could use roses, tulips, daffodils …"

"Sure." Defeat overtook me; I couldn't pick anything.

He looked at me, waiting for clarification.

I sighed. "Tulips and daffodils. Plus, lots of greenery. Something that looks alive."

"Of course."

'Of course' seemed to be Mr. Watts' favorite phrase.

"Now, as far as the casket is concerned, we have a few options."

He stood, and I followed him from his office to the showroom. We reached a large display area in the back, where I was sure the more removed mourners would never go. The room was filled with an array of caskets. He spread his arms as he stood in front of them.

"This one is our most popular. It is pretty weatherproof, and all the fixtures are stainless steel, which will withstand rust a little longer than some other models."

I saw myself visiting Dan. Driving out to the graveyard at night with Chinese food he couldn't eat, digging through the earth to get to him. When I hit the coffin, perhaps I could say, 'Ah, Mr. Watts was right. These fixtures have resisted rust quite nicely, and now I can open the lid and see my husband—oh! Too bad the mortician's work didn't last as long as the casket!'

My stomach turned. *What was wrong with me?*

"This model is six thousand."

"Oh!" I hadn't meant to gasp out loud. "Would you mind showing me something a little less ... "

"Of course." Mr. Watts nodded deferentially and motioned towards another casket, this one a sleek grey. "This one is just a step down from the one you just saw. It's four thousand."

It was still more than I wanted to spend.

NEGATIVE IMAGES

I felt a little guilty, but it wasn't as if Dan knew or cared what he was in. He wasn't here anymore. How many times had Dan picked the cheapest option for everything? Cheapest hotel, best deal on seats to the game, cheapest beer. Dan had never been a luxury person. I was the one who would push him to splurge now and again.

My eyes strayed to the next casket over.

"That one is made of wood," Mr. Watts said plainly. "It will not be resistant to weather or the elements."

"You mean it will disintegrate in the ground quickly." And Dan, too.

"In a word, yes." He gave a short laugh. He had his hands clasped behind his back, and the way he smiled at me said that surely I wasn't the sort of woman who would bury her husband in a cheap coffin.

"How much is it?"

"Two thousand," He said after a short pause. He knew I was going to choose it, maybe even before I did.

The morning of Dan's funeral, I woke with a start. Thunder rumbled in the distance, and I relaxed into the mattress, allowing my muscles to uncoil. I rolled over instinctively to reach for Dan, but his side of the bed was empty, the sheets untouched, no indent of his head on the pillow.

I wasn't used to him being gone. I would give anything to see him again. I lay in bed until 7:30, just listening to the wind and watching the room change from grey to pink. My garage door rumbled, but I wasn't going to trick myself into thinking it was Dan again.

Monica had checked on me every day since he died. That first night, she had picked me up from the hospital. She stayed in our guest room down the hall, and I cried myself to sleep.

We hadn't spoken about work but formed a silent understanding that I wouldn't be going in. Monica stopped by every evening to have dinner with me and see if I needed any help.

Overall, I thought that I'd handled the funeral arrangements and the sudden onslaught of family as well as I could. My parents hadn't come in early—no surprise there—and Dan's parents had made up for it, giving opinions and too much advice. No one knew what Dan would have wanted.

He and I had talked about death only twice: when we'd decided to start trying for a baby and seen a lawyer about our wills and when we debated what Negative Images were.

Aaron Ellsworth, Carrie's husband, had been on the news. He stood in front of their house to report on her condition.

"I'm not sure why my mother-in-law came back as an NI, and I think that's the angle we should research. What causes someone to come back? I know they attach themselves to the person they were closest to, but I never realized that Carrie was that person for Elaine," Aaron mused, his flushed cheeks matching his hair.

I'd shuddered and leaned into Dan.

"What's wrong?" he'd asked. "It must be tough to hear about Carrie, huh?"

"It's not that, exactly. It's just what he said about Carrie being the closest person to her Negative Image. Can you imagine? What if the person you loved most had an incurable illness? You'd have this idea of

NEGATIVE IMAGES

them returning to you as an NI hanging over whatever time you had left."

Dan had squeezed me tighter. "You really think these Negatives are the people they claim to be? Not something else? Personally, I think whatever these NIs are, they're not the people who passed. Carrie's Negative Image is not her mother. I think her real mother is in a better place."

I'd nodded into his chest. "I want to believe that too."

"But?"

"I just don't. I think the NIs are who they say they are. Or at least some part of that person."

"Part of them? A fragment of their former selves? Let's hope I'm right and you're wrong." He'd laughed, a throaty chuckle that filled me with comfort.

"I do hope that, even if I don't think your theory is right."

"Well, I'd never come back to you. I can promise you that."

"Don't even joke about something like that! It's not funny." I'd swatted at him, and he'd laughed again.

A quiet tapping on the door jolted me.

"Anita? Honey?" Monica came in, carrying a cup of coffee. She pressed it into my hands. I took a sip, allowing the rest of the fog in my brain to clear.

"I need to find clothes." I left a tangle of sheets on the bed as I walked through the bathroom to my closet.

Monica parted the sea of hangers. She looked impeccable as always—a black pencil skirt paired with a sweater and a simple strand of pearls around her neck. Her hair was slicked back from her face and coiled in a low bun. Her take-charge attitude was forceful but quiet. She'd taken the lead in my closet, and I could let my brain rest, knowing that she would make sure whatever I chose looked right.

I have a lot of black clothes, but I use them for work. Black sets me apart from the guests at the events I help plan; it lets me fade into the background but stand out to people looking to make a complaint. I didn't want to contaminate my work clothes. Whatever I wore to Dan's Funeral, I knew I could never wear again.

Finally, I found a dark dress at the back of my closet. I realized it was the same one I'd worn to my grandfather's funeral, and I had to stifle a laugh. It seemed I had a funeral dress, after all.

A rustling came from behind me, the swish of satin among my skirts and dresses. I turned around to show Monica my dress, but all I saw were a few hangers swinging slightly, as though someone had just run a hand through the garments.

"Monica?" I called out. She walked back to the closet from my bedroom.

"I was just picking out a little jewelry for you to wear." She gave me a reassuring smile. "Nothing flashy."

"Thanks." I felt thrown. I still had the sense that someone had been beside me just now. It couldn't have been Monica. My jewelry was in my dresser, in my bedroom. I shook the feeling off and put on my funeral dress.

Once I got to the church, the service flew by in a blur. It was crowded—Dan's large, extended family had all come. Somewhat surprisingly, my cousins, aunt, and uncle had come, even though we hadn't seen each other in a long time. My mother gave me a brief hug and a murmured condolence.

NEGATIVE IMAGES

My family had never really known how to mark any important occasion, so it wasn't surprising that they looked uncomfortable now.

At the cemetery, I concentrated on the cold breeze so I wouldn't have to listen to the prayers spoken over Dan's coffin. If I concentrated hard enough, the people around me, my parents, Dan's parents, and our combined families, all became a buzz. Nothing more than a group of loud bees, and when they touched me, all I felt was the absence of cold instead of warmth.

Afterward, many people pressed their arms against me and offered words of condolence before making their way to their cars. My parents and Dan's lingered.

"I just want a moment," I said.

Reluctantly, they retreated. I exhaled a long sigh that let me relax as much as I thought I would be able to for days. This was my last moment with Dan. Only it wasn't, really. We'd had our last moment in the hospital.

I stood there, waiting for some emotion to pass through me. I wanted to feel like a widow should. Grief-stricken, emotional. But I felt empty.

I reached over and touched the casket.

"You don't know how to say goodbye."

I whipped around, catching a glimpse of what might have been a shadow but was more likely just another headstone—maybe even just a tree.

But I knew that voice.

I shut the thought out of my mind and wrapped my coat more tightly around myself as I walked back to the car.

CHAPTER FOUR

Four days had passed since the funeral. The flower arrangements I'd brought home wilted a little each day.

The casseroles my mother had made were all frozen and too big to thaw for just myself, so I was forced to leave the house. I wheeled my shopping cart around the grocery store, wandering up and down each aisle. Instead of making a list, I'd put a random collection of food in the cart.

I walked down the snack aisle and picked up a box of Oreos. How many times had I bought a box for Dan and I, thinking it would last us several days, only to find that he or I ate them together almost immediately? I put them in the cart with a sigh.

"Oh, I envy you your Oreos. Try not to eat the whole box in one sitting, though. Remember how we were supposed to clean up our eating?"

I froze mid-exhale until the remaining air demanded out. The muscles in my arms tensed as I gripped the shopping cart. Standing perfectly still, with nothing amiss in front of me, left me wondering if maybe—please,

NEGATIVE IMAGES

God, maybe—I had imagined it. Something had to be wrong with my head. It was the grief—some misplaced sense of guilt over the Oreos. Yet, the voice had come from behind me: Dan's voice, or *almost* Dan's voice. I was dying to turn around and check. But at the same time, I didn't want to look.

"It wasn't real," I whispered to myself. "Just check out and go home."

My sweaty hands slid over the plastic handle as I quickly pushed the cart to the end of the aisle, then made a sharp left turn, rounding the end cap.

"Hey!" a lady barked at me. Two boys were with her, staring at me openmouthed.

"I'm sorry. I didn't see you there."

"You can't just go running through the grocery store like that!" Pink blotches sprung up over the woman's cheeks like poorly applied blush. "You nearly smashed your cart into my son."

I willed myself to be still—really still—instead of this frantic person who could barely look at them. When I saw she was right, guilt took over my fear.

"I'm so sorry."

"You have to be careful with kids." The voice behind me laughed, mocking. "Not that you'd know."

I tensed up when the woman's eyes fixed on some point behind me. She gasped. She grabbed both sons and pulled them close to her, one on either side. Her face went from red to purple. Without another word to me, she grabbed her cart, turned it roughly around, and disappeared down the aisle.

Was I the monster, or was there one standing behind me?

Tears blurred the edges of my vision. With a deep breath to steady myself, I wheeled my cart towards the front. One of the wheels started squeaking. When I got to the register, everyone stared.

All those eyes scared me. I could guess what they were looking at, even if I wasn't brave enough to look for myself. As soon as they registered the presence behind me, they looked at me differently.

The cashier, just a high school kid with braces, showed her fear plainly. When I approached, she stepped back from me like she thought I had some contagious disease. It made it difficult for her to scan everything. I did my best to look normal.

The boy who was supposed to be bagging my groceries instead grabbed his phone from his pocket and angled himself to get me and the cashier in frame.

"John, what are you doing?" the cashier squeaked.

"I've gotta put this on YouTube." He was nonchalant and completely unapologetic, as if it was his right to film me.

It felt like I was folding in on myself—I wanted to take up as little space as possible. No one's face showed compassion. Only fear, anger, and disgust. Was that the way I'd looked at Carrie all those days ago?

The bagger wasn't the only one filming. So were some of the people at the front of the store. A man paying at the next line over was taking a picture. As was the employee at customer service. I couldn't breathe. What would they do with this? Who would they show my face to?

"Please stop! I just wanna get her outta here as fast as possible," the cashier complained.

John the Bagger ignored her request.

NEGATIVE IMAGES

"I'll do it," an older man groused. "Just stay over there." He put his hand up in front of him, not letting me put the bagged groceries back in my cart.

"That'll be $43.15."

Her relief that I would pay and leave was palpable.

I put my card in the chip reader. She spoke again, an urgent whisper, her eyes wide. "He's looking at me. Why is he looking at me?"

"Who's looking at you?"

She scowled. "As if you don't know what you have."

Bile settled at the base of my throat as I took in everyone around me, all of them listening to what I would say and the no doubt feeble explanation I would give. John the Bagger still had his phone up to catch everything. If shame were visible, I think it would have been a burning red rope tethering me to the presence behind me. Everyone's reactions made me almost certain of what was behind me. But I was holding onto hope that I was wrong.

"Please." My voice was just above a whisper. "He just showed up for the first time." I struggled to keep my tone even. "What does he look like?"

"Um ... he's tallish? A white man with brown curly hair? His eyes are—they're just ... all black."

Dan.

My stomach lurched. I fumbled my wallet and dropped it on the floor. When I stood up, I banged the back of my head on the card reader. No one asked if I was all right.

The cashier tapped her foot on the floor while she waited for my receipt to print. Finally, the machine spat it out. My coupons printed out separately and were left forgotten, a nice bonus for the next customer who checked out without a Negative Image attached to them.

"Does he go with you?" The cashier seemed nervous, and I didn't blame her. I didn't want to be stuck under this thing's gaze for the rest of the day, either.

I shrugged, trying my best to act casual, but my shoulders were stiff. "I don't really know."

She looked at the floor.

Neither of us wished the other a nice day. I pushed my cart out of the store, the wheel squeaking the whole way. I only looked where I needed to. Finally, I made it to my car, loaded the groceries, and got in the car.

With my eyes closed, I locked the door and let out a deep breath. Maybe I was safe. Maybe he'd gone away. Maybe there was no monster.

I opened my eyes. A shape in the rearview mirror made me scream, and I clapped my hands over my mouth.

Dan sat in the backseat. I watched him wave at me in my rearview mirror. His eyes were large and black, completely unreadable. The blackness appeared swollen, like an overripe berry about to burst.

I recognized the shape of his smile. In life, it would have been his sarcastic smile, but now his upper lip seemed to curl up a little too high, forcing his smile into a sneer.

"Darling." His voice was recognizable as his own but amplified and warped—just different enough to make me question if it was really him. "I thought you'd be happier to see me."

CHAPTER FIVE

I gripped the steering wheel so tightly that the muscles in my hands hurt. Sweat pooled in my armpits before coursing down my arms to my elbows. In my rearview mirror, Dan studied me with those strange bug eyes. I turned around to look at him directly, but he was gone. I whirled back around to the front, but he wasn't in the mirror anymore, either.

"Dan?" The tears I'd been holding back in the store came gushing out.

Frustrated, I struck out with my fists, slamming them over and over against the sides of the steering wheel.

An older man tapped on my window.

"Are you all right?"

"I'm fine."

I wiped some tears from my face. My hand came away streaked with mascara and mucous. Lovely. I offered a small wave and started the car.

When I got home, I was surprised to see the garage door closing behind me. I popped the trunk of the Corolla and squeezed myself in the space between the bumper and garage door so I could collect my groceries, which were scattered all over the trunk. Plastic dug into my arms as I maneuvered myself so I could shut the trunk. I walked into the house and locked the door behind me. I wanted to slide down the door and collapse into a puddle on the floor and cry.

Instead, I took a deep breath and unpacked. This was simple organization, something I could do in my sleep. Yogurt belonged in the dairy bin—milk on the shelf.

Then I saw the Oreos. My stomach twisted uncomfortably, and I just made it to the kitchen sink before I threw up. My legs trembled, and I cleaned my face with a damp paper towel. I tried not to look at the Oreos as I threw them in the trash.

My legs gave out, and I sat with my back against the kitchen island. I was looking at the floor when I saw a pair of sneakers. A scream worked its way up my throat, already raw and sore from vomiting, and I forced it back down. I was alone in the house, with no one to hear me except this ... *thing*, and I didn't want to give it the satisfaction.

"What do you want?" I asked as if it were that simple.

Dan sat down on the floor across from me, his back against the stainless steel fridge. He smiled, and I noticed again that it looked more like a sneer. Maybe he (or it) wasn't capable of smiling.

"Maybe I just missed you," he said in a sandpaper voice.

Of course, that wasn't the answer; it couldn't be, but I nodded. I felt his gaze on me, and as much as I didn't want to, I met it.

"I miss my husband," I said after a long while.

I thought back to the hospital. He'd never woken up. I'd never even gotten to say goodbye properly.

My vision swam, and I dropped my gaze to the tile. "You were there. At the funeral."

"Of course." He scoffed. "You think I'd miss my own send-off?" My mind whirled. Dan, in the coffin, pumped full of formaldehyde, rotting underground. Dan, in our kitchen, his eyes focused only on me.

"If you were there ... that was four days ago. Why did you stay away so long?"

His upper lip lifted to expose his teeth. "Don't act like you missed me. You don't. You were afraid when you heard me at the grave, and you've been relieved every day to wake up by yourself." His eyes were unreadable pools of black, but something in the way he stared at me stole the breath from my chest. Then he moved, crouching right in front of me so we were occupying the same space.

"All this grief. The wallowing. You think you miss me. But you know what? I think what you really miss is everything I did for you. Even now, my suffering, my death, is weighted against how it's affected you and your precious business." He pointed, his finger hovering a millimeter from my chest.

"I don't know what you mean, Dan. Of course, I appreciated your help, but it wasn't why I loved you. Is that why you're here? You think I didn't care about you?"

He vanished.

I lay crumpled on the floor between the island and the fridge. Now that he was gone, I could almost believe I'd imagined everything. The check-out girl at the grocery store already felt like some stereotype of teenage-hood in my mind.

I had to keep going and find a way forward. I needed normalcy and order. Since Dan died, I'd let everything in the house pile up in a weird tribute to the time I'd spent without him. The floral arrangements from the altar, brightly colored roses and greenery, had started to wilt. I'd gotten flowers sent before the funeral, too, and a pungent smell stirred up as I moved them into trash bags. Some of them were in vases, the water clotted with suspicious-looking substances as I poured them down the drain. I left them to parade around the countertop. What were you supposed to do with leftover funeral vases?

"Are you trying to purge me? Get all this death out of your system?" When I turned away from the sink, there he was, blocking my way.

Dan's voice was harsh and sarcastic. He'd always been so playful. Even if he were serious about something, he would always throw in a joke, so I knew he wasn't too upset with me. My mind searched for the sound of his real voice, but I couldn't find it.

"You don't have to start your tears now just because I joined you," he said.

I swiped at my face. My hand was wet; I'd been crying without realizing it like my eyes were a leaky water bottle. I tried to push Dan out of the way, to get past him, but my hand went through his midsection. I gasped and pulled back, expecting to see some injury, but I was okay, aside from a cold, tingling sensation.

Dan chuckled. He raised his hand, and I flinched before he attempted to tuck my hair behind my ear. That tender, everyday gesture of Dan's was defiled by this ... this thing. Dan always complained that my hair fell in my face. He said he wanted to be able to see me.

"Please." Tears fell down my cheeks despite my best efforts to hold them back. "I don't know what you want, but please leave. You're not Dan. Not *my* Dan."

"But I am, Anita. I am your Dan. I always have been, and I always will be." He sounded almost caring, except for the gravelly, unnatural tone.

"You're not him."

He shook his head, one eyebrow raised.

"What do I have to do to get you to leave?"

He leaned in close, his lips almost touching my ear. "Nothing. No matter what you do, I'll be here.

"Not gonna lie, I would love to have you back. But are you sure you're ready? You sound a little ... I don't know. Off." Monica always sounded busy, and it was weird to hear her slow down to voice her concern.

"I think it would be the best thing for me. I have to try to get back to normal sometime, right?" I bit my lip, knowing that with an NI, I might not see normal for a long time.

"You want something to take your mind off your grief."

"Yes. Exactly." It was, at least, partly true. I couldn't stand to be alone in my house with Dan's Negative Image.

"Okay. Sure. It'll be great to have you back, if you think you're ready. But you know how we do business. I can't take your events or give them to Tricia if it's too much. That's not what we're about."

I rolled my eyes. Of course, Monica would remind me of this, even though we'd come up with the idea together. Working with her at Legendary Events was a blessing and a curse. We were co-owners, and we wanted to differentiate ourselves through one-on-one service.

"I'm ready for it. Promise. I'll see you tomorrow."

I should have told her, I thought after I hung up.

The following morning was bright and clear. I could almost forget it was the end of January and I had a Negative Image lurking somewhere, waiting to make his appearance.

Dan's Negative was nowhere to be seen while I got dressed. He wasn't waiting for me in the kitchen, and as I stepped into the garage with my thermos in hand, he didn't appear in the car to join me on my commute.

I walked around holding my breath without realizing it. Each time I turned a corner or opened a door to find the space unoccupied, I let out a sigh.

Sunlight beat through the branches of our tree-lined street, the bare arms jabbing up and out at me as if in accusation. Without the leaves to filter the light, I squinted in protest. When I reached over to the glove compartment to grab my sunglasses, I thought I saw a shadow in my rear-view mirror, but when I looked again, it was gone. My heart stuttered, and my hands shook as I pressed the ignition button.

When I arrived, Tricia and Monica stood stiffly in the hallway, making me think they'd been waiting for me. They eyed me as I walked down the hall, then stepped towards me at the same time, enveloping me in hugs with conflicting scents of florals and musk. Tricia's silk blouse rubbed against my neck, and Monica patted my back.

"Anita, I am so sorry," Tricia said. "You know, we all thought Dan was just wonderful. I can't imagine what you're going through right now."

You really can't, I thought, picturing Dan's Negative with his large black eyes.

"If you need anything, we're here for you, Anita," Monica chimed in.

My heart welled with gratitude. I knew they meant it. They were two of the kindest people I'd ever met.

"Let's chat for a bit," Monica said as she opened the door to her office. "How are you really?" she asked once the door was shut.

I shrugged. "Not great, but getting better, I guess. What have I missed?"

Monica pursed her lips, and it was several seconds before she spoke. "It's been slower than usual. We've had some postponements and cancellations because of the NIs. Some vendor problems, too."

"How about Carrie?" I asked. It was thin hope, but I'd been praying I'd at least have a message from her. She'd been on my mind more since the grocery store trip.

Monica shook her head. "Nothing. I wouldn't expect to hear anything. However, we do have a new client coming in at 9:30. I don't want to swamp you, but I'd love it if you could work with him—he asked about you. I have a list of vendors he sent over. He wants to repurpose some choices for an existing event."

"Oh. So, is it a totally different event now? What was it before, and what's he changing it to?"

"I'm not sure, but I thought you could at least feel it out."

"Okay, I'll go look through these, but I wanted to talk to you about something—"

Monica screamed and fell out of her chair. I couldn't see her, but she gasped for breath, and I heard her muttering to herself. "Oh no, oh no, oh no."

A moment later, she peered around the desk, still trembling in fear. She took a moment to collect herself. She looked up at Dan's NI and clenched her jaw. "Damnit, Anita! You have a Negative Image?!"

Monica looked at me with the same fear as those people at the grocery store yesterday, making me feel like a threat. My lungs collapsed in on themselves; the next breath I took was painful.

"I wanted to tell you—"

"But you didn't!" Monica yelled from her hands and knees, her head and shoulders peeking out above her desk.

"I'm so sorry." I buried my face in my hands.

"How long have you had it? Him?" Monica stood up and practically threw her desk chair back into place.

"Not long. A day."

I felt like I was on trial. Monica stood in front of me, breathing heavily, her hands on her hips in indignation.

"Wow. You didn't think to mention this when you called yesterday?"

I sighed, realizing that the reason I'd given myself sounded incredibly childish. "I didn't want to tell you over the phone."

"Right. This is so much better. The visual here really helps explain everything. God, Anita!"

"I'm sorry!"

Air by my ear stirred. "You sound like someone who is very sorry that Mommy has caught them. But you'd do it again. We all know it. Beg forgiveness instead of asking permission, right?" Dan's Negative sneered at me.

NEGATIVE IMAGES

"Please! Can you just shut up? Just let me have this conversation!" I snapped at him, then clapped my hands over my mouth. What would Tricia think of all this shouting? Our office was almost spa-like in its quiet.

"What's he saying?" Monica asked. She sat back down slowly, her eyes fixed on Dan's Negative Image. She sounded wary now instead of accusatory.

"What do you mean?"

"I see his mouth moving, but I can't tell what he's saying. It's like listening to someone with a bad phone connection."

I'd forgotten Monica wouldn't be able to understand him. I remembered how Carrie had screamed in the conference room when hers first showed up, the horrified look she'd had on her face. It was because she'd understood her Negative, just like I could understand mine.

"You can understand him, right?" Monica asked.

I nodded. "He sounds like Dan, only his voice is a bit ... off. He agrees with you, I think. That I should have told you earlier."

Of course, that wasn't entirely true.

"I can't expect you to give an accurate translation, I guess," Dan's NI chimed in.

Neither of us spoke for a moment. I had no desire to repeat anything this thing had to say.

"I'm sorry, Monica. Okay? I'm sorry I didn't tell you, and I'm really sorry he showed up here. I'm not sure why I thought he wouldn't."

Monica laughed, a bitter sound coming from deep in her throat. "So, you see him, get creeped out, and the first thing you decide to do is show him where you work?"

"I'm sorry. I shouldn't have. But I can't control when he's with me and when he's not."

Monica cleared her throat and rested her hands on her desk. "What do we do now?"

I shrugged.

"He's not with you all the time," Monica mused, her head tilted back and eyes on the ceiling.

"No. Thank God."

"Huh. That's interesting." She turned to face me, looking more like the confident Monica I knew. My own posture straightened automatically. "Why don't you just work in your office whenever he pops up?"

"It's not like he gives me advance notice."

"Well, for now ... I think that's better than nothing."

For the next hour, I attempted to work while Dan's Negative worked at distracting me. He sat in the chair across from my desk, so I couldn't help but see him in my peripheral vision as much as I tried to focus on looking up the vendors on my computer.

Then he moved closer. His presence was like a draft from a vent hitting the back of my neck. My fingers stilled on the keyboard. I couldn't bear to look at him. If he were real, his breath would be on my neck, and I'd feel his warm chest leaning into my back, the way he had done a thousand times during our relationship—our marriage—and then he would put his hands over mine, to prevent me from working any more.

NEGATIVE IMAGES

My chest constricted, a hot ball of fire pulsing within me. I saw Dan's hands hovering over mine, emitting no warmth, no cold, no sensation whatsoever. It was wrong. I pulled my hands into my lap and clasped them together. Dan's Negative chuckled softly behind me and moved his hands away.

I swiveled my chair around and peered up into his face. He smiled down at me with Dan's smile, and a part of me wanted to return it.

"I bet you miss that, don't you? You miss me holding your hands, kissing you. Me."

"Of course I—"

He let out a laugh, mocking and harsh.

"I miss Dan." I clarified too late.

"I'm much better than that paltry version of myself you loved so much."

"You're not."

"I am. I'm honest."

"Honest?" I wanted to slap him. "You're cruel."

He bent over me then, his hands resting on the arms of my office chair. He placed his mouth close to my ear and whispered, "Every time I did that, that little gesture that you loved, it was out of desperation. I hated how much you worked. If I wanted your attention, I had to take it. And I'll do whatever it takes to get it now."

CHAPTER SIX

When Dan's NI finally left, I was distracted. Instead of looking at vendors, I looked at pictures on my phone. It was good to see Dan's face, even if it was just in a photograph. I kept swiping and saw pictures of Carrie's event that Tricia had sent me. She'd taken some of the people milling around, and I caught a glimpse of a woman in a purple dress. I zoomed in closer and recognized the woman from the parking garage. There was no doubt in my mind now that she had a Negative Image with her that night.

A rap on the door startled me. Tricia poked her head in without waiting for me to answer.

"Mr. Maguire's here. I set him up in the conference room."

"Thanks," I said and cleared my throat.

"Oh!" Monica called from across the hall. "Hold on, I'll go with you."

She raised her eyebrows at me in an unasked question; I shook my head briefly and walked down the hall.

A man in a navy blue sports coat was seated at the table with his back to me. Seeing the conference room brought back more thoughts of Carrie and her NI. I closed my eyes for a moment, hoping to clear my head.

Monica opened the door. "Joshua! It's so nice to see you. I'd like to introduce you to Anita."

The man in the sports coat turned towards me, and my brain locked up for a moment. In my head, I saw him again explaining his views on Negative Images while he leaned against a hospital vending machine. He'd said something was wrong with the people who had them. Vending Machine Guy. Great.

I shuddered. Surely now, I thought, Dan's Negative would appear.

Joshua looked over at me, and his face shifted from a prepared mask of distant politeness to puzzlement. Clearly, he recognized me, but he said nothing.

"It's a pleasure to meet you, Joshua." I slapped a smile on my face as some self-preservation instinct kicked in. Given what I remembered of him and his thoughts on what I was starting to think of as my "condition," I didn't want him to know about my Negative Image.

"*He'll know.*"

I gasped and whipped around to look behind me before noticing a shadow by the window behind Monica.

Monica and Joshua exchanged an uneasy look before they both stared at me.

"Sorry." I tried to laugh it off. "I think the cleaners left a pin in my blazer."

"Oh!" Monica exclaimed.

"I have it now, it's fine." I pantomimed pulling a pin out of my sleeve. What was I going to do with this nonexistent pin now? I decided to slip it into my pocket. "Please, go on."

Monica cleared her throat and shifted her weight as she focused on Joshua. "Well, Anita, as you know, Mr. Maguire wants to alter an event he had been planning."

"Yes, I was able to reach out to some of the vendors. Was it originally a wedding?"

"Yes. But now, well, it's an event to honor her memory," he said.

My politely interested smile stayed fixed on my lips, but I shot daggers at Monica. Surely she wasn't about to recommend me to coordinate this event for a man going through a loss?

Monica's mouth fell open, and she mouthed, *I'm sorry* from her position behind him.

I knew she'd soon be begging my forgiveness, but I also knew I was probably going to get stuck with this event anyway.

"I'm so sorry for your loss." It was a struggle to set aside my own grief and find some sincerity.

Joshua sighed. "Thank you. You see, she was in an accident. We were supposed to get married in a few weeks, but instead ... well, her parents planned the funeral. It was a beautiful service. I don't think it's what she'd have picked, but I don't think she had any ideas in mind anyway. Not at her age." He was rambling a little and pursed his lips together before continuing. "It's just that I still have all these things from the wedding, and I thought since it's too late to cancel, we could have a gathering for her. In her memory."

Monica cleared her throat and looked at me pointedly.

NEGATIVE IMAGES

"Well, Joshua." I fumbled, struggling to come up with what to say. "I think what you're trying to do is admirable, to say the least."

"And thankfully, Anita has good relationships with most of the wedding vendors in town," Monica added before I could bow out. "I'll leave the two of you to get started. Joshua, please accept my condolences." She backed out of the room, avoiding my gaze, and shut the door behind her.

Joshua pulled out his chair and unbuttoned the top button of his coat with a practiced gesture. He poured himself a glass of water while I flipped through my planner until I reached the notes section in the back and found a blank page. I uncapped my pen and wrote *Joshua Maguire* at the top. It was a little gesture, but it grounded me. It also bought me a few moments to consider how to start our conversation.

It felt like some weird challenge or test: Plan a memorial event while trying to hide your own grief and recent loss and pray that your Negative stays away until the meeting ends.

"Usually, I begin these meetings by talking through your vision for the event, but maybe we should start with your fiancé. What was she like? What parts of her personality do you want to shine through at the memorial?"

Joshua took a long time to answer. He fiddled with the sweat dripping off his water glass before taking a long sip. I was about to apologize when he finally spoke.

"She was ... well, I don't know if I understand what you're asking. But Ainsley was very social, very bubbly and fun. She spent a lot of time with her friends."

Joshua got a faraway look in his eyes, and I wondered if I'd gotten too personal too quickly. I was thinking of what I might want to be asked if the situation were reversed, but maybe Joshua wasn't much of a talker. After another moment, I moved on.

"This is probably difficult to talk about, and I'm sorry. You mentioned wanting to repurpose some of her wedding plans. I reviewed some of the information you sent over already."

Joshua grimaced. "Ainsley did most of the planning, but it wasn't very well organized."

I leafed through the pages Monica had given me. Ainsley's handwriting was precise and small, with large loops in her cursive l's. What sort of person had she been?

"I spoke to a few people this morning to see who has the flexibility you want. Janet has been great about the flowers. If you'd like, she suggested modifying your original selections to a color scheme of white and pale pink.

"What was it before?" he asked.

"Bright pinks, peach, and yellow," I said with a forced smile. It was annoying how he knew so few details of his own wedding. Well, none, actually. It was a sharp contrast to the experience I had with Dan when we planned our wedding. We had planned everything together; Dan was especially enthusiastic about cake sampling.

"I think we can keep it the way it is."

I circled the brighter color scheme in my notes. "I'll let Janet know. I understand that you want to keep most of your fiancée's choices, but you might want to consider some changes. Like keeping the flavors she chose for the cake but changing the design. Why don't you tell me a little about what you envision?"

Joshua let out a long sigh and shifted his focus to the window. Morning light bounced off the windows of the neighboring buildings.

NEGATIVE IMAGES

"Listen, I really don't know much about what goes into all the planning, and I can't visualize anything right now. Is there a way for you to just sort of ..." He made a pushing gesture with his hands. "Can you come up with something for me?"

"Of course." I capped my pen and closed my notebook, ready for this meeting to be over.

"Wait a minute. I know you," Joshua said, and when I glanced up, he was looking at me differently, as though he'd figured out a puzzle.

"I don't think so." I smiled a little out of politeness. I didn't want to talk about that time in the hospital waiting room when Ainsley and Dan had both still been alive. He'd been a bit ruder in the waiting room, even dismissive in our conversation about Negative Images. If he knew my husband had come back as one, would he insist that something was wrong with me?

"This will sound odd." He chuckled. "But by any chance, were you a nurse? Or a nurse's assistant at some point?"

"No."

"I swear I know you from a hospital."

I tried to keep my face blank when I looked up at him. He annoyed me. He struck me as too self-important or entitled, even in his insistence on continuing this conversation that I was trying to politely decline.

"Monica mentioned that you'd requested to work with me specifically. You probably saw my photo online. Or maybe you remembered me from one of your friend's events?"

I expected him to nod and drop the issue, but he didn't.

"No, the reason I requested you is because Ainsley selected you as her first choice to be our wedding planner. You were unavailable. I saw your name and company in her notes, so ..." He gestured at the room.

"I'm sorry I didn't get the chance to know her." I was surprised to realize that I meant it. Thinking of her writing my name in her wedding notes, even though it was the smallest of connections, filled me with regret.

Joshua smirked as he drummed his fingers on the table. "I know you. I know I know you, and you know me, too. You just won't say." The smirk on his face vanished as it drained of color. "You have one."

I'd finally gotten a little comfortable in the meeting, but now the air around me felt different, as if the pressure had dropped. I knew Dan's Negative must be leering at Joshua. Joshua clenched his jaw tightly and pushed himself back from the table.

"Don't you think you should have disclosed this thing?"

"He's a nuisance," I admitted. "But he doesn't affect how I do my job." I tried to look capable, but I felt ridiculous knowing Dan's Negative was behind me. Tricia walked past the conference room and stopped short, running into the edge of a table. She'd seen it. Great.

"Are you sure about that?" Joshua had noticed Tricia, too.

Tricia looked behind me at Dan's Negative Image. Her cheeks were blotchy. Joshua, too, was looking behind me. I didn't want to, but I turned around to look. Dan's alien eyes gleamed. He lifted a hand and waved at Tricia while a smile played across his mouth.

Tricia squealed and ran back the way she'd come.

"You're so ashamed of me," Dan's Negative said with a sigh.

"What is he saying?" Joshua's voice resonated in the small conference room.

"Nothing, really." I felt a little like a child. I could barely look Joshua in the eye anymore—my whole body itched with shame.

NEGATIVE IMAGES

Joshua rolled his eyes. "He obviously said something just now. He's looking at me. What does he want?"

"He says I'm ashamed of him." I gave a slight shrug and looked at the floor.

"Who is he?" Joshua asked. His eyes roved over the Negative Image, taking in all the details like he'd never seen one before. For all I knew, he hadn't, aside from the YouTube clips he was so fond of.

"*This*," I pointed, "is a crappy Negative Image. It's posing as my husband, Dan."

Joshua stayed silent for a moment, the murmurs from the hallway filling the space. I should have found time to tell Tricia about my Negative Image this morning. I massaged my temples. *Stupid.* I guess a part of me thought Monica would tell her, but it wasn't her responsibility. It was mine.

And all of this was going on in front of Joshua, our brand-new client. This wasn't going to help business. My head felt like someone had placed a tight band around it and squeezed.

"I should go," I mumbled.

I swept my computer and planner off the table and walked out of the conference room, ears pounding. In the hallway, Monica comforted Tricia, who thankfully had her back to me. I ducked into my office long enough to grab my car keys. When I stepped out, Monica had maneuvered Tricia out of the tiny hallway so I could squeeze past them. It sounded like Tricia was hyperventilating. Monica glared at me as I grabbed the door to our office and headed for the elevators.

I pushed the down button repeatedly.

"Just like a two-year-old," Dan's Negative quipped.

"Shut up."

Dan had always chided me during my more impatient moments, but always with a joking attitude, never harsh critique.

The doors finally opened, and I stepped into the elevator, glad to be away from Monica, Tricia, and Joshua. The stainless steel doors slid shut, and I saw Dan's Negative standing in the reflection next to me.

"Alone at last," he whispered. The air by my ear felt cold, and I swatted at it to move him away like I would a bug.

Goosebumps broke out across my arms. I pressed the button for the lower level to get to the parking garage, but it didn't light up. The elevator didn't move.

I swiped tears away from my cheeks.

"Come on, come on, come on ..."

"Yes, good thinking. Talking to machines and pushing those buttons hard will get this elevator moving in no time, Anita. Such a smart toddler."

"Stop it!" When I screamed, I could see the air coming out of my mouth—why? Was it the late January chill or Dan's Negative Image making that happen? "Please just stop. Just let me get home. Let me be alone," I muttered under my breath.

"You'll never be alone again, Anita."

The elevator lurched as it finally moved toward the parking garage.

"You have me, remember?"

The doors opened, and I bolted for my car as if I could outrun my Negative Image and leave him behind for good.

I sprinted across the parking garage in my heels. A sheen of sweat covered my whole body, and my heart raced. I finally reached my car, expecting some reprieve from the torture. Instead, I was horrified to see Dan's Negative in the passenger seat.

NEGATIVE IMAGES

"Ready to go home, darling? Did you have a tough day?" His tone was simpering, and he grinned at me, knowing full well that he was responsible for everything that had gone wrong.

Blood pounded in my ears. I wanted to scream and cry, but I didn't want to give this thing the satisfaction of seeing me upset. I clenched the steering wheel of my car as I pulled out of the parking lot.

"Why are you here?"

"Touchy, touchy. Obviously, I'm here to spend time with you. You know, if I had to bet, I'd guess that most grieving widows would be ecstatic to spend more time with their husbands. But you? You're so cold, and it's really making me feel unloved, Anita. I don't think you were even sad to see me die. You don't even miss me."

"I miss Dan every day. If you'd leave me alone, I'd have a chance to really miss him. Right now, with you here, I feel fear more than anything."

"Do you?" He leaned over the center console. "Cause I know fear. I don't think you're experiencing enough of it."

He pressed his face closer to mine so that his nose was practically against my cheek. Distracted, I had to slam on the brake as the yellow light suddenly turned red. My body lurched forward, and the seat belt tightened across my chest. Dan's Negative Image stayed completely still.

"Did I touch a nerve?" Dan's Negative eased back from me a little and smirked. Seeing Dan's gestures and facial expressions come to life on this creature killed me.

"Why are you here? What do you want from me?"

"I just told you." He chuckled and looked out the window.

"No, you didn't. You're some ... *thing*. I don't know what to call you. But you're not my husband. I would love to spend time with my actual husband."

"You are spending time with your husband." He reached over and put a hand on my knee.

I flinched, even though I couldn't feel anything. Dan used to do that to me all the time if I was upset. Something in his touch always calmed me down. He used to rub small circles on my kneecap. This Negative Image was doing the same thing, even though I couldn't feel it. The light turned green, and the car behind me tapped its horn. I was glad to have a reason to keep my eyes off his hand.

I wanted to come up with a snarky comeback when a detail about him came into focus. He looked normal, aside from his black eyes. Why didn't he have the same injury that Dan did?

I was so distracted by this thought that I almost drove into the semi that had stopped in front of me.

A coffee shop was just across the intersection, and I pulled into the parking lot.

I glanced at the empty passenger seat. When had he vanished? I was glad he was gone but bothered that I couldn't pinpoint when he'd left.

Maybe I could go inside and get a cup of green tea; it might be good for me. Dan and I had met at a coffee shop—not this one, but whenever I grabbed a coffee, it made me smile to think of our serendipitous meeting.

But as I started to open my door, I saw a man running towards me in my side mirror. As he got closer, I recognized him.

Joshua.

He hadn't been happy to find out I had an NI, but was he so upset about it that he needed to follow me?

I closed my door again and pressed the ignition, but I'd forgotten to step on the break. My window for leaving was gone. Joshua rapped sharply on my window.

NEGATIVE IMAGES

For a moment, I sat with my hands on the steering wheel and my eyes fixed on the building in front of me. But he was impossible to ignore, especially since he was still tapping on my window like a bird. I rolled my window down a couple of inches.

"Yes?"

"Anita. I wanted to talk to you about something." His tie had whipped over his shoulder, and he struggled to put it back in place. He breathed heavily and kept glancing back from where he'd come. He'd lost his cool, composed demeanor.

"About what? After your reaction to my husb—Negative Image, I assumed you wouldn't want my help with your event."

He clenched his jaw. "I've been on the fence about whether it was a good idea at all, actually."

I stifled a groan. Monica would hate to hear this. I'd lost a new client already.

I rolled down my window a little further and turned to face him. "You signed a contract. You don't have to work with me, but we do have other people who can help you."

"Look. It's hard to explain. The real reason I wanted to host this memorial wasn't just to honor Ainsley's memory."

"Okay." I sighed. "Did I misunderstand your idea for the event? Maybe this is something Monica and I should work on together."

Joshua shook his head. "That's not it. I know this will sound weird, but I have to talk to you. It's more important than you realize."

"Whatever you have to say, just say it."

"Look, this involves you. And me, too," he added. "But it's not something I can talk about out here."

I glanced at his car in my rearview mirror. A petite blond woman stood next to the passenger door with her arms crossed.

"Is she the reason you don't want to have the memorial anymore?" I jerked my thumb behind me.

Joshua's face turned beet red, and he muttered under his breath before speaking. "Yes, she is. But it's not like I've moved on quickly or anything if that's what you're thinking." He took a deep breath. "I have one." He paused. "I have a Negative Image."

Chapter Seven

My mouth fell open, but before I could say anything, he continued, "You've seen the news. You must be keeping up with the developments." He studied me. "Aren't you?"

I pursed my lips together, and from the corner of my eye, I saw Joshua's brows furrow. In truth, I hadn't looked at the news much since Dan died. It was just too hard. Besides, there wasn't very much that I could do about any of this right now. When something big came up, I knew I'd overhear someone talking about it.

"You're not?" he asked, his tone incredulous. "You've got to see the latest break in this story. For people like us, it's essential."

Every inch of me wanted to flee. I never did well with the sad stuff—that was part of why I'd gone into event planning, so I could help people craft perfect moments in their lives. As much as I wanted to shift my car into reverse and leave, I couldn't; Joshua's hand was still stuck in my window. I was stuck. I pulled out my phone. "Look, can you just send me the link?"

"I could, but I really need to talk to you about this. In a way, it's a relief to know that you have one of these things. We can help each other out. Please, just come with me."

"If you think I'm going someplace with you, you're crazy." I paused for a moment. "I suppose we could go in the coffee shop, though, if you insist."

"Anita, I'm sorry. If I didn't have that—" he gestured behind him—"I would never suggest it. I promise I'm not some creep, and I kind of guessed after this meeting that there's something about me you don't like." He shook his head, then stared at me intently. "It's like you were already mad at me about something the first time we met."

"Well." I stifled a laugh. "We didn't meet for the first time at the office."

"What do you mean?"

I sighed and looked in the rearview mirror at the blonde, who was still next to Joshua's car. "That woman, she's your Negative Image, right?"

He nodded.

"She's your fiancée, Ainsley?"

He swallowed and nodded again.

"So, is it still your opinion that the people with Negative Images, people like you and me, did something to deserve it?"

He narrowed his eyes.

"That's what you said the day that we met. In the waiting room? At the hospital? My husband was in surgery because, according to some idiot, Dan stole his parking space." My eyes welled up with tears. "It's not even like it was marked as a reserved spot or something. But even if it was—"

I started crying harder and leaned over the steering wheel. I'd worked so hard to block out all the anger and sadness that came with this part of

Dan's death. I still couldn't believe that a parking choice had led to him losing his life.

Joshua patted my back—an awkward gesture through the car window—and a moment later, I heard him whisper, "It's gonna be okay."

I sat up straighter and wiped the rest of the tears from my eyes.

"Why didn't you say anything?" Joshua asked quietly, his eyes on the ground.

I shrugged. "I can't stand to talk about that time in the hospital, especially with the opinions you shared; I just didn't want to bring it up."

He nodded, eyes still on the ground. "I guess I can see your point."

Joshua glanced up at me with a crooked smile, and then we both caught a movement in the side mirror. Ainsley's Negative was on the move now. She walked towards my car in the flip book movement I'd seen with Carrie's NI. When I looked at Dan's Negative, he moved smoothly. Ainsley looked like bad stop-motion animation. She jerked a little as if something had shocked her and brought her back to life—or was trying to. Her red-lipped smile and swaying hips didn't match up with her gait. And then she sped up, closing the distance between her and Joshua until she was at my window, too.

She raised a hand in greeting, then placed it on Joshua's shoulder as if she were laying claim to him. Her black eyes looked flat and vacant, different from the shiny, inky look I saw in my Negative.

"Have you changed your opinion now that you have one?" I asked Joshua as I started my car.

"No, I haven't." He ran his hand through his hair in frustration. "I'm not the only one with that opinion, either. Please. If you won't come with me, will you at least follow me to my place so we can talk for a little bit without having to worry about anyone else?"

I glanced at the coffee shop in front of me. Going to the house of a man I'd just met wasn't typical for me. But what was normal about our shared situation? Besides, he made such an effort to talk to me; it must be important.

"Fine. But I'm driving myself."

Joshua pulled his red Nissan into the single-car garage. He lived in a duplex with a crisp white exterior. I'd imagined a larger home, a place where he and Ainsley would have started a family. I parked behind him in the driveway, got out of my car, and followed him inside. Joshua closed the garage door, and I followed him through a short hallway and a laundry room before we got to the living room. Ainsley's Negative, for the moment, was nowhere to be seen. While Joshua appeared polished, his home was a sty. The smell alone was overwhelming: spoiled pizza and stale air.

"Sorry about all this." Joshua stepped over several books and a pile of mail as he made his way through the room. "I haven't had anyone over in a while."

He continued into his kitchen, which looked slightly less like something had blown up but smelled worse. Joshua emptied his garbage can and took it back out through the garage, but the smell lingered like it had soaked into the walls and the furniture. I was dying to open the windows for little light and fresh air. A few moments later, Joshua returned and sat down.

He had a television on his wall by the kitchen table. I tried not to let my distaste show. I'd never enjoyed TVs in places where conversations should flow. Joshua leaned forward, his back hunched over and shoulders pulled up to his ears. He pulled up his DVR and quickly found what he was looking for.

He pressed play on our local channel, complete with downtown Omaha visible through the window behind the anchor, Paul Peterson. "Sad news from Argentina. Maria Vasquez, the first person to come forward with a Negative Image, has passed away. Although she was known to be a private person before her husband's NI appeared, she became even more reclusive once the presence attached itself to her."

The camera cut to an Instagram video.

"My mom was a very loving, very caring person. I would trust her with anything because I knew she would keep it in her heart for me." I recognized her son, Eduardo. When I'd seen him on the news, Dan had watched with me. "My mother left a note, and she gave very clear instructions for us. I could tell by her words just how passionate she was about this, how important it was that we share this with the world, so anyone else who is suffering as she did might have a better understanding." The young man took out a piece of paper full of creases, which had been folded over many times.

"Living with a Negative Image has become unbearable," he read. "People in my life who I trusted with almost anything, I cannot trust with this. It's a curse, a constant pain. What has been worse is the way I have been treated by my own family and friends. The phone calls are gone. The dinners are over. No one wants to look me in the eye anymore;

they're all ashamed to know me. He attacks me constantly, whether I am awake or dreaming. It's too much for me. I go now, with the hope that I might find peace somewhere else at last."

Eduardo folded the paper up again and put it in his pocket. "I had no idea what my mother was going through was so hard. My brother and I did our best to be there for her and help her through this. It's clear we didn't do enough."

Paul Peterson came back on screen. "Maria Vasquez took her own life two days ago. She was fifty-six. While the family has not gone into further details about her death, they have been transparent about the fact that their loved one chose to end her own life as a direct influence of having a Negative Image attached to her. On another note, no one has seen the Negative Image of the woman's husband since her death."

Joshua paused it. Peterson's face froze in a look of practiced concern. "Well?"

"Well?" I crossed my arms over my chest. Joshua continued to stare at me as if he had been expecting more of a reaction. It was, of course, a bit shocking and sad, but no more than so many of the other tragedies reported daily.

"Doesn't it bother you? I think the whole point of sharing this story was for everyone with one of these things to know what they're up against."

"No." I was determined to be optimistic. "I mean, I do see your point. It's kind of a cautionary tale, but I don't think it's being shared to make us feel hopeless. It might be a call to offer support to people like us."

Joshua laughed, an uneven, loud sound. "Wait till I show you the comments." He retrieved his laptop and pulled out a chair at the kitchen table for me.

NEGATIVE IMAGES

I shook my head. I was glad he'd removed the trash, but I didn't want to linger. "The internet is full of trolls. That doesn't mean it's how most people think."

"Don't tell me you've never left a mean comment before." He logged into his Facebook account and searched for Channel 4's Facebook Page.

"I haven't, actually." I leaned against the island behind me.

"You have no online presence? As an event coordinator?"

Legendary Events had an Instagram account, and I only used Pinterest so clients could share ideas with me. I hated posting anything, though. "Monica handles all the social media stuff for work."

With a sigh, he pivoted his laptop towards me. He'd pulled up the same video we'd just watched. The top three reactions people used were wow, sad, and angry.

"See how many people are angry?" Joshua asked. He had the demeanor of a prosecutor cross-examining a witness.

"At least more people are saying wow or sad," I pointed out.

"For now. Let's look at the comments."

"I really don't think that's an accurate way of gauging how people are feeling—"

"That's because you have a weird relationship with the internet." He scrolled for a moment. "Here's a good one. Angela says, '*She deserves to go to hell for killing herself. Clearly brought her husband's NI on herself.*'" Joshua looked up and shrugged. "That wasn't as bad as I thought it would be. Oh, here's one. '*Anyone with an NI should just off themselves and spare the rest of us from having to see* this *things. They're creepy AF.*'" He accentuated the misspelling for my benefit.

"No one would say that to us in real life."

71

"Maybe not yet." Joshua paused. "This is just the beginning. She was the first person to have one of these. Now she's the first to die."

"Maybe she'll be the only one to die." I rubbed my hands over my arms. "Someone on there must have said something positive. Neutral, at least." I pursed my lips as Joshua scrolled.

"Yes. You're right. Jessica Saunders. *'This poor woman! I can't believe she was so burdened she felt she didn't have any other way out than suicide. Clearly, we need to treat everyone who has these with more compassion.'*"

"See! I told you people weren't all so bad. I think that's why her son shared her letter. So other people will be kinder to us."

"Do you want to hear what people's replies to her comment were?" Joshua sounded practically devious. I knew he'd read them no matter what I said.

He cleared his throat. "*'Don't you get it? She killed herself out of guilt. Something she did caused her husband to come back as an NI, and she couldn't take it anymore. She deserved it.'* Next up, *'Everyone with an NI is going to wind up killing themselves sooner or later. It's probably the only way to get rid of them.'* Oh, here's a really sappy one. *'I feel terrible that she had to end her life, too, but I'm sure she felt like she was doing the right thing. Now her family won't have the burden of having someone with an NI in the family.'* More?"

I felt colder now than I had outside. "That's awful."

Joshua turned in his chair to face me. "Tell me you don't think things could get dangerous for us very quickly."

"If people *know* we have Negative Images, they won't be kind. But would they be dangerous? No."

Joshua let out a laugh and quickly covered his mouth. "What do you mean *if* people know?"

NEGATIVE IMAGES

"What?"

"Look. I feel bad admitting this, but I've been following this guy on YouTube. He shares videos of people."

"Oh, not him again."

Joshua gave me a quizzical look as he scrolled through the videos on his computer.

"The hospital," I reminded him. "You were watching videos that Greg somebody posted."

"Oh. Wow. I'd forgotten about that, but yeah ... I guess I've been keeping up with him for a while. Take a seat."

I perched on the edge of the dining chair next to him.

"Look, I really hate to do this to you, but I found this while I was waiting for the elevator after I saw your Negative Image in the office. It's the first thing that came up when I searched for you. He adds location info to his videos. I don't want to show you, but you need to know this is here."

He clicked play, and shaky cellphone footage showed a scared-looking teenage girl at the grocery store check-out counter and me fumbling with my wallet. Dan's Negative was behind me, looking at the camera and waving. While in person, I always saw him move fluidly, but in the video, he had that awful stop-motion quality to his movements, and I lost my breath. I saw myself drop my wallet, and the video zoomed in on Dan's Negative.

His black eyes gleamed when he moved, and the sharp fluorescent light hit them, a tiny little pinprick of white in that unnatural darkness. I clapped a hand over my mouth as I watched Dan's Negative wink—all for the benefit of the camera.

"Excuse me."

I ran for the sink and was just able to determine which side had the garbage disposal before I heaved.

Joshua followed me and brought out a bag of frozen peas. "Put that on the back of your neck. It helps."

I did as he suggested. He rinsed out the sink, ran the disposal, and got me a bottle of water from the fridge.

"Thank you."

"Sure. I'm really sorry—but things like this ... not knowing doesn't mean that it's not there."

"You're right. It's just ... I remember that day so clearly. It was the first time I had to deal with him. I honestly hadn't seen him before. And he just followed me around harassing me ... and I remember that kid. The video was shot from the bagging area. He was supposed to be bagging my stupid groceries, not filming me so I could get ridiculed on YouTube later."

"Yeah. I'm sorry." He guided me to the table, and I sat back down in the chair. So much for a quick exit.

"I don't get it, though," I pressed. "How can you go around in public, just living your life, without worrying about your Negative following you everywhere? When you saw mine at work, you looked startled, almost like you hadn't seen one before." I'd been speaking quickly and only just stopped myself from going on a full-on rant.

I forced myself to slow down and took a large sip of the water Joshua had given me. He was slightly red in the face, and I hoped I hadn't upset him.

Then he looked up at me and shrugged.

"Why do you think my place looks like this?" Joshua spread his arms wide, inviting me to examine the filth around me.

NEGATIVE IMAGES

I shrugged. It felt awkward being invited into someone's home when it looked so messy and, even worse, being asked to comment on it.

"It's obvious, isn't it?" Joshua flashed a wise-ass grin. "I can't open my windows. I can barely take my trash out on garbage days. She's always here. At first, I thought she'd be with me wherever I went. I thought that's how it worked. I didn't know they were ... selective. I used up all my vacation days and most of my sick days at work for the year, so I had to go. I had to show up. And guess what? It was heaven. She wasn't there. She was waiting for me when I got home, though." He laughed. "It's just so ironic."

"What?"

He waved my question away. "Another time, maybe." He looked at me for a moment, and his smile faded. "Today was the first day she appeared outside. And she's not here now, either."

"Maybe it's because you're home less often than you used to be."

"I don't know what to do about that. I have to work."

"How long have you had her?"

"I don't know."

I sat down in the chair next to his. "How do you not know?" After my fiasco at the grocery store, I didn't think I'd ever look at a package of Oreos the same way again.

"Everything after Ainsley passed away just feels like a blur. I remember coming home from the hospital. They'd worked on her for a long time, but in the end, she couldn't pull through. This place felt off to me even then, but I didn't see anything. Sometimes, I'd wake up in the middle of the night, and I thought I'd see her shape in bed next to me, but when I sat up, she'd be gone. Then, one day, she was just there. And she stayed."

Ainsley struck me as manipulative, her presence a slow burn or a long con.

I wondered if Ainsley had died on the same day as Dan or if she'd had more of a battle before she succumbed to her injuries.

My phone rang, and I was so lost in thought that I jumped. It was Monica, calling from her office phone. I debated for a moment before letting it go to voicemail.

Joshua looked at me, waiting for me to respond.

"Since she's spent most of her time here, do you think she's looking for a way to connect? Is that why you were thinking of having your event?"

Joshua shrugged. "I don't really know what I was thinking. I was hoping it might bring her some peace. Remember when I told you about the funeral? Honestly, I know Ainsley wouldn't have chosen any of it. It was surprisingly low-key, maybe because of the suddenness. I'm not sure. But, if you can tell from her wedding choices—"

"She wasn't subtle. She wanted the wow factor."

Joshua chuckled, then caught himself. "Yes. But then, I wonder ... would she make the same kind of choices for a funeral? Maybe it's not enough for her—what her parents chose, I mean. Maybe she's attached herself to me because I haven't grieved her properly."

"Wait," I said as I leaned forward. "What do you mean? Do you think if you had planned the funeral, she would have come back to one of her parents? I don't understand how her coming back to you is related to the funeral."

Joshua threw his hands up and walked away. "It's probably not. But on the other hand, what do I have to lose, Anita?" he asked, his back to me. "There's no solution for me. The wedding Ainsley planned will never happen. And I can't help but wonder if having some version of what she wanted would help her to, you know, move on. And it's right around the corner; it's not like I can postpone it."

I swallowed. He had multiple good points. If he was right, and the NIs were all back because of unfinished business, then this could help not only him but everyone. In his case, it seemed like a relatively obvious solution, too.

Of course, I couldn't help but think of Dan and wonder what unfinished business he might have. And with the aggressive nature the Negatives had, I wasn't sure it would be easy to find out. Maybe that was the point.

"Well? What do you think?" Joshua turned around to face me, looking so hopeful and somehow just as anxious that I couldn't disagree.

"I don't know, but like you said, you have nothing to lose."

His shoulders relaxed, and he took a seat next to me again. "So, you'll help me?"

"Yes," I said with a small sigh. "As much as I can. I mean, you did sign a contract with us, after all."

He held out his hand, and I shook it—the start of a tenuous alliance.

Chapter Eight

A few days later, I knocked on Joshua's front door, trying to juggle the fabric samples in my arms. Joshua opened it and welcomed me in.

"Come on in. Sorry about the mess. I think it might be a little better than last time, although it's hard to tell."

Joshua ran a hand through his hair and stepped back to let me in. He looked a little embarrassed, even though, as he had pointed out, I'd seen the mess before.

"No worries." I stood in his entryway awkwardly until Joshua seemed to remember that he should lead the way.

We went to his kitchen; his laptop was on the table, just like last time.

"Thanks for meeting me here. I didn't realize you'd have so many samples with you today—I wouldn't have made you go to so much trouble."

I smiled and nodded but couldn't meet his eyes. The last few days had been tough. Monica had been upset about how I'd handled everything with Tricia.

NEGATIVE IMAGES

"I really thought, after your NI showed up, that you would have found, I don't know, thirty seconds to mention it to Tricia." Monica had said when I'd gone in yesterday. "I ended up having to give her the rest of the day off."

"You're right," I'd said. "I definitely should have explained it to her, and I'm sorry."

I'd hoped that would be enough—usually, if Monica was upset, taking responsibility was all she really wanted. But that didn't quite seem to be enough now.

It wasn't so much the fact that I'd made a mistake or that Monica had seemed more distant after what happened with Tricia. There'd just been a shift in everything work-related.

"Are you okay?" Joshua asked. "You look upset."

"Oh, it's nothing." I tried to bat away his words like a fly before taking my laptop out of my bag.

"No, it's something. I struck a nerve, I think. I'm sorry. I didn't mean to."

"It's okay." I pulled out fabric swatches for the tablecloths and napkins from my bag.

Joshua handed me a tissue—quick to notice that I was holding back tears.

"Do you want to talk about it?"

I'd been dabbing my eyes, and I froze. We were in a similar situation, sure. But did I know him well enough to go into detail about this sort of thing?

I stared into his earnest brown eyes, still holding onto my crumpled Kleenex.

"I've been working from home a lot more lately," I spoke slowly, trying to test out how much I should say to him.

Ever since Dan's NI appeared at the office, he'd been showing up more often. It had only been a few days, but this thing had put me in a very awkward position.

"Our assistant complained about the NI being in the office. She didn't speak to me about it, just Monica."

"I'm so sorry."

I nodded, once again weighing how much to say and fighting the urge to spill the whole messy story.

"He has been around a lot, especially in cramped areas like the kitchenette and the shared bathroom in the hallway. Tricia basically said she was too uncomfortable to work around me. And, well, we need her help, especially since I'm not very helpful right now.

"She also told Monica that she thought it would affect our business." I let out a loud sigh. That, more than anything, bothered me the most. This wasn't Tricia's company; it was mine and Monica's.

"Has it affected business?" Joshua asked.

"No. Maybe."

Joshua's brow creased in confusion, and I couldn't blame him.

"See, Negative Images—in a general sense—have affected our business almost from the beginning. There's been fewer events, vendor issues ..." I shrugged.

Joshua looked lost in thought. He rose suddenly, and I got the impression that he had something else on his mind as he asked me if he could get me something.

"Water? Coffee? Tea?" He opened his fridge and stared at the contents. I noticed that it was almost as empty as mine.

NEGATIVE IMAGES

"Oh. Um ... tea would be nice."

Joshua shut the fridge door a little too hard. Half-empty condiment jars rattled against each other. As the door swung, I caught another flash of movement, and Dan's Negative appeared in the space where the open door had been.

"Ah. Company." Joshua's lips set together in a thin line, and I saw the muscles in his jaw clench as he got some herbal tea out of the pantry.

Dan's NI smiled at me vacantly. His eyes seemed darker and emptier than usual.

"Anyway," I continued. "I don't know for sure, but usually, if we have a client, I go into my little office and shut the door. A client wouldn't have seen him. I've been very careful. I don't see how he—" Dan's NI lifted a hand in greeting—"would have directly affected business."

Joshua was quiet, and I worried I might have blabbered too much. The truth was, I hadn't been able to speak to anyone about this. He may not have been the best person for me to talk to, but he was the only person I had.

"Joshua?"

"It sounds like Tricia knows she has leverage. Monica probably thinks that she has to take Tricia's concerns seriously; otherwise, she might be out an assistant."

"Plus, it means Monica wouldn't be stuck looking at this thing." Now that we'd talked all this through, I could easily picture Monica using Tricia's concern as a convenient way out of the situation for herself, too.

Dan's Negative grinned at me, flashing Dan's perfectly straight, white teeth. I turned away from him.

"That could be part of it," Joshua said. "I'm sorry, Anita." His back was to me as he filled the kettle, but his voice sounded dejected. "I've had my own share of complaints at work. Some of my coworkers are asking me to resign." Joshua spoke as though I'd dragged it out of him.

"That's drastic, isn't it?"

Joshua flicked a knob on his stove, and after some clicks, the fire jumped up. He set the kettle down and lowered the flame so it danced just underneath it. Was he the cook, or had it been Ainsley?

"Well." He turned to face me and leaned against the countertop. "Ainsley's been showing up a lot lately, especially during meetings. She'll literally sit down on the conference table. Or she'll sit in the chair next to me, which is awful when a real person needs to sit in it because the other spots are occupied. I don't know what's going on half the time. It's ridiculous."

"Can't you just phone in? Like from another room?"

Joshua let out a sigh. His expression was hard to read—he kept his eyes on the floor. I wondered if he thought it was a bad idea. Or, more likely, he'd already tried it.

He was still silent, so I pressed him a little. "Why do they want you fired? Why not just work from home?"

"Well ..." His voice trailed off. "Some of this you probably know."

I shook my head.

"The way Ainsley died ... it was very grisly."

This wasn't the direction I'd thought the conversation was heading. I stilled. "I knew she was in a car accident."

"It was a wreck. I don't honestly know how she made it to the hospital alive. It would have probably been a blessing if she'd died instantly."

I felt like I was missing something. "I don't understand why this would lead to your coworkers wanting you to resign ..." I'd seen Ainsley's

NEGATIVE IMAGES

Negative. She didn't look like someone who'd been in an accident, just as Dan's Negative didn't look like someone who'd been shot.

"It was my involvement in the crash." He spoke so softly that I wasn't sure what I'd heard at first. He still hadn't looked up.

I thought back to Dan's surgery. Joshua had annoyed me so much that day, but physically, he'd seemed fine. He couldn't have been in the car with her.

Joshua gulped, and his breath hitched unevenly as he spoke. "I thought you probably would have seen this if you researched me before taking me on as a client. I guess you didn't."

I couldn't imagine what he was going to say next.

"I was the other driver."

With terrible timing, the tea kettle whistled on the stove. I froze, gripped by Joshua's story. He didn't move; it was as if he hadn't heard it. I rushed to turn off the burner. The kettle's loud shriek became a whine before it quieted.

"Anita?" Joshua's voice was a whisper. "Say something. Please."

"I'm so sorry. That must have been awful." A morbid part of me wanted to press him for details. *Was he drunk? Was she? Whose fault was it?*

"Thanks." He finally looked up at me. His brown eyes were filled with tears, but he also looked relieved. "It was. I mean, it was bad enough at the time, but for some reason lately, a lot of people have been asking me about why we weren't together that night. As if two people can't have separate interests or something."

"Hmmm." I chewed on my lower lip as Joshua poured the steaming water over the bag of herbal tea, making citrus scents waft upward.

"Wouldn't it have bothered you?" he countered.

"Of course. Were you guys apart a lot of nights? Or was there something special about this night? Why would people even ask?"

"Well. It wasn't unusual for us to have different schedules, if that makes sense."

"Yeah, I get it. I have a lot of late-night events. Sometimes Dan helped out, but it was hardly quality time, and we were both tired." I sighed. I was trying to bring up a less-than-perfect moment for Joshua, but speaking ill of my relationship in any way felt like a betrayal.

Out of the corner of my eye, I noticed Dan's Negative Image shift to a more upright position, like a dog going into attack mode. Shit. I should've known better than to bring up our relationship. He walked over to me slowly, his black eyes boring into mine.

"Oh yes. Remember how we always talked about having a quiet night in? Learning how to cook back when we were dating?" Dan's Negative reached my side in three steps. "I wanted us to take a class. Do you remember?"

I nodded.

"It would have been fantastic. You doing the prep work, you know, chopping up the veggies." He leaned over the island, mimicking the quick motion of a chef dicing up vegetables. He continued his chopping motion, running his hands over mine as if he were slicing me up, too. As I watched him, the edge of my vision tinged with grey, and my hands started shaking. I took a step backward, and Joshua put a hand on my back to help steady me. My hand swiped the countertop, and the mug shattered on the hardwood floor. I gasped as boiling water scalded my legs and feet while steam rose from the shards.

"Look at you." Dan tsked. "So clumsy."

I swallowed hard and reminded myself that this wasn't Dan. Dan didn't care about cooking.

"I know, I know, you thought I didn't care about the cooking." Dan's Negative put his hands up in a gesture of surrender. "And you're right. I didn't. At least, not enough to make a big deal out of it. I always thought that you and I had more time. Time to do what I wanted to do, Anita. Or, you know, time to do at least one thing on our list. All of our little 'couples' activities were things on your agenda."

"My agenda?" I knew I shouldn't take the bait, but I couldn't help myself. "They were necessary things, Dan! We agreed that the house had to go at the top of the list. It's not my fault that it needed some work!" I wanted to push him; I had never been a physical person, not like this. I took a step, and a shard from my mug embedded itself in the ball of my foot.

I gasped and hobbled to the kitchen table with Joshua supporting me.

"I hope you're enjoying those paint colors. And the garden you didn't grow anything in last year. And the cabinets we stained." He stared pointedly at the trail of blood I'd left on the floor.

I was really crying now. Tears dripped onto my pants as I huddled over myself. He was spoiling everything. I saw Dan and I, messy and sweating, half laughing and half crying over the realization that we'd managed to paint a good portion of our baseboards because the painter's tape was too thin. Or ribbing each other about which podcast we should listen to and how ridiculous he found my obsession with *Serial* back when we were dating. We'd eaten pizza on the front porch when it was ninety degrees, just to escape the paint fumes in the house.

Had he really hated doing all of that with me? Was he so angry about the nights I worked events or the days I came home exhausted and just wanted time to myself?

Dan's Negative crouched in front of me, forcing me to look at him. "You just think about it. Do you remember my face every time we started a project? Did you catch the sighs of disappointment? Or were you too wrapped up in yourself to notice? I'll admit, I always thought I did a good job keeping you happy. I always thought to myself, 'Someday she'll repay me. Someday she'll put me first.'"

My pulse quickened. His nose practically touched mine as he said, "Even when I lay dying, I don't think you considered what I was feeling. It was just your own feelings and fears that you thought of."

I flinched as if he'd spat in my face and closed my eyes tightly, trying to block him out. When I opened them, he was gone.

Moments passed.

"Anita? Anita?" Joshua shook me slightly. "Are you alright?"

My mind was barely functioning. I had no words. I felt so tired. So old.

"Dan," I said finally.

"Dan's Negative."

"Right."

My breath was ragged, as if I'd just run a race. I leaned back in my chair and pressed a palm to my slick, sweaty forehead.

Joshua cleared his throat. "What happened? It was bad, wasn't it?"

I shook my head. "It was ... different. He brought up very specific instances. All these things Dan didn't get to do, and how it was my fault. And ... I think he had a point. But I'll never know if anything he said is true."

"Of course, it's not true." Joshua's voice was smooth and even.

"You're probably right. But it felt like this thing was speaking the truth. Like everything he said was the truth, and all my memories were a lie."

"That's what they do."

"So, all those weeks you spent at home with yours, did you feel the way I do now?"

"More or less." He paused. "I have a theory about this, actually. I think that in the beginning, they take time to observe us. I felt like Ainsley's Negative studied me to figure out what I missed the most about Ainsley. This Negative wanted to pack powerful punches, you know?" He let out a bitter laugh. "She brought up all these moments, some of the best moments of my life, and she's killed them for me now. I don't think I'll ever look back on them happily."

I shuddered. "Please don't say that. I was really hoping you would give me a pep talk. Tell me it gets better."

"I can't do that."

It was almost midnight, but I couldn't sleep. Instead, I limped into what used to be the dining room but now served as a makeshift office and opened my laptop. I hadn't been doing much—well, any—work while working from home. But now that Joshua had fully committed to his event, I had a lot to do with little time. I needed to review Ainsley's food choices and email the caterer. I doubted that all the guests who'd initially

RSVP'd would attend, and I needed to see if the amount of food could be reduced.

But instead, I opened my laptop and googled Negative Images. The news story and vicious trolls Joshua had shown me online stuck in my head.

Headlines echoed the story of Maria Vasquez's suicide. One article went into detail about the scientific research doctors and scientists were doing—apparently, MRIs weren't as helpful as doing an autopsy might be. My mouth filled with bile when I thought about how they'd take her apart piece by piece to find out what was different.

The search result that stuck out to me the most didn't mention her suicide at all. A YouTube video showed footage of her son.

"My mother was a very strong woman. She always had this calm, self-assured energy. But once my father came back to her, she changed. She stopped coming outside. She stopped calling. I think about her all the time. She was barely living her life at the end. And that's why I and my family agreed to donate her body to science—to help other people dealing with this problem."

He turned away and blinked a few times to clear the tears from his eyes. I paused the video. I couldn't watch it anymore. It was too easy to imagine someone saying the same thing about me. Only who would do that? Who would speak for me? My in-laws hadn't been in touch since the funeral. My husband was already dead. Tricia was exceedingly creeped out by me.

And the most obvious choices—my parents, Monica ... I sighed. I hadn't heard much from my parents since the funeral. They lived two states away. And while we'd never had a big fight or falling out, we'd grown apart. They were quiet people who led simple lives. And I'd wanted more. I'd wanted to create a life for myself that was full of friends and was worth celebrating.

I hadn't even told them that Dan had come back as a Negative. For that matter, I was pretty sure my in-laws didn't know either.

As for Monica, I'd created some friction between us. It may not have been wholly my fault. But it was still there. Something that would require more than a Band-Aid to fix.

I was about to click the back button to see the rest of the search results, but instead, my mouse hovered over the comment section.

My neighbor has one. I feel bad for her, but it's really hard for my kids to have to see that thing.

I wish my neighbor would move away. He makes no effort to hide it. We have kids, too. It's fuckin awful. Get it under control or go somewhere else!

It felt like a slap. Wasn't it obvious we had no control?

I need to know why these people have these NIs attached to them. Like, what the fuck did they do? They've gotta be some bad people man...

People are really overreacting to all this. Poor guy just lost his mom! It could happen to anyone. We need to be supportive and tolerant. You could be next!

You must have one if you're spouting all this feel-good shit.

We need a way to identify these people.

"If I were you, I'd click on that one." I saw Dan's Negative Image reflected in my computer monitor. His hands rested on the back of my chair. "See the link underneath that comment about identifying yourself?"

"What?" My voice rasped, and I cleared my throat. He chuckled at me.

"Well, you did Google this, right? And the whole point of that would be to know something. I think you'll find some interesting information on that website."

"I don't want to."

"Oh, Anita, I'm sure that's not true. You were thinking about it, weren't you? But suddenly, because I ask you to, you're not interested. Just click on it."

I stared at his reflection on my screen. "No."

"There was always so much you didn't want to do for me."

My stomach cramped. I did want to click on it. Everything he said was true.

I clicked. In my monitor's reflection, Dan's mouth split open in a grin.

The website was titled nidatabase.com. Below the masthead read, "It's up to us to identify them."

"Oh no," I mumbled.

"Oh, yes." Dan's Negative answered with a smile. "It's a good idea, isn't it? A directory of anyone living or dead associated with a Negative Image."

"How did you know what it was?" I turned in my chair to face him, craning my neck.

He shrugged and leaned over until he was centimeters from my face. Goosebumps covered my arms. My whole body felt cold—my lungs ripped apart by ice with each inhale. His black eyes glistened at my distress.

"Damnit!" I screamed. "Answer me!"

Dan's Negative opened his mouth wide and laughed. I stood to face him; I didn't realize I'd pushed my chair away until I heard it hit the floor.

NEGATIVE IMAGES

"What are you?" I was sick of this. Sick of being tortured by the love of my life, sick of having to relive every goddamn thing I'd done wrong in the last few years, sick of hiding in my house.

I leaped at him, swinging my fists to land a punch somewhere, anywhere. My arms flew through him. My legs tangled in the chair. Before I knew it, I was falling, my forehead smacking against something hard.

CHAPTER NINE

The house was dark, the light from my computer monitor glowing above me. Only a few minutes had passed, but it seemed longer. I tried to sit up but was too dizzy. I lay back down, and my phone poked into my hip. After twisting painfully, I was able to get it out of my pocket.

I needed help. I should have called Monica. Maybe it was the stupid reason I'd hit my head—lunging at something that wasn't there—but I dialed Joshua.

"Hello?" His voice sounded thick with sleep.

I must not have answered right away. Annoyance crept into his voice. "Anita? Is this a drunk dial? Really not cool—"

"Joshua?"

"Yes. What do you need?"

"I'm sorry to call you so late. I hit my head. I think I'm okay, but it was really weird ..."

I eased up from the floor and leaned against the wall. My head pounded harder with each movement.

"Can you come over?"

"She's a wreck."

"Should we move her? Try to wake her up?"

My eyes fluttered open. I heard two voices, but it should have been one. The light hitting my eyes was brutal. I took in Joshua, looking rumpled in jeans and a hoodie, and Monica, who somehow looked put together in a coordinated tracksuit. I hadn't called her, even though she was my best friend. I squeezed my eyes shut so I didn't have to look at her.

The two of them grabbed me by the arms and helped me to the sofa in the family room. My head lolled against my shoulder, and it was Joshua, not Monica, who seemed concerned about keeping my head still.

"Let's get her some water." Monica's authoritative voice was reassuring. I opened my eyes once I was away from the harsh lights. Monica took the lid off the ottoman and grabbed a blanket for me. Once I was tucked in, she touched the plump skin on my forehead, reaching out with one finger. She winced more than I did.

"What the hell happened to you?" She perched on the sofa next to my legs and took my hands in hers.

"I don't know."

"Try to tell us. Please?"

Joshua appeared next to Monica with a glass of water in his hand. I downed it.

"You didn't do this to yourself on purpose, did you?" Joshua's voice was stern.

"I didn't mean to. It was Dan—Dan's Negative. He was strange. Taunting." I remembered the eerie light shining from my laptop in the dining room. "Could you get me my laptop? I could show you."

Monica kept fussing over me. The vanilla and musk of her perfume made me feel nauseous, and I waved her away as Joshua came back, laptop in hand.

He held it out towards me like a strange beacon as Monica propped me up with a few pillows.

I frowned. The screen saver was still on. My computer usually showed photos of Dan and me, along with destinations we'd visited or wanted to visit. In the photo onscreen now, we looked fresh-faced and happy. We'd just started dating. I pressed the space bar to wake up the computer, but another photo slid onto the screen instead. Our whole relationship started to fade in and out of the computer screen, all in chronological order. The two of us at the church altar when we got married, our honeymoon in Turks and Caicos. Selfies, date night photos. Then it got weird.

A photo of us sanding down the kitchen cabinets before we stained them popped up. Dan didn't look particularly happy, but he could have been focusing on what he was doing. My back was turned to the camera. In the next photo, we were carrying cartons of Chinese food. Dan's mouth was set in a straight line and I was looking back at him. Then, there were some of us working at events I'd helped coordinate. Monica was in some of these, too. It almost looked like she was lobbying for Dan's attention. Meanwhile, Dan looked ... angry. I looked up at Joshua and Monica. They were squinting at the photos.

NEGATIVE IMAGES

"When were these taken, Anita?" Monica asked. She pointed to the event photo.

"I've never seen them before."

More photos flooded the screen. There we were in the hospital, Dan covered in blankets, resting, while I held his hand from the chair next to him. My eyes were two black orbs.

I screamed and pushed the laptop away from me. Monica grabbed it before it could hit the ground.

"Did you like my gift?" Dan's Negative appeared at the other end of the couch. "You always wanted everything to be picture perfect. Even in death."

"Go away! Stop it!" Joshua and Monica pushed down on me. I wanted to go for him all over again, arms swinging, legs kicking like a child throwing a tantrum.

He sighed. "I'll go. For now. You're no fun when you're hysterical." He vanished.

My whole body shook. I could barely breathe. Monica and Joshua shushed me, rubbing my arms and gently pressing my head back against the sofa cushions.

"He's gone," Joshua reminded me.

I nodded. I knew that, but what was it he'd said to me? *I'm always here. I'm always watching.* I covered my eyes with my hands like a small child trying to hide.

"We didn't take those photos." I pointed at the laptop, now sitting harmlessly on the coffee table, the screen dark. "The ones in the house ... the ones in the hospital." I pulled the blanket up under my chin. "I wouldn't have wanted any pictures of him like that. It's not right."

"What?" Joshua seemed alarmed, and with good reason, I thought. "I knew the last one wasn't real, but ..."

"The screensaver was all wrong, too. Usually, it's other pictures. It's like he took it over. How?"

Joshua and Monica exchanged a look, and I wondered if they thought I was crazy. Even for a Negative Image, this wasn't normal behavior.

"Does yours ever do anything like that?" I asked Joshua.

He shook his head. "No. At least not yet."

"Wait." Monica looked from me to Joshua. "When did this happen? You have one, too?"

Joshua ducked his head and rubbed the back of his neck. "Well, yeah. I do. It's my fiancée, Ainsley."

Monica offered me a Kleenex. My cheeks were wet.

"I suppose that's why you were at his house the other day." Monica sighed. "You know, you could have mentioned something to me, Anita. I'm on your side."

"I know, but ... I guess I just thought you should hear it from Joshua."

Monica glanced at him, then softened. "I suppose that's fair."

"What were you saying about the laptop, Anita?" Joshua asked.

"He wanted to show me something. A website. I'd been looking up news about people with NIs, and he just ..." I couldn't say what happened. I was embarrassed.

For a moment, I'd forgotten that he was a Negative Image playing tricks on me. I'd thought I could take him down in a tackle, even though I'd never tackled anybody before, least of all Dan.

Joshua picked up my laptop. "Do you mind if I take a look?"

I shrugged.

Within a few clicks, he'd found the website. "NIdatabase.com. Oh shit."

"What is it?" Monica got up to look over Joshua's shoulder.

"'If you have information on people in your area with a Negative Image attached to them, please submit it here. We verify every claim before updating our directory. If you have pictures, this process will be expedited.'"

"What? Is this even legal? Shouldn't this be a violation of privacy? I'd sue if I were on here." I was glad to see that Monica was sticking up for our rights.

"See if we're listed," I whispered.

Joshua typed. "I'm on here. Kind of. They list me as possibly having a Negative Image. Some fucker on here says, 'I can't get a picture of him with his Negative Image, and to be fair, I haven't seen it. But he's been behaving so oddly ever since his fiancée died. He barely leaves his house and never even opens his windows. He works downtown. If anyone can get a pic, that'd be great. Don't want one of those creeps in my neighborhood.'"

"Wow," Monica and I said at the same time.

"They list my company. And the name of my neighborhood. So, if anyone was bored enough, they could probably trail me during the day, hoping for some pictures." The room was quiet except for a few clicks as Joshua looked through the site. "You're in a different section, Anita. Confirmed NI. They have your home address, where you work ..." He paused and continued to scroll through the page. "They've got a link to that YouTube video I showed you. Pictures, too."

Joshua passed me the laptop and pointed at a section on the screen. There was my car, in my own driveway, and someone had captured

REBECCA SCHIER-AKAMELU

Dan's NI sitting in the back seat. I looked like myself—they had my profile—and I was probably concentrating on pulling into the driveway. But I didn't look frightened. It didn't look like anything out of the ordinary was going on.

"Keep clicking. There's more." Joshua and Monica exchanged another glance, and I was worried about what they'd already seen before handing me the laptop. I clicked the arrow, and the next picture slid onto the screen. I was about to get on the elevator at work. This picture must have been taken from the parking garage. Was it Tricia? Or just someone else in the building?

"I can't believe someone in our building posted this about you."

"I can't believe one of my neighbors did."

I hit the back button, not wanting to see any more information about myself. Joshua had filtered the website to results in Omaha, and I saw Carrie's name and picture. Underneath that, I saw the woman from the event that I'd seen in the parking garage. Her name was Destiny Wallace. I wondered who else I might know on the website; I couldn't bear to search anymore.

I passed the laptop back to Joshua. I didn't want to see anything else, at least not until I was feeling stronger. The bright light from the screen had seared my eyes.

"You probably have a killer headache. Do you think you can keep down some ibuprofen?" Monica asked.

I nodded. She went into the kitchen and came back a few moments later with two capsules and a glass of water. She'd been over a lot after Dan died, but I was surprised she remembered where I kept the Advil. She hadn't had to look—I would have heard all the cabinets opening and closing as she went through them. "Thank you." I swallowed the pills and sipped the water slowly.

"There's another section to this website." Joshua looked up at Monica, and she tensed. "It's for allies."

Monica rubbed her temples. "Let's hear it."

"It lists you as a likely ally. Monica employs Anita Matthews at Legendary Events despite knowing she has an NI attached to her. She's also working with Joshua Maguire as a client, who is listed on here as possibly having an NI.'"

"I'm not an employee," I griped.

At the same time, Monica asked, "Who would know that you were a client?"

She looked pissed off, but then she grew quiet, her hand covering her mouth. I realized she was scared because the only people who would have this information would be those who worked with us. A vendor or Tricia.

"They're just listed as EVJ72," Joshua said with a shrug.

"Why do they list the allies?" I asked.

Joshua raised an eyebrow.

"Look, I'm sorry if I'm a little slow, but I probably have a concussion, so cut me some slack."

"True. So, at the top of this page, they say, 'Although they don't have NIs attached to themselves personally, allies make life harder for the rest of us by supporting those who do. Avoid doing business and socializing with allies of people with NIs. Give your support to regular people just trying to get by instead.'"

"Oh great." Monica laughed. Her eyes grew dark, though, and I knew that no matter how much she was trying to laugh this off right now, she was someone who wouldn't just forget this or let it go. The idea that anyone might avoid her now simply because of her relationship with me—and Joshua, for that matter—made her cringe. She'd worked so hard to build up our business, and while I'd always respected her instincts, I can't say it didn't hurt to see the thoughts running through her head. I could practically see her weighing her friendship with me against this business and her reputation.

"Oh crap." Joshua scrolled and clicked through the site. "The guy who made it is the same guy I've been following on YouTube. Greg Patisis. He's been collecting all this information for a long time. I mean, he started posting about this right after Maria Vasquez's story broke."

I nodded. "You've mentioned him a few times. You liked him."

"Not anymore." Joshua scoffed and shook his head.

We sat in silence for a few minutes as Joshua clicked through the rest of the site.

"This makes things a lot worse. For all of us," Joshua said. "Anita." He ran a hand through his hair. His eyes were puffy. "Tell us again. What happened? How did you get hurt?"

I chewed my bottom lip, dragging out the moments before I answered. "I lunged at him. I just wanted to punch him. He insisted on getting me to look at that website, and I ..." My vision grew blurry, and my cheeks felt hot. I couldn't look at either of them. "I don't remember exactly what he said or did that got me so mad, but for a moment, I forgot what he was. Of course, I didn't hit him—there was nothing there when I lunged."

"Okay. So, he didn't physically hurt you."

"No."

"But he knew that this website existed ... and he manipulated your computer somehow to change the pictures on your screensaver. That's weird."

"Well, what's considered normal behavior for a Negative Image, anyway?" Monica asked. "I mean, I hear about these things constantly on the news. I know that the number of people stuck with one is going up and that they have weird black eyes and aren't physically present. No one can understand what they say except the person attached to them."

"Names," I corrected. "Other people can understand when an NI says their name."

"I haven't had mine interact with anything like that." Joshua pointed to my computer. Both of them looked at me as if I could somehow explain how or why Dan's NI was able to do what he did.

"Has Ainsley ever known about something that you didn't? Try to tell you about it?" I was hopeful that maybe Joshua would remember something she'd done that might be similar. At least now Monica's gaze was fixed on Joshua instead of me.

"I can't think of anything right now. I'll let you know if I do."

I sighed. They were both looking at me again, waiting to say something. I just wanted to pull the blanket over my head. "This is the first time that Dan—his Negative Image, I mean—has done this. Before, he would always just show up and threaten me."

"Ainsley doesn't threaten me. Not exactly."

"Well, what is she like? What does she do to you?" This was like when I had chickenpox as a kid. I'd caught it from my friend. Hers were mostly on her torso and hidden beneath her shirt. Mine were all over my face for everyone to see. I'd only seen Joshua's NI a handful of times.

"Ainsley is a lot like how she was in life," Joshua shrugged. "She's more upset, of course. Oh, and her simple presence is poisoning everyone I know against me." I could tell he was going for sarcasm, but his attempt to lighten the discussion only made me angrier.

"Mine threatens me directly. He says I'm not afraid enough yet and that I deserve this. I've almost gotten in car accidents a few times."

"I mean, mine makes me feel like a horrible person. Besides, I felt like a horrible person anyway because of the accident. You don't have to feel that way, at least."

"Why doesn't she torment you the way mine does?"

Joshua shrugged. "Maybe they're just finding out different ways of torturing us. I don't know."

"Has yours ever caused you to hurt yourself like mine just did?"

"No. I haven't had any physical injuries."

I put my face in my hands and massaged my temples. My head throbbed despite the medicine Monica gave me.

"Joshua, you've expressed the view before that people who have NIs must have done something to deserve them, right?"

"I did. Before I had one of my own."

"So now you've changed your mind? Even though, ironically, you're the one who actually did do something to deserve it? I mean, you fucking ran into your fiancé's car and killed her."

A vein pulsed in Joshua's forehead, and his hands clenched into fists. "Just this once, I'll give you a pass. You probably have a concussion. But I'll be damned if I race over here in the middle of the night to help you again." He practically spat the words as he walked past me.

Joshua slammed the garage door, and a moment later, his car started and then his tires crunched over leaves on the street.

Monica looked at me and sighed. "You know you've basically lost your only other friend now, right?"

"Shit." *What was wrong with me?*

Monica stood up. Her eyes were red and puffy with lost sleep. "I should probably go too, Anita. Do you think you'll be okay? Do you want me to help you upstairs?"

I shook my head and leaned back. "I'll just stay here."

Monica nodded and walked into the kitchen. She picked up her purse from the island.

"I'm sorry, Monica." Suddenly, I didn't want her to go. It felt like I'd fractured something between us, too, when I insulted Joshua. "I'm really sorry. I know this must be hard on you, too, and I didn't mean to wake you tonight. I had no idea Joshua was going to call you."

She shrugged and fiddled with her key fob. "It's no big deal."

I pushed myself back up onto my elbows. "Why *did* he call you?"

Monica stiffened and stood up straighter. "He couldn't get the door open. No key."

"Oh." I tried to get up, but my head thrummed with the sudden motion. "You don't have a key, though, either. You gave it back to me after the funeral. Remember?"

Monica opened her mouth and shut it. Then she shook her head as if to clear it and moved towards the door. "I remembered you kept a spare key in that fake rock."

"Oh." I tried to get up, but my head pulsed again in protest.

"No, no, stay where you are. And don't worry about tomorrow. You should rest." She looked worn out. So exhausted and almost frail.

I remembered Monica's face when she heard Joshua reading about her on the 'allies' page of the website. And how when I needed someone, she hadn't been my first thought.

"Monica?"

She turned around to look at me, her hand grasping the doorknob.

"Do you not want me to come in to work anymore? I mean, once I'm feeling better?"

She gave me a weak smile. "If you want to, of course. It's not like I'm your boss. I'm sorry if you thought I was mad at you. I do think you owe Joshua an apology, though. A big one." She sighed and opened the door. "If you need help with anything tomorrow, let me know."

The door closed behind her, and I was alone again. I sank down into the pillow under my head, and when I dreamed, I was surrounded by keys.

CHAPTER TEN

My eyes burned. Too much light seeped through the thin skin of my eyelids. I cracked open one eye—I hadn't closed any of my blinds last night, and a beam of winter sunlight shone right at me.

I'd been expecting messages or missed calls from Monica or Joshua, and I didn't have any. No one wanted to see how I was feeling this morning. I know I'd said a lot of things, but I was still a little surprised. And hurt.

I forced myself to get up, and while I was making coffee, I remembered the website. Thankfully, my laptop was just on the coffee table. A couple of quick clicks showed me the pages Joshua had gone over last night, and hitting back eventually took me to the comment section that had led me to the page.

And Eduardo Vasquez's last video.

If anyone knew what we were up against, it would be him. But how to reach out? After a lot of digging, my head was pounding, but I had an email address. I'd found it in several different comment sections online. I didn't feel great about reaching out—if people had disclosed it online like that, he probably had a lot of hate mail. I wasn't emailing him with hate mail, of course, but I wanted information from him, which still didn't seem right.

I added information to the beginning of the email to let him know that I had a Negative Image myself and included a link to the database. I asked a few questions, feeling bad knowing that others were probably asking him about it every day.

I wanted to know two things in particular: First, what he hoped an autopsy would show and when he thought they'd get results. Secondly, if he'd seen his father's NI since his mother passed and whether his father's NI had manipulated any technology like mine had.

It was difficult, but I finally sent it. I couldn't quite explain why, but it scared me to reach out like that. Perhaps it was a mixture of sending a message out into the world that admitted what I had or just the idea of seeking answers, but reaching out unnerved me.

It was almost as hard as my next task. After looking through the site, I remembered what I'd said to Joshua.

I'd blamed him for Ainsley's death, something he and undoubtedly Ainsley's Negative already did. It wasn't like me to be so vindictive. Dan's Negative must be poisoning me. Or, maybe it was just me. I'd been so mad to see all the details about myself on that website when Joshua wasn't even listed in the confirmed section.

I'd messed up. I'd messed up so badly it was probably beyond repair. As much as I hated to admit it, I needed Joshua. Somehow, in just a short period of time, he'd become a friend I could count on to be there for me, even in the middle of the night. And I couldn't stand the thought of him not being in my life.

NEGATIVE IMAGES

Eventually, I calmed down enough to call him and at least try to apologize. I dialed before I could talk myself out of it. The phone rang once, twice, three times. He wasn't going to answer.

"Anita." He said my name on the exhale of a sigh. He didn't want to hear from me, and I didn't blame him.

But he'd still answered.

"I'm so sorry—"

"I don't want to hear from you today, Anita, unless it's about the memorial. And I think you can just email that, right?"

"You're right, I could, but that's not the real reason I was calling, and I think you know that. I was just so upset, but I should never have taken it out on you. I know that sounds cliché, but I mean it. I was just so mad about having my whole life out there, and I snapped. Your life seemed so ... normal compared to mine, and I was jealous. Even though I know your Negative has taken a different approach. And I know that lately, she's been more visible at work. What I did was so wrong, and I'm—I'm incredibly sorry."

I could barely breathe while I waited for him to respond. I'd gone on such a rant, but I just wanted him to know that I meant it.

"Maybe it's just the power of suggestion," Joshua said, blowing past my apology, "but Ainsley's been harping on me all morning. She's much more aggressive than usual."

"How so?" I wasn't sure if I was forgiven.

"Well, basically, what you said last night. That it was my fault that she died in the accident. Nothing I didn't already know, but, you know, she has a different perspective than either of us. So, I got to hear all about the agony I caused her." Joshua's voice sounded off, as if he was trying and failing to tell this as a funny story. Or maybe he just didn't want to let his guard down around me yet.

A new thought made me feel even guiltier: The change in Ainsley's behavior could be my fault. I thought again of Dan's Negative Image. *I'm always watching.*

"Can you come over?" I asked abruptly.

Joshua made a weird noise. Was he stifling a laugh? "Are you serious?"

"Yeah. I have an idea I want to run by you."

"What's wrong with right now?"

I sighed and reminded myself again that I had called to make amends, not ask for favors.

"Sure. Do you think they watch us? You know, when they're not visible. It's just something Dan's Negative said. About always watching me. Otherwise, how would Ainsley know about our conversation? How would she know how to torment you with that information today?"

"I don't know." Joshua sounded skeptical, like he was brushing me off. "It's possible. I think I mentioned to you that my house felt different after Ainsley died, even before I saw her Negative."

I was just beginning to enjoy the normal banter of our conversation, and then we lapsed into an awkward silence.

"I'm gonna go for now," Joshua said. "Oh, how's your head?"

"Terrible. I think you were right about that concussion. Everything is too bright."

"Sorry. I had one once. You should avoid trying to read or watch anything. Try a podcast, maybe. And stay hydrated. At least, that's what my doctor said. You probably shouldn't go see yours, though." He laughed. "I'm really glad we didn't take you to a hospital last night. God knows how they would have treated you. I've heard the medical professionals, in particular, don't like having us in hospitals."

"What do you mean?"

"Oh, just, you know ... having a bunch of Negative Images in the waiting room isn't a good look. Too many dead people—high mortality rate and all that."

"Is that a serious answer?"

He was quiet for a minute. "Okay, you know what? Just stay put. I'll bring you coffee and something to eat if you can get up to let me in."

I wanted to question him or at least say thank you, but he'd already hung up. He'd been so mad—and rightfully so. How was he able to set that aside so quickly?

I thought again about last night and how Monica came because she knew where I kept my spare key. I wanted to ask him about it—after all, wouldn't he have seen where she got it from? But instead, I texted him the code for the garage door.

I leaned back against the pillows on the sofa. I should get dressed and brush my teeth, but the pull to burrow myself in a cocoon was too strong to resist. I rolled over, away from the bright light, and closed my eyes. The wind gusted, making the windowpane shake. Something creaked upstairs. Dan. No, he's gone. The sump pump in the basement ran, then stopped. The heat kicked on, and in the quiet moments between the sounds, a heavy silence settled in. I wanted to open my eyes, but I couldn't. I burrowed further, squeezing my eyes shut like a small child. Each sound was too loud, too near. *He was here.* My heart thudded, and my breath came faster and faster. Tears leaked out of my eyes, and my hands began to shake. I thought I might burst, but I couldn't bear to open my eyes; I couldn't make a sound. If I could just stay here—quiet—I'd be safe. Some rational part of me knew that wasn't true, but that part was a million miles away.

The garage door rumbled as it rose. Then I heard the other door open. Joshua must be here. But I still couldn't sit up or open my eyes. I was on the verge. I just knew if I opened my mouth, I'd start screaming. The garage door gave a loud bang as it descended, and my heart leaped again. Footsteps sounded in the kitchen; then, I heard a faint gasp.

"Anita? Are you here? I see your, um, friend."

I still couldn't answer. My hands shook, clutching swathes of the blanket. Someone grabbed them. I pulled back. I had to stay covered. I had to stay safe.

"Anita? It's Joshua."

He pressed his hand over one of mine and pried the blanket from my grasp. "Jesus. What did he do to you?"

I still couldn't make a sound, but I forced myself to take deep breaths. One, two, three. In. One, two, three. Out.

Finally, I opened my eyes and looked up at Joshua. Dan's Negative hovered over his shoulder, leering, too many of his teeth gleaming in his wide grin. My face grew hot with shame. Dan's NI hadn't said a word or made a sound, but I'd been so terrified I hadn't been able to move.

"Anita?"

"Sorry." I made myself focus on Joshua. His brows were pulled tight together. "I don't know what happened. Honestly."

Joshua glanced over his shoulder and then turned back to me. "I have a good idea. I'm guessing he tried one of Ainsley's tactics." He reached for a cup on the coffee table. "I hope it's not too cold."

"Thank you." I took a sip. He'd gotten me some kind of latte. Usually, I drank black coffee, but with my nerves fried, I was glad for something a little sweeter.

"Sometimes, especially early on, just being in Ainsley's presence gave me a panic attack. A lot of times, she'd get so close, especially when I was just waking up. The first thing I'd see was her face, hovering maybe an inch above mine. It was paralyzing. And then, other times, I thought I was having a heart attack. It was like ... somehow, she changed the mood of the entire house."

My gaze had drifted to the window, but now my focus snapped back to him. "I'm so sorry for what I said yesterday. I had no idea what you'd been dealing with, and now, I guess I do." I gestured to Dan's Negative, still silent. He fixated on me, his head moving whenever I did. He was practically mirroring me in order to stay in my line of sight.

Joshua nodded but didn't say anything.

"Please forgive me. I never knew your fiancée, and I certainly didn't know anything about your relationship."

Joshua's jaw clenched. "No. You were right to assume."

I waited and took another sip of my latte.

"I didn't kill her. Well ... what I mean is that it wasn't intentional. Ainsley was a very sociable person. It was typical for her to go to happy hour with her work friends, and she usually didn't invite me along. I work long hours sometimes, so it wasn't always a big deal.

"The night she died—it was a Thursday. She'd been at a sushi place with three of her friends. They said she had sake bombs and a California roll. One of them told me that she hadn't seen Ainsley eat much during the day, and then she obviously didn't eat much at the restaurant. I mean, a California roll isn't filling, right?"

He gave me a half smile, which I returned. Then, he drank some of his coffee, perhaps to give himself a moment before continuing.

"She called me to come get her. But my phone was on silent. I don't know why she didn't just get an Uber or ask a friend to drop her off. Her friends said that when she couldn't reach me, she stopped drinking. I guess to sober up."

Joshua's eyes were distant, his tone of voice bitter.

"I stopped for a burger on my way home and was on the same road she was, which is the worst thing. I mean, I was coming from one direction, she was coming from the other, and I hadn't gotten to our turn yet. She'd driven past it."

Tears welled up in his eyes for a minute, but after a sniffle, he pushed ahead with his story.

"I didn't know it was her when it happened. It's a narrow road, and she drifted into my lane. I honked and swerved to the shoulder, but she just kept coming. There are all these trees right up to the side of the road, so I couldn't get off the road without running into something. I thought the best thing was to speed up and get around her quickly. But she hit the back half of my car.

"She wasn't wearing her seatbelt and got ejected through the windshield. I still feel so stupid, but even when I called 911, I didn't realize who I'd been in an accident with. I mean, it was dark, and the car was obliterated. Even when I told them about it, and I said it was a silver Honda Civic, I never thought it could be *her* Civic.

"Then I was stumbling around in the dark, trying to find her. I told the dispatcher she wasn't in the car, and he asked if I saw her but told me not to move her or even touch her. When I finally found her, her face was half in the ground. She looked so ... anonymous.

"Black pants and jacket. Shoes gone. Somehow." Joshua's voice grew husky, and he took a moment to contemplate the coffee cup in his hands.

"I saw that she had blonde hair, but so many women have blonde hair." He looked up at me and gave me one of his ironic smiles. "Not you, though."

I ran my fingers through my hair subconsciously. He continued.

"Police came at the same time as the ambulance. They took my statement. Then the EMTs turned her over, and I saw ..." He swallowed and looked away. When he spoke again, I could barely hear him. "Her face. She was bloody, especially on one side, but I could tell it was her. Of course, the cops were instantly suspicious.

"I wasn't charged with anything, but they interrogated me for a long time. It wasn't until the next morning that I made it to the hospital. I'm amazed I made it there at all. But people still blame me, I think."

"She was drunk."

He shrugged and ran his thumb along the grooves in the lid of his cup. He looked up at me then; his eyes were hard and unforgiving. "Ainsley was drunk a lot, apparently. But I didn't notice. When I think about it now, there were signs I missed ... at the very least, I should have noticed how much she drank when we were together. Sometimes, I did think it was excessive. But I never said anything to her about it. I didn't want to cause trouble.

"Her parents are sick over it. Understandably so." His hand shook as he put his empty cup down. "They used to like me. I thought they respected me and trusted me. But they've always asked why I wasn't charged. It's hard to tolerate someone when they want you in jail. Even though she was very, very drunk, they keep insisting it can't be that bad.

Sometimes, her mom says they must not have accurate results; they keep denying that part of it. And they just can't stomach me."

"The memorial. Is it for them?" I had a sudden urge to hold Joshua tightly. In my own loss, I'd felt nothing but love, comfort, and sympathy. People trod carefully around me and gave me a wide berth to process my grief. I couldn't imagine what it was like to grieve while people suspected you were a killer.

I took in the worry lines on Joshua's face, the redness in his eyes from tears or another sleepless night. His back was slouched. He looked nothing like the imposing figure I'd seen in my office the day Monica put me in charge of his event.

And I'd contributed to mowing him down with the hateful things I'd said to him.

"The memorial *is* for Ainsley. But, I suppose, it's also for them." He shook his head as if trying to get a particularly unpleasant thought out of his head. "I don't think they ever really thought I was good enough for her. And, now that she's gone, I guess I proved them right."

The corners of my eyes pricked with tears. Joshua's face looked pinched; his mouth twisted in a grimace. He looked away from me, and I dabbed the corners of my eyes, embarrassed at crying over his story.

"Even though I can't change what happened," Joshua continued, his voice unwavering, "I want them to know that I loved her, that I miss her."

I reached towards him and gave his hand a squeeze. "I'm so sorry, Joshua. For everything."

"It's okay. I can't blame you. We all say things we regret when we're not at our best. I mean, I've definitely been more of an ass now than I ever was before." He let out a harsh laugh.

NEGATIVE IMAGES

A loud, garbled sound broke through that startled us both. When I looked up, I saw Ainsley. It sounded a little like she was trying to speak underwater. Her hand was on her hip in a defiant gesture. Then she focused on me, and even though I was becoming used to the blank, black gaze when it came from Dan's Negative, hers had a different effect on me. It was like looking into a pit. Maybe it was because I couldn't understand her, but at that moment I felt threatened.

Joshua turned bright red.

"What did she say?"

"She says I'm really doing the memorial for myself so I can feel less guilty about what I did to her. And that I never would have brought her coffee if she wasn't feeling well. She also says the memorial won't make her leave."

I glanced at him—the thought had crossed my mind, too.

"I *had* kind of hoped ..." He shrugged. His face was red. "No one has gotten rid of theirs. Have they?"

It was a sign of desperate hope that he was asking *me*. I obviously wasn't as informed about this as he was.

"I emailed Eduardo Vasquez. I thought he might have a better understanding of Negative Images than just about anybody else," I said.

Joshua gave me a big smile. "I'm shocked. It doesn't seem like you to reach out to a stranger like that."

"It's not. But I don't want to live like this."

"The only problem is that his mother never did get rid of hers ... maybe we should reach out to other people listed on that website," he suggested.

"It's not a bad thought. We can find out what other people have tried."

"How about her?"

My head was pounding. We'd been searching through the list of people on the NI database for two hours. At first, we just called every person, starting with others listed in Nebraska. I'd told him about the woman from the parking garage that I'd recognized, Destiny, but she hadn't answered. Despite that, we kept going, wanting to take advantage of our NI's absences, even though most people didn't want to talk.

"Julia Crowley. Iowa. Worth a shot, I guess." Joshua didn't sound hopeful.

I dialed her number.

"Hello?" The woman who answered sounded tired and frail.

"Hi, is this Julia? My name is Anita, and I was hoping I could talk to you about the NI database? We have—"

I heard shuffling sounds and a muttered conversation before a man's voice spoke through the phone.

"Julia doesn't want to talk to people like you. She's had enough heartache. It's a terrible thing to lose a child, no matter how old they are. And it's ten times worse knowing that our daughter's not at peace. How do you think I feel, knowing that our only child came back for her?"

Joshua jumped into the conversation. "That's exactly the kind of information we'd love to hear about. We're also victims of this website, and we believe the only way to counteract it is by posting our own information about what it's like to live with a Negative Image. Plus, a list of strategies others have tried to get rid of them. People blame us all the time, but no one understands unless they have—"

"No, you don't understand!" I recoiled from the phone as the man shouted. "We've talked to people just like you. That Greg Patisis—promising us a sympathetic ear and a positive side to our story. You know what? It's bull! They take what we say and make everything even worse. They paint Julia as a bad mother and grandmother. They speculate about whether she was neglectful or abusive when our daughter was younger. They mock our pain, and I won't give you any ammunition to use against us!"

He hung up, and Joshua and I let out twin sighs of defeat.

"No one has ever called me to ask about my NI," I said. "It's weird. I really thought that people would be glad to hear from us, to take control of what people are saying about them. But they're all just so ... scared."

"I haven't gotten anyone calling me either, but maybe it's just because we haven't had ours as long. I mean, look." He pointed at a date on Julia's page.

My mind was stuck on Julia's husband. Sure, he'd been mad about us calling, but when he spoke of their daughter, I'd caught a hint of something else. Jealousy, perhaps?

Joshua clicked through different pages, comparing our information. "You and I have only been listed on the NI database for about a week."

"Still ... the idea that someone is just reaching out and harassing people on top of the website just seems a bit much. I mean, the website is very damaging as it is."

"It would be better if we could visit people in person," Joshua mused. "That way, we could actually prove that we are who we say we are."

I squirmed a little in my seat and tucked a strand of hair behind my ear.

Carrie had been on my mind. She was the ideal person to contact. We already knew each other, and she was nearby, which made her the best choice we had.

But, on the other hand, she'd never returned my calls or emails—or Monica's. And I'd run out on her when she was in a vulnerable position. Sometimes, I still thought about that meeting and wondered what she would have done if Monica or I had been the one to get an NI.

One of the things that always impressed me about Carrie was how she managed to help others almost effortlessly. Would she have held her composure and offered water or a shoulder to cry on? Or would she have run, too?

I'd wanted to get Carrie's business, not just because we needed it for our company, but because I truly admired her. In a way, I envied her.

"I think," Joshua said slowly, eyes still on the screen, "that we'll need to look at people who don't have confirmed NIs or people who are out of state. Unless you want to look again at the ones we'd vetoed first to see if there's anyone we should reconsider."

Our veto list consisted of people who seemed hard to reach, like Kim Brandt, the anchor Dan liked. But when I saw Carrie's name on the confirmed list, I'd insisted on vetoing her, too, telling Joshua only that she was a client. I hadn't told him anything more than that.

He gave me a questioning look and waited patiently for a reply. I let out a shaky breath and turned to face him.

"Maybe we need to prove to people that we're reaching out because of the reasons we're stating. Maybe we should wait until after your event." I'd had this thought a little earlier, but it seemed mean to suggest it at first—it felt like offering Joshua as bait.

"How would they know, though? You mean ... record it or something?"

I let out a sigh, glad that he'd said it instead of me.

"What do you think? You suggested sharing what others had tried. This is a pretty big attempt ..."

"We'd have to put it on YouTube. Maybe some other social channels. We might as well."

I was surprised by the lack of emotion in his voice. He spoke so matter-of-factly.

"But are you okay with that?" I pressed.

"You said it earlier when you mentioned Eduardo. We can't live like this."

Chapter Eleven

I was grateful that there were still three days before Joshua's event. It bought me a little time to get comfortable with our online plan. I still didn't love it—I never would—but it made me feel better knowing I didn't have to be in this initial video. Joshua created accounts for us and even posted some teasers on Instagram about his upcoming event.

I'd been obsessively checking my email, hoping for a response from Eduardo, but there was nothing yet.

Finally, the day arrived. Joshua was disheartened by the number of people coming. Ainsley and Joshua's guest list was made up of at least seventy percent of her friends and family. In fact, from what I could tell from names alone, Joshua hadn't invited any family. But he still had around 50 people coming. Crucially, Ainsley's parents had decided to attend. I knew the memorial event was for them as well as Ainsley, but it was nerve-wracking to know they'd be in attendance.

The memorial would have made a lovely wedding reception, and seeing it all come together made me hope that Joshua was right and this would give Ainsley closure so she could leave.

If only it would be that easy to get Dan to go. I couldn't imagine a service for him that I hadn't already had. I'd planned his funeral the best I could, knowing how he felt about certain things, so it would leave me in a perplexing situation if Joshua turned out to be right.

Joshua greeted each person who came in with a warm handshake and a smile, but I could tell it was stressful for him to hold it together. People were trickling in slowly. I watched as Joshua greeted a couple in their 60s. He looked especially stiff, and they seemed like they would rather be anywhere else in the world. These must be Ainsley's parents.

I kept to the back of the room, observing and ready to offer any help. Monica was here, too, but in charge of filming.

"Can you believe he did this for her?" a woman whispered at one of the back tables.

"No. But also, oddly, yes?" said another woman who must have been her friend.

They giggled.

"Same," said the first woman. "I just can't tell why he's doing it. If I were Ainsley, I wouldn't forgive him for running me off the road. He should be in jail."

"Shhh, Jess, not so loud," the second woman hissed.

"I'm just saying. It's like he's trying to buy her off."

"Look, regardless of what you think of him, we're here for Ainsley, remember? In case this turns out to actually help her move on, we want to support her."

I walked away from them as they looked at the menu. Ainsley's friends were sharp and quick; I'd have to watch out for them. I scanned the room and approached the entrance to see Joshua.

121

"Most of the attendees are here," I said. "You might want to go up and say a few words of welcome and then maybe offer the microphone up to others who want to talk about Ainsley."

He nodded, jaw locked, and approached the makeshift stage by the quartet. As he picked up the microphone, Ainsley's NI appeared. People gasped in surprise, even though they, of course, knew what she was. "Thank you for coming," Joshua began, but it was hard to hear him over Ainsley's NI's shrieks coming through the microphone. It was a horrid, mangled static, worse than any normal microphone feedback. Joshua lifted the mic high in the air and put it on the stool before stepping away from it with his hands raised. "Um, I don't think Ainsley wants me to do much talking tonight, but please come forward to share your memories of her throughout the dinner." The string quartet had stopped playing. Otherwise, I don't think anyone could have heard him.

The room's attention seemed split between Joshua at the mic and Ainsley's parents, who had chosen a table in the middle of the room. Ainsley's mother was openly weeping.

After Joshua's introduction, it was a long time before anyone was brave enough to speak. The room had a tense atmosphere with her Negative Image watching over what should have been her wedding reception. Eventually, a brave soul stood up and walked to the mic.

"Hi." The man gave a small, awkward wave. "I, uh, I guess I'll introduce myself. I'm Caleb, a friend of Joshua's. We've been friends since high school, and one of the things that always struck me about Ainsley was her cheerful nature. She was a sweet and warm-hearted girl, and I know she was looking forward to starting a life with Joshua. Ainsley, I hope you can see that Joshua is still trying to make you happy, even now."

NEGATIVE IMAGES

There was a small smattering of applause, and Caleb hugged Joshua afterward—one of those manly ones with the clasping of arms. It was quieter immediately following his short speech, leaving it all the more obvious that Ainsley's two friends had found something to be upset about. It wasn't much—just whispers and snickering as they hid their faces behind their hands, but I wasn't the only one to notice it. As more people stared at them, they quieted down, duly chastised.

A woman came up next. She had long brown hair that she kept moving out of her eyes as she spoke. "I'm Kim, a friend of Ainsley's from college. Ainsley was a driven person. She was outgoing and friendly, and what I remember most about her was how she'd go out of her way to get you to loosen up if you were a little uptight. She was like a stress reliever in human form." She chuckled. "But I will say, I don't think I—or Ainsley, for that matter—" She gestured at Ainsley's Negative, who must have said something in response. Kim looked taken aback amidst the staticky sounds. "Um. Sorry. Right, I was saying that I don't quite know if this will give Ainsley what she needs, but she's here to see it, so here's hoping."

A few other people approached the mic and formed a short line. The mood started to shift away from memorializing.

"I don't think this is right," another of Ainsley's friends said into the mic. She got a smattering of applause for her remark. "I don't think she would have wanted this—it's just a mockery of what should've been her wedding day. And to be honest, Joshua, I thought more of you than this. Ainsley was already laid to rest, and this seems like something you aren't doing just to honor her."

Ainsley's mother nodded emphatically.

I walked toward the stage but was too far away to get there before another woman grabbed the mic.

"I think what Joshua is doing is very honorable. I think it's obvious that he's doing it for Ainsley—he doesn't like seeing her like this and is doing everything he can think of to help her move on."

I finally made it up to the mic and asked for it. "I'd just like to remind everyone that the reason we're here is to pay tribute to Ainsley, and if need be, I'll moderate this to make sure that that's what we're coming up here to say."

Suddenly, no one wanted the mic anymore; debates about the merit of the event were happening at each table.

"What is he playing at?"

"If she was already given a funeral, how is this gonna help her?"

"I think he's just doing it to try to get rid of his NI."

"It's a nice gesture, and I can understand why he did it."

"It's a kind way to mark the occasion, I think."

While at other tables this might just be lively dinner conversation, the two women I'd noticed earlier were getting more vocal.

"If he'd really cared, he would have been there when she called. But he put work first, again," said the one called Jess.

I looked around for Monica—this was getting out of hand. I didn't see her anywhere. I was shaking as I went back to the front and picked up the mic.

"We can appreciate that everyone here has opinions, but we respectfully ask that you discuss them after the event. As someone who has worked closely with Joshua to put this evening together, I can tell you that his goal has been to honor Ainsley. He kept as many of her reception choices as possible this evening so that so that all of you could still experience what she wanted. If anyone would like to share memories of Ainsley, please come forward."

NEGATIVE IMAGES

For a moment, there was silence. Then Ainsley's father stepped forward. My hand was still shaking as I passed him the microphone. He'd come here, which was hopefully a positive thing, but I was worried about what he might choose to say.

"I'd like to thank everyone who came this evening," he began, as though it were his event and his idea. "It means a lot to me to know that so many of Ainsley's friends are concerned about her finding peace and gaining closure. It's been a horrible thing to know that my daughter has come back as a Negative Image. I've spent countless nights praying for her spirit.

"Ainsley was an extrovert. She loved people, loved making new friends and learning about others. When she and Joshua shared their engagement with us, I was a little surprised. Joshua, for those who don't know him, can be quiet. But, I thought they could balance each other out nicely."

He paused and dabbed at his forehead.

"Joshua assured me that he would always take care of my Ainsley. I suppose, in his own way, he's trying to do that through this event. Of course, not everyone knows—" His voice cracked, and he paused to compose himself. "Not everyone knows all the circumstances surrounding Ainsley's death. And the truth is that Joshua knows them all too well. And I can't help but wonder if my daughter had chosen someone else ... if she might still be here today."

There was more murmuring around the tables, but Ainsley's dad wasn't done.

"But, I know there's nothing I can do about this now. I just ask you to be kind to one another and think of my little girl today."

He took his seat, and I watched him rejoin his wife, who gave his hand a squeeze. I glanced at Joshua, sitting at his own table with just two other people. The one who'd come up to speak first was leaning over—it looked like he was trying to whisper some words of encouragement. Joshua's face was red, and unless I was mistaken, he was holding back tears.

I'd gotten stuck holding the mic, and as I stood there awkwardly, combing the crowd for a sight of Monica, I heard Dan's Negative.

"I don't think this event is one of your best," he hissed, his mouth on top of the mic. "I'd rate it a zero out of five stars."

People clapped their hands over their ears, and I realized they must have gotten another dose of bad feedback from the microphone. I put it down carefully. Luckily, I'd caught sight of Monica, who was still filming.

But, to my horror, I realized she wasn't the only one. We'd planned to upload a selection of clips from tonight, but we wouldn't be able to control this narrative.

I joined her at the back of the room. "Should we pull the plug? Try to end it early?" I whispered.

Monica looked unsure, which was a first. "I don't know, Anita. I think you should ask Joshua. It's only been a half hour, and the entrees haven't even been served yet."

"I doubt he'll care about the food, but I'll ask him."

I was making my way over when someone else grabbed the mic. One of the women from that back table. Jess. She tapped it with her hand as if there were any questions about whether it was working.

"I want to talk about Ainsley," she said. "She was one of my best friends. And she was always down to hang out after work. But do you

NEGATIVE IMAGES

know why she was? Why she was always free? 'Cause her fiancé was too busy."

Shit.

Jess swayed on the stage. She was drunk.

"He was always working. And I think she was lonely. I think she just needed a connection, you know?"

I walked as quickly as I could to the front, but it felt like an agonizing amount of time.

"If she were here today, I don't know if she'd be really happy, you know? Like, I know she wanted the wedding and she was so excited, but after that? I don't think so. She just needed to be around people, 'cause she was just such a nice person. Really nice."

I'd finally reached the front and took the microphone gently from her hands. I turned it off and motioned to everyone to be quiet.

"At this point, we'd like to thank you for coming, but we're going to ask everyone to please head home at this time," I said as loudly and as clearly as I could.

Dan's Negative talked over me the entire time. Of course.

"Fail. Fail. Fail. You failed, Anita. No one in their right mind will work with you now, Anita. And you sure as hell didn't solve any problems today."

Heat rushed to my face as he spoke, and I watched everyone stand up. No one needed to be told twice. The only person I didn't see in the crowd was Joshua.

It was only after everyone left, including Monica, that I saw him. His eyes were redder than I'd ever seen them, and his whole body looked like it was vibrating in shock.

"Joshua. I'm so sorry."

He didn't say anything—he just stared at the empty room, the uneaten food, and sad-looking decorations.

I went up to him and wrapped my arms around him, and after a few moments, he hugged me back.

CHAPTER TWELVE

I paced back and forth in front of Joshua's front door. It was freezing, by far the coldest day we'd had so far, and my teeth chattered. "Joshua?" I rang his doorbell again and banged on the door.

I'd barely heard from him the rest of the weekend after the memorial, and I was worried. I heard shuffling footsteps and was relieved to hear the door unlocking.

"Anita. Hey."

"Hi. Can I come in? I brought some things for you," I said, gesturing to the grocery bags on the porch.

"Sure."

He stepped aside, and I made my way through with the bags. He plopped himself down on the sofa and barely seemed to care as I went through his cupboards to unload the food I'd brought for him. I'd seen him upset before; I'd seen him when he was unsure. But I'd never seen him quite so reserved and distressed.

"How are you?" I asked as I sat next to him. I'd drawn my own conclusions about his wellbeing, but I wanted to get him to open up.

"I know you didn't get what you hoped from the event," I said after a moment. "I'm so sorry."

"Thanks," he said after a long pause.

"What can I do for you?" I asked when it was clear he wasn't planning on saying anything else.

"Nothing. There's nothing anyone can do."

I'd seen the videos online. Ainsley's friends posted them—big surprise there—and none of them were very flattering to Joshua.

"We could post some of the speeches that your friends gave."

"You mean the one speech?" he asked.

I shrugged. "I think there were two." I was trying to lighten the mood, but it didn't work. "I was just thinking we could follow through on your idea. You know, sharing tactics that others have tried to get rid of their Negatives. Maybe today, we can try reaching out to more people from the database. I could contact the woman from the parking garage again. Or we could focus on people who've had their NIs the longest."

Joshua stayed silent, his expression unreadable.

"I know your memorial didn't work out the way you wanted it to. But we still learned something about these things: they don't seem to be looking for closure. That's important."

Joshua finally turned to look me in the eye. I still couldn't tell what he was thinking. "'Didn't work out the way I wanted it to?'" he said, throwing my words back at me. "It was a fucking disaster, Anita. I never should have gone through with it."

"You said it yourself earlier, though. What did you have to lose? I know it didn't give you what you wanted, but at least you tried. I think that's so important."

NEGATIVE IMAGES

He let out a sigh. "I don't know. What was I trying to do? Get Ainsley's friends to be even angrier with me? Get her father to hate me more than he already does? If people didn't blame me before, they do now."

"For what it's worth, I don't blame you. And I heard what everyone there had to say, and I've heard the story from you. It wasn't your fault."

I grabbed Joshua's hand in mine, and he squeezed so tight that my knuckles cracked.

"Can you stay awhile?" he asked.

I nodded. "As long as you need."

'As long as you need' turned out to be a whole day. I actually dozed off on his couch that afternoon and woke up to sounds in the kitchen.

Joshua was cooking something. Scents of chicken and onion wafted over.

"It's nothing fancy," Joshua said, seeing that I was awake. "Just chicken, veggies, and rice."

"It sounds perfect."

"Hey, um, thank you. For coming over to check on me. I think I needed it."

"Of course. That's what friends are for, right?"

Joshua nodded and brought over full plates to the family room.

"So," he began after a few bites. "You still want to reach out to people?"

"Yeah. I think it's more important now than ever." I paused and took a sip of water. "I heard back from Eduardo over the weekend."

"That's huge! What did he say?"

I was glad to see that my big news had had the desired effect on Joshua. He was more animated, more himself, even if his eyes were still rimmed red.

"Here, you can read it."

I passed Joshua my phone.

Hello Anita,

Sorry for taking a long time to get back to you. I've had a lot of messages lately. I appreciate your condolences. I'd heard rumors that America was keeping track of people with Negatives, and I'm sad to see the database you shared with me. Nothing like that is here, yet.

It's hard to talk about my mother, as I'm sure you understand. I don't know if you're aware, but I'm the one who found her. She actually had a faint pulse, but she died before medical help arrived.

My family and I will continue to share updates on what doctors can learn from my mother's body, but since you asked, I can tell you that it hasn't been as helpful as we'd hoped. So far the medical examiner has found nothing unusual. We were so hopeful that we could learn something from her.

And no, I haven't seen my father's Negative since my mother passed away. While he was here, he didn't manipulate any technology or other objects. I haven't heard of any Negative doing anything like that before.

I wish you luck as you look for a cause—I think the idea of sharing what others have tried to do to get rid of theirs, or any common threads, might be helpful. Please keep in touch, and I will do the same.

Thank you,

Eduardo Vasquez

"Huh. I mean, I guess it's good that he responded. But it's not quite as helpful as I hoped it would be," Joshua said.

NEGATIVE IMAGES

"Still. He thinks reaching out to others would be helpful. I think he's right."

Joshua sighed. "Okay. We'll have to be more visible, then, warts and all."

I nodded.

After dinner, we uploaded some of our experiences on YouTube—the kinder speech videos that Monica took at the event, plus one Joshua had me film of him to explain what we were trying to do and what he'd learned from the event. While he'd mentioned me by name, I was grateful that I hadn't had to appear in a video. Yet.

Next, we had to figure out who to approach now that we had something to share with the world. We dove back into the database after dinner, and I suggested reaching out to Destiny again, as the thought of contacting Carrie was still too difficult. I punched in her number, took a deep breath, and waited.

"Hello?" The woman's voice was faint.

"Hi, is this Destiny?"

"Speaking."

"My name is Anita. I don't know if you'll remember me, but I saw you in the parking garage a few weeks ago after the auction for St. Anthony's? I didn't know it at the time, but a Negative Image was harassing you?" I struggled to get the information out and made every statement a hesitant question.

There was a long pause, and I checked to see if we were still connected.

"I remember you," she said finally. "Your husband didn't see him, just you."

"That's right. We got into a little disagreement about it."

"What do you want?"

I recoiled a little, surprised at the hard tone that had crept into her voice.

"Well, since that day, my husband has died. And he's come back as a Negative, too. I was hoping we could talk."

I heard Destiny breathing into the phone. It seemed to take her a long time to decide.

"Tomorrow. 9:00 a.m. You can come to my house."

She gave me her address and hung up, leaving me unsure of whether I wanted to do any such thing.

The next morning, Joshua and I met at Destiny's house. We both parked on the street, and I noticed the flick of a curtain on the first floor like she'd been watching and waiting for us to arrive.

I waited on the sidewalk for Joshua, and as we approached the door, it swung open. Destiny stepped back, giving us ample space to enter.

She was shorter than I remembered and looked smaller inside a gigantic grey sweatshirt. Her large brown eyes traveled back and forth between us.

"Thank you for meeting with us, Destiny," I said when she remained silent.

"I can give you a half hour," she said, her voice matter of fact.

"Thank you," said Joshua.

"What did you want to talk about?"

We followed her into a living room that was the polar opposite of Joshua's. There wasn't a speck of dust on any surface.

NEGATIVE IMAGES

"Well, Joshua and I both have Negative Images, and we're trying to figure out how people get them and document the methods they've tried to get rid of them."

"I just posted several videos," Joshua added. "My biggest attempt to get rid of mine was through a memorial event."

Destiny nodded. "It's a smart idea. Especially with all the information that's being gathered about us online."

"The database."

"Of course. Not to mention other videos and posts online," Destiny said.

"Would it be okay to interview you? And then share it on our YouTube channel?" Joshua asked.

Destiny considered for a long moment. "I looked you up after you called. I saw your earlier videos. I'll want to see this video first and approve it."

"That's more than fair. I can film you right here if you're comfortable with that," I said.

Destiny nodded, and she and Joshua positioned themselves on the sofa. Joshua and I had discussed our approach last night after our phone call; we'd come up with a brief list of questions for him to ask, and I'd record. I was just grateful that he seemed comfortable with being in another video after what he'd posted about his event. "Thank you for speaking with me today, Destiny. If you don't mind, I'd like to start by asking who your Negative Image is and how long you've had it."

"It's my father. I was one of the first people to get a Negative."

"Do you have any ideas on what might have caused your Negative to attach to you?"

135

Destiny pulled on the sleeves of her sweatshirt until her hands were no longer visible. "I'm not really sure. Our relationship was strained. It had been for a long time. But that said, he always made it a point to tell me that I was the most important person to him since I was the only family he had left. I know he had disappointments, though."

"What do you mean by that?" Joshua asked.

"Well, my father was in the military. I know he was unhappy with what I chose to do with my life. He said as much while he was alive. I think he wanted me to go into the military, too, but I became a graphic designer after college. He'd have liked me to be more regimented in my daily life. You know, make my bed every morning, stick to a strict schedule, exercise."

"I see."

"By nature, I'm just a disorganized slob; at least, that's what he used to tell me."

As Destiny spoke, I couldn't help but look at our surroundings. The room was impeccably neat and didn't reflect what she'd said about herself at all.

"Have you tried anything specific to get rid of your Negative Image?"

Destiny nodded. "I've taken everything my father said he wanted me to do and done it. I decluttered my whole house. You should have seen how much I carted to Goodwill. I set up a schedule for myself, too."

The half-hour she'd allotted for this conversation made more sense now.

"I keep the house clean, exercise for an hour every day, and try to dress neat when I leave the house. This sweatshirt was one of his. I've been wearing it because I want him to know that I loved him, that I miss him, and I'm trying to make him happy."

NEGATIVE IMAGES

Destiny smiled as she fiddled with the sleeves of her sweatshirt.

"Has it helped?"

Her smile faltered before she could fix it back on her face. "I still have my Negative Image, if that's what you're getting at. And he still finds things that he's unhappy with. But I'm trying. And if I didn't try, I wouldn't be able to hold on. Do you understand?"

"Absolutely," Joshua said. "Just one more question, if you don't mind."

"I have time for just one more."

"When you do things to try to make your Negative happy, does it help? For instance, does he appear less often, or do his attacks get less severe?"

Destiny shook her head and gave a small smile. "He tends to stick to a schedule. He comes every hour, on the hour. He hasn't missed a visit yet. Sometimes, though, he stays longer than other times. I'm trying to figure out what causes that."

"Destiny, thank you so much for your time."

"You're welcome. I hope this is helpful in some way."

I stopped recording.

Joshua and I reconvened at my house to review the video.

"It's crazy to me that she's done so much to try to make her Negative happy and hasn't seen any results," Joshua said.

"I can't imagine living for weeks on end in a way that didn't come naturally."

We sent Destiny the video, as promised, and in less than ten minutes, she called.

"Destiny? Is everything all right? What did you think of the video?"

"You can't use it." Her voice was harsh, as if she were moments away from screaming at us. "My father didn't like it. He says it can't go up online, or he'll never leave. Do you hear me? You can't post it, please."

Her voice was shrill and desperate—she almost sounded like a different person than the woman we'd met with, who had been so calm and helpful.

"We won't. I promise."

"Good, thank you." She took several deep breaths. "I can't help," she said quietly. "He says I can't do anything that might help. I'm sorry. I wanted to."

"I understand, really."

"No, you don't. Not yet. He'll get so much worse, your husband. Just you wait."

I wasn't sure what to say to that.

"Please, whatever you do, don't post my video. And do not contact me again."

She hung up, and I stared at Joshua, who'd caught every word since I'd put her on speaker.

He looked at his phone and sighed. "I thought it would have been a really good video to share," he said.

I nodded. "It would have. She was direct and articulate, and she had a clear tactic that she was committed to."

Joshua handed me the phone, and with a lot of reluctance, I deleted the video. I didn't want to be tempted to go back on my word later.

138

CHAPTER THIRTEEN

Hours later, we were no closer to finding anyone else to meet with, and I wished I could reach back out to Destiny and beg her to reconsider. This was an all-or-nothing moment to help others. We were almost out of options. I decided to suggest the one person I'd vetoed and knew personally. We were coming up empty everywhere else.

"We can try Carrie." I swallowed. I couldn't stop playing with my hands.

Joshua furrowed his brow, probably perplexed that I wasn't saying more.

"Your client?" he asked finally.

"Yeah ... there's a bit more to the story," I told him everything, starting with the conference room and ending with our failed attempts to contact her. By the end of it, my face felt hot, and I wanted to drink a gallon of water. I'd never been so ashamed of my actions.

For his part, Joshua sat on the sofa, unmoving except to nod his head or purse his lips in response to something I'd said.

"So ... you don't want to reach out because you think she's mad at you?"

I shrugged and looked away. "I'm assuming she is. I mean, if she feels generous towards me at all, she might cut me some slack since she was one of the first people to get one. I literally had no idea what I was seeing. And to be honest, I'm not even sure how aware she was that I ran off. She looked like she'd passed out. At the very least, she was dazed."

"Right." Joshua stood up and walked into the kitchen with our dishes. It was touching, considering how messy his home was the first time I saw it.

I stood up and stretched. My head was aching. We'd been online all evening, and I wasn't sure how much longer I could keep at it.

Joshua came back and went straight for the computer. I couldn't help peeking at Carrie's picture when Joshua pulled up her page. Her blonde hair was styled in an effortless-looking blowout. It might have been used for one of their organization's websites.

"She looks rich," Joshua said.

I couldn't disagree. She did have a sophisticated look that implied wealth. Besides, I had guessed as much myself. Her job, as far as I knew, was serving on the boards of several charities.

"Her NI is her mother?"

I nodded and closed my eyes to block out the bright light, but instead, I saw the white-haired woman standing behind Carrie again in the conference room.

"It looks like no one's seen her lately, and it also says that she's suspected to be one of the firsts. Her address is listed."

I stopped breathing for a second. Joshua couldn't be suggesting that we show up at her house, could he?

"I think we should visit her," he said after several silent moments.

"You mean ... without calling?"

He shrugged. "If she hasn't responded to you yet, why would she start now? But, since she knows you, I think there's a good chance she'd open the door to you at least."

We stared at each other. Joshua broke into a grin as he realized I wasn't protesting.

"Come on. You think it'll work, too."

"Yeah, I think it might." I didn't love it, but it was the best lead we had. "When did you want to go?'

"We're not exactly busy right now, are we?"

"Well, no, but it's late. I know she has a family. How about tomorrow morning?"

"First thing?"

My head was screaming. "Call me when you wake up. Let's plan for 9:00."

"I'll pick you up." He strode purposefully to the door; I trailed after him to show him out. He seemed reinvigorated—a man on a mission.

I slept later than I meant to—it was 8:30 when Joshua's text woke me with the reminder he'd be here at 9:00. I hurried into the bathroom to get ready.

I'd just washed my face and picked up my bottle of contact solution when I caught sight of Dan's Negative in the mirror. I jumped. The bottle flew up and behind me, landing with a thunk on the tile.

"Wow," he said, giving himself a congratulatory chuckle. "I was starting to think you were getting used to seeing me everywhere, but I guess it's all in the timing."

He strode across the room and crouched down, his rear hovering directly over my bottle of contact solution. "Isn't it a little soon to be taking a new lover, wife of mine?"

"It's not like that," I spoke through gritted teeth.

"Isn't it?" Dan's NI pressed. "I saw how you reacted when he came by the other day. And what? He brought you coffee? You're so easy. I would know, seeing how we met at a coffee shop. All it takes is a sugary snack or some caffeine. Wasn't it just a few days ago you were loathing him? I guess sometimes the best sex is with people you hate." He gave me a wink.

I refocused on getting ready. I still had my glasses, at least. I ran my brush through my hair.

"We won't be doing that. Absolutely not."

He laughed. "He really fooled you with that sob story about his wife. And you believed him, you idiot! Don't think for a minute that he doesn't know exactly what he's doing. Let's hope you don't end up like poor Ainsley."

"Enough." I turned around and crouched down to grab my contact solution. I needed it, but I couldn't bring myself to reach under him to get it.

Dan laughed, his black eyes glistening. I'd never seen them shine so brightly. "You can't bear to touch me, can you? You always were frigid."

He vanished. The bottle of contact solution rocked slowly back and forth across the tile like a breeze had just come through and disturbed it.

NEGATIVE IMAGES

What had he meant? I'd never thought our sex life was anything other than normal. Maybe normal hadn't been enough.

My phone buzzed on the counter—a text from Joshua. *I'm here.*

How had this conversation with Dan's Negative taken so long? I texted back, *Come on in. I need 10.*

I took a breath and crouched down again. With a quick reach, I swiped the bottle off the floor as if Dan's Negative might come back to lay claim to it again.

A few minutes later, I came down to find Joshua. He looked at home on my couch as he scrolled through his phone and sipped coffee.

"Hi," I said, greeting him with a small smile.

"Hey. You look great, Anita. The bump is hardly noticeable, now," he said as he reached towards me. His fingers grazed my hairline. "Oh. Here. Brought you some coffee." He handed me a cup from the coffee table.

"That's so thoughtful. Thanks."

We stood for a moment, and I took a sip, more to have something to do than anything else.

"Shall we?"

I nodded, and we left through the garage. Joshua opened the passenger door of his Camry, and I hesitated with my keys in my hand.

"I thought maybe we'd take one car so we don't take up too much of the street."

I slipped my keys back into my bag. "Good point."

I walked over to the Camry—he was still holding the door for me.

"Thanks," I said as I got in. Then I remembered what Dan's NI had said about me being easy to please.

Joshua got in a moment later. "You okay? Nervous?"

"I'm fine." I was. I wasn't worried about Joshua. All the same, I felt a pang of guilt when he pulled away from my house. What was I doing? I hadn't even told Monica my plan. And Carrie wasn't *my* client—she was *our* client. Calling would be awkward with Joshua in the car, but I could at least text her.

Joshua and I are going to try to see Carrie. Looking for others with NIs to counter the Patisis site.

I saw three dots pop up on her side of the conversation, then disappear. Then reappear. Joshua drove slowly through my neighborhood and I was grateful that Carrie lived on the other side of town.

Why??? I would have come with you if I knew you wanted to do something like this. Be safe!

I sighed, unsure about what to say in response.

"Everything okay?"

"Huh?"

"You look worried."

"Oh." I shrugged. "I just wanted to let Monica know what we were up to. Since it's business related, you know, at least kind of."

Joshua nodded. "I'm guessing you didn't like her response?" He gave me a quick glance as he made a right turn.

"I think maybe she's feeling left out? I'm not really sure." This part wasn't completely true, although I didn't elaborate on my thoughts to Joshua.

What had Monica meant by 'be safe?' Did she have some concerns about Joshua?

I wondered if she, like Dan's NI, assumed that Joshua would be some sort of rebound for me. My stomach flip-flopped as we merged onto the highway. I closed my eyes and took deep breaths. When that didn't help, I resorted to rolling down the window and leaning towards the fresh air.

"Please don't get sick in the car." Joshua sounded like he was only half joking.

"Sorry." I turned to look at him. "I won't. Texting in the car was a bad idea, I guess. I was just feeling a little bad I didn't tell Monica about our plans sooner."

"Well, she's not your boss. And she doesn't have a Negative Image like we do."

"Still."

I'd always leaned on Monica. She took care of the parts of our business that I struggled with. And I balanced it out with flare. We were such a good fit most of the time that working together felt intuitive. And she'd helped me so much the day Dan was shot and with everything that came after. Reaching out to family, planning the funeral ... and how was I repaying her? By going behind her back.

Cars zipped past us on the left-hand side. After a few minutes, I was able to close the window. I kept thinking of Monica's concerns and the jabs Dan's NI had thrown at me. Plus, Joshua was so unusually quiet that I couldn't tell what he was thinking. Was he regretting this trip? The car ride started to feel like sharing an elevator with someone for a very long time.

Joshua put on his blinker and shot me a quizzical look as he checked his blind spot.

"I hope I'm not the one making you nervous."

"What? No, of course not," I scoffed.

"Okay. I just had to ask. Because honestly, after everything we talked about, I thought maybe you were nervous about being in the car with me."

For a second, I thought he was joking, and I was glad I stole a glance at him before trying to laugh it off.

"No. Honestly, I can tell you that that thought hasn't crossed my mind."

The tension eased in Joshua's jaw, but he seemed to be choosing his words now carefully.

"I guess I just thought... I don't know. That you might be more excited about this."

"I am, I mean, I want to be. But I'm kind of dreading seeing Carrie after what happened before. What if Carrie doesn't even agree to see us?"

The car behind us tapped its horn, and Joshua waved his hand in apology.

"Look, Anita, I get it. I really do. I don't think I told you how my relationship with Ainsley started, did I?"

"No, not really."

"We met while we were in high school." The hint of a smile played around the corners of Joshua's mouth. "I convinced her to study with me for an English test, and we talked for two hours straight. We never opened a textbook. So, unsurprisingly, we failed." He grinned widely and chuckled a little. "Needless to say, her parents were kind of pissed at me."

From the back seat, I felt a strange pull and wasn't entirely surprised to see Ainsley's flat, black eyes staring back at me.

"Winning her parents over was hard work, and anytime something bad happened, they were quick to revert to their old position. Like I said,

NEGATIVE IMAGES

I don't know if they ever thought I deserved her, but they accepted the fact that we were getting married."

Ainsley's mouth split open in an ugly snarl, and a crackling noise came from her red lips. Joshua winced at whatever she was saying. "Anyway," he continued, raising his voice to be heard over her, "I guess my point is that sometimes you just have to be persistent. Even if it sucks, this'll be worth it. And I'm here to back you up."

"Thank you." His hand was resting on the gear shift, and without much thought, I reached for him. As I turned his palm over in mine, Ainsley let out a loud whine, like feedback coming from a microphone.

"She doesn't like that."

Joshua dropped my hand and placed both of his on the steering wheel.

CHAPTER FOURTEEN

I pressed the doorbell of Carrie's house, and a melody chimed. I looked back at Joshua. He shrugged. The neighborhood was quiet, and I took in the large, manicured yards of the other houses. Ainsley's Negative had been speaking to Joshua the whole way over, and her garbled complaints continued. After a few moments, I pressed it again. Maybe I'd talk to her through her doorbell camera and hope that she was watching the feed. A moment later, I heard shuffling footsteps.

The door only opened a crack—enough for me to glimpse a blue eye, heavily lined in black (tattooed eyeliner, I guessed), and an ashen complexion.

"Carrie?" I took a small step forward so she could see me better.

Her brow wrinkled. "You're that event planner."

I ducked my head in an effort to hide my embarrassment. I'd tried to get Carrie's business for ages and practically revered her, and it stung to know that she didn't remember my name. "Anita. Yes. From Legendary Events."

Carrie frowned. "I thought it was obvious that I didn't need any more of your services. You know what I have."

My breath caught. Carrie's voice had an edge to it. Had she remembered being left in the conference room?

"Actually, I'm not here for work. You and I are on a website that lists people who have Negative Images. My friend Joshua and I both have one."

Carrie's one eye narrowed into a glare. "Where?"

I glanced back at Joshua, but Ainsley's NI had conveniently vanished. I hadn't seen Dan's Negative since this morning. Of course, they were gone the one time it would actually benefit us to have them. "They've left us for a moment."

She raised her eyebrow. "That's convenient."

I sighed. "You must get a reprieve from your mother's Negative Image every once in a while. Don't you?"

"How did you know mine was my mother?" Carrie's eyes widened.

"Well, I did see her in person, although I wasn't sure she was your mother. That detail is on the website I mentioned."

Carrie opened the door a little wider. In the sunlight, I noticed that her skin had a gray tinge to it, and she had heavy shadows in the hollows of her eyes. She glanced up and down her street and motioned us to come inside.

A wide entryway led into a formal sit-down area with a large dining room to the left. She led us past a second sitting area to a spacious kitchen. She wore a white bathrobe with silky blue pajama bottoms visible from the knee down. Her hair was pulled back into a ponytail, and the shorter pieces had fallen out and looked lank and dirty. She looked nothing like the poised and confident Carrie from a couple of months ago.

Carrie motioned for us to sit, so we took seats at the table.

Her kitchen was pristine. Carrie grabbed two glasses from a cabinet, and I noticed that everything matched, even the coffee mugs. It looked nothing like my hodgepodge collection at home. This would have been my dream kitchen—something to aspire to when Dan and I bought our next house. Even now, as I pulled my chair in closer to the table, I was still a little envious.

Carrie placed the water glasses in front of us and hesitated slightly as though she couldn't decide which chair to use. None of us spoke. Carrie's eyes flitted between me and Joshua.

Finally, Carrie broke the silence. "You said there was a website?"

"Yes," I cleared my throat, unsure where the conversation was heading. "It's called NIdatabase.com."

Carrie pulled out her phone and typed in the address. Joshua's knee bounced up and down, and I tapped him, willing him to be still. Carrie pursed her lips as she scrolled through the site. Her brow furrowed, and the vertical lines between her eyes deepened.

"It's me," she said, her voice just a whisper. She put her phone down and slid it off to the side.

"Yes. I'm sorry."

"I had no idea that was out there—that it existed."

"It was a shock to me, too." I rubbed my forehead, realizing too late that I might've rubbed off the makeup covering my bruise. "You can look me up. Joshua, too."

Carrie nodded. She looked small. Frail. "That explains the phone calls. Aaron told me not to answer the phone anymore."

"Yes, people have been getting harassed. My Negative is my husband. He was shot in a parking lot." My voice broke, and I reached for my water

NEGATIVE IMAGES

to cover it. "Joshua's Negative is his fiancée, Ainsley, who died in a car crash."

I hoped Carrie would talk about her Negative, but she stayed quiet, just looking at us. I had no idea what she was thinking. My palms started sweating, and I looked to Joshua for help moving the conversation forward. Just then, I noticed movement out of the corner of my eye, and I saw Carrie's Negative Image coming towards the table.

She wore a ratty-looking house dress and matching house shoes. As before, her poufy white hair drew my attention. It had been teased and filled with hair spray to hide the thinness and resembled a helmet. She shuffled forward, her unsteady gait made worse by the flickering, stop-motion quality of her steps.

Carrie kept her eyes glued to the table.

I wondered if she was afraid—her mother's NI walked over and sat next to Carrie, staring at her, although Carrie did her best not to look at it. Its effect on her was palpable as she began to tremble.

Then, the Negative focused its gaze on me. I couldn't tell what she was saying, but watching her look at me and listening to the garbled noises she made was enough to keep me quiet. Thin lips trembled as she spoke, and I saw a small glimmer of teeth.

"Please. Go ahead." Carrie's voice was so quiet I almost wondered if I'd mistaken hearing her.

When she looked up at me, her hollow eyes shone fiercely. "If we don't continue our conversation, then this is just another thing that she's won. That she's taken from me."

I nodded and did my best to ignore Carrie's Negative. "Um, Joshua and I, and I'm sure you probably have as well ... uh, we've experienced a lot of hostility. We're trying to figure out how people get a Negative Image and if there's any way to get rid of them.

"Seeing that website just made us realize how much people hate us. And it's not our fault. I know everyone has a different philosophy, but I truly believe that we didn't do anything to deserve what we're going through right now."

Carrie pursed her lips. "I'm not sure I can agree with you there."

Joshua and I exchanged a look. I wasn't sure if Joshua's opinion had changed, but I hoped he wouldn't voice it.

"Please, go on." Joshua prodded.

"My mother died in a nursing home. *I* put her there. I really thought it was the best thing for her. She didn't live there very long. Only three months."

I reached across the table and took her hand. "I'm so sorry."

Carrie's Negative made growling sounds mixed with static noises. I didn't mean to, but I recoiled and dropped Carrie's hand. A tear trailed down her cheek, and she clasped her hands together on the table.

"Every day, I question what would have happened if I'd made a different decision." Carrie's voice quivered, but she fought to maintain her composure. "Would she still be here if we'd asked her to move in with us? Or if we'd had a caretaker come to her home? I wonder if the place I chose for her had any red flags that I missed, if it was too much change for her too soon, or if I should have consulted with other professionals ..." Carrie slumped in her chair. "I just can't shake the idea that she's here because I didn't do enough for her."

"I'm sure it wasn't an easy decision."

"Of course, it wasn't easy. But ... we made it quickly. We felt we had to."

NEGATIVE IMAGES

Joshua glanced over at me, and he seemed to have the same thought on his mind. Should we press her to find out more or shift the conversation?

"What do you mean?" I asked.

Carrie sighed in a futile effort. She glanced out the window to her left, but her Negative shifted in front of her, a gnarly finger pointed in Carrie's face.

"Um." Carrie took a deep breath and closed her eyes. "I just need a moment."

"I'm sorry," Joshua began. We shouldn't pry—"

"No. No, it's okay. I've had this on my mind for a long time. You see, my mother ... our relationship was complicated. I mean, whose isn't, right?"

I gave a small smile, my mind drifting to my own mother. Complicated was certainly a good way to describe our relationship. We had completely different thought processes and values; I never quite understood where she was coming from.

Carrie continued, "She could be stubborn, you know? Aaron and I asked her to move in with us years ago, but my sister was convinced it was the wrong move. So, Mom stayed put, then later she fell, which led to the hospital and eventually rehab. And unsurprisingly, she didn't do well when she got back. After another accident, even my sister realized that she couldn't live alone. She needed so much extra assistance at that point, and stairs were a no-go. We don't have a first-floor bedroom, so we would have had to put in a stair lift, which just ... besides that, we just felt like with the boys and their little messes and our work schedules, we didn't think we could have her live here comfortably. So we found a really nice place."

153

The sound of white noise amplified, and the hair in my ears rose up. Carrie's NI had her mouth open wide in a scream—a deep, black cavern that matched the dark pits of her eyes.

"I wish I could take it back. I wish I had fought harder years ago to have her stay here. She wouldn't have had those falls, she would have been okay, she ..." Carrie stared at the floor, and the screaming faded like a radio signal getting farther away.

"I'm sure you did what you thought was the right thing." I leaned forward. "If it helps, I've had similar thoughts about my husband. About the shooting. Would he still be here if I hadn't called him? If I hadn't gotten him so involved in my business? I had no idea what I was sending him into. Please, you can't blame yourself."

Carrie nodded. "I know. Deep down, I know you're right. But then I wonder: Why is she here?"

"We know it's a lot to ask, but we want you to help us." Joshua leaned towards Carrie, practically pleading. "You could take your experience, all that she's done to you, and use it to help others."

"So ... what? You want to know why I think I have one? What I've tried to make her go away?"

"Yes, exactly," Joshua said. "We're posting all this on YouTube, hoping that collectively we can come up with something that works. May I record our conversation? No video, just audio?"

Carrie hesitated a moment. "I suppose ... it can't hurt me worse than what others have said about me."

Joshua began recording. "You were one of the first people to get a Negative Image. Do you have any thoughts on why that might have happened to you?" he asked.

NEGATIVE IMAGES

Carrie's eyes were dark. "The simplest explanation was that she died two weeks before I got her Negative. And when I got mine, forgive me for saying so, but your NIs were still living people, weren't they? I don't think there's much more to it than timing."

Joshua's face had gone red, so I asked the next question.

"What did you do when you got your Negative?"

"Well, as you said, I was one of the first. I saw the news about Maria Vasquez and knew, of course, that it was no joke, no prank." She sighed. "Looking back, I was so naive. I called my therapist and my doctor. I asked them for help, and of course, they knew nothing. As weeks went by, I tried different things. I visited her grave. I went to the home and was allowed to visit her old room—I tried talking to her there."

My heart sank. I'd been considering visiting Dan's grave myself.

"Did you ever get a break from your Negative after trying these things? Any hint that you might be on the right track?"

Carrie let out a bray of bitter laughter. "Of course not. She was usually with me, reminding me that it wouldn't work, that there was no getting rid of her."

I stilled. So far, this wasn't a hopeful conversation.

"Is there anything you've observed about your Negative, anything that gives you hope that she might go away?" I pressed.

Carrie tapped her fingers on the table as she considered. "I have to believe it's possible to get rid of them. But I have no idea how. The only thing that I can say is, well ... she is my mother. At least, she's part of my mother. She knows everything that my mother knew. But my mother was never this vengeful in life. It's like a part of her is missing from this thing."

An alarm rang on Carrie's phone, and she quickly silenced it and rose from the table. Joshua stopped recording.

"My husband and boys will be home soon from Jack's basketball game. I need to take a minute to change. I know they probably don't expect much from me anymore, but I don't like them to know that I spend the day like this. She pulled on the fluffy collar of her robe.

Joshua and I began to stand, but she motioned for us to stay where we were.

"Please. I'll just be a few minutes. Stay here."

She went upstairs, leaving us alone with our water in her massive kitchen.

After fifteen minutes of sitting silently and awkwardly with Joshua, Carrie returned.

Her face looked brighter—blush brought color to her gray complexion, and her dark under-eye circles were gone. She'd styled her hair in a low bun with every strand tucked neatly into place.

Not a moment later, a back door opened, and the chatter of boys' voices filled the kitchen.

Carrie's husband and sons walked in, and when they saw us, silence filled the space. The man looked around fifty—paunchy, with a beer gut preceding him and a belt underneath to support it. His mouth was slightly open, and his eyebrows drew together in suspicion. The boys were skinny and shy, and the youngest was hiding behind his father.

"Mom?" the older boy spoke. "You're downstairs?"

NEGATIVE IMAGES

Carrie nodded, and I realized that though her Negative had followed her up, it hadn't come back down with her. She walked over to her sons and gave each one a hug. The older boy tensed, his shoulder hitching up as he tentatively raised his arms and circled them around his mother. The other child looked several years younger, and he was quick to give his mother a big squeeze.

Her husband glared at us. I remembered seeing him on the news.

"Aaron, I want you to meet Joshua and Anita. They're like me. Anita, Joshua, this is my husband and my sons Ben and Jack." The boys gave meek waves.

"Why don't you two go upstairs and play for a little bit?" Aaron suggested.

The boys took off, needing no further explanation.

Carrie gestured for Aaron to join us at the table.

"If you're like her, then where are your *things*?" He didn't even want to say the word.

"They're not with us at the moment." I tried to sound matter-of-fact, but under Aaron's scrutiny, I knew I sounded meek.

"Carrie, did you see them?"

"Well, no, not yet."

Aaron hunched over, face to face with Carrie. "They're just like those people who called you last week," he said, his voice level and soft. "You can't give them access to you, Carrie."

Carrie shot me a pained smile. "Aaron, this is Anita. I know her from the auction that took place right before I got the NI."

Aaron glared at us from beneath his brow, his mouth practically disappearing in a grimace. "What's that supposed to mean? Aren't they the same people who kept harassing you with emails and phone calls while you were dealing with this monster?" His stomach shoved the table towards us as he stood up. Water sloshed out of our still-full glasses. "I think you should leave."

"I don't know what people you're talking about, but we're not trying to exploit Carrie. We're here because we want to get rid of them. We told her about this website—all of us are on it. You can look us up if you don't believe us."

"It's true," Carrie chimed in. "I saw. There's a page about me. There are pages about them."

Aaron sat back down, but his shoulders stayed hunched up, and his posture was stiff. I was grateful that Carrie had claimed to see our pages. There was no way she would have had time to get ready and look us up, so I guessed she was lying.

Joshua and I looked at Carrie, unsure how to pick up the conversation.

"Aaron, they're trying to help. We spoke about our loved ones, and Anita and I actually had similar experiences, questioning whether we could have done something more for them—"

"You told them that?" I noticed beads of sweat on Aaron's brow. "Carrie ... I want to believe them—and you, of course—but what if that's not their real intention? I just don't think it's wise for you to trust them. For all you know, they might have recorded you just to mock you online." Aaron swiped at his brow. "Carrie, maybe you should go upstairs for a little while. Let me have a chance to talk to these people and see what they really want."

He took Carrie's arm and tried to pull her up from the table, but she shook him off.

NEGATIVE IMAGES

"Aaron," she said. She peered up at him until he returned her gaze. "Don't you think I know what I'm talking about?"

"Of course, sweetheart. I'm sorry. I'm sorry," he repeated, this time apologizing to Joshua and me. "We don't really have anyone on our side anymore. Forgive me if I'm not the most trusting person."

"Aaron does have a point," Carrie added. "The neighbors avoid us. My sister hasn't spoken to us since Mom died, and we don't have any other family. Not anymore."

Joshua inched his phone into the middle of the table. "You can look through it. I don't care. We just want Carrie's help to tell the world what we live with."

Aaron looked frozen—I couldn't tell if he was hearing us or not.

"They mess with your head," I added. "Every day, my husband's Negative tells me that I deserve this and that I'm to blame. I would have done anything to save him, but there was nothing I could do." A lump in my throat stopped me from continuing. I could have done things differently. But I didn't know what would happen. I couldn't have known. So, who was right? Him or me?

I cleared my throat and forced myself to continue. "He's ruining my life. That's what they do. They're trying to destroy us!"

Carrie looked at me. "Yes. She says things like that. I've told you, Aaron: she blames me."

Aaron gave up and sat back down, his mouth slightly open and his face still unreadable. Carrie's Negative chose to reappear at that moment, just as the tension had been lifting. Her garbled, static noise was hard to ignore, but I took a deep breath and pushed forward.

"Joshua and I want to create something to counter the NI database," I began as though I were leading a client presentation. "We've posted some initial videos with details about what we've tried to get rid of them."

"I had a memorial. Our videos so far are about that. It didn't work," Joshua added.

Carrie's Negative paced behind her, still making crackling sounds that reminded me of a radio searching for a signal.

"People get Negatives all the time," I said over the noise. "It will keep happening. And so far, no one has figured out a way to get rid of them."

Joshua nodded emphatically. "Aaron, Carrie, I'm sure you're aware of all that's happening, just like we are. It's awful to realize the medical and scientific communities don't have an explanation for this. And who knows how long it will take them to find one?"

"We want to offer people options. And hope. So they don't feel like the only way out is by taking their own lives like Maria Vasquez."

It was like we'd flipped a switch. Carrie's Negative went from a constantly unsettling presence to a real threat. She bore down on Carrie, jumping from the area behind her to the middle of the table so she could get in Carrie's face. She flickered like film reels spliced together and sped up.

My arms prickled in goosebumps—I'd never seen a Negative Image do that. Carrie's mother started yelling. Carrie flinched and sank lower into her chair, but I didn't know what to do for her. Fat tears leaked from her eyes, and her shoulders shook with sobs.

We couldn't intervene and ask the Negative to leave her alone. We couldn't remove Carrie from the situation. And I wondered if staying here, listening to her sob, was making things worse.

NEGATIVE IMAGES

Aaron must have felt the same way; he motioned for us to follow him out of the room. Joshua looked at Carrie, then at me. I guessed he felt as badly as I did about leaving her alone in the kitchen to cry, but he started to follow Aaron.

I looked back at Carrie before we left the room. She'd covered her ears, and in between her cries, I heard her beg.

"Please, Mom. Stop."

Tears pricked my own eyes, and I tensed up. Even though I'd experienced the same thing, watching Carrie go through it was worse.

"So nice of you to corner a former client in her own home and make her cry. She's hysterical." Dan's Negative winked a black eye at me and nudged me with his elbow as we walked down the hall. Anytime he tried to touch me, I felt nauseous, even though I didn't actually feel his touch.

"You really do have one." Aaron turned and looked Dan's NI up and down, his eyes huge. "I haven't seen one aside from Carrie's."

"Yeah. I get it." I sighed.

"Where was he before?" Aaron asked.

"I don't know, but if I did, I'd make sure he stayed there."

"I can't get over the sound they make when they speak," Aaron said as he sat down and motioned us to sit on a sofa opposite him. "Reminds me of something out of *Poltergeist* or *White Noise* or something."

"Yeah," Joshua and I said in unison. I felt weary, and spending time explaining our situation to Aaron seemed like a waste.

We could still hear Carrie crying in the kitchen. Joshua looked back towards the hall every time she gave a loud sob. I could tell he was uncomfortable leaving her alone.

"Mr. Ellsworth, it's obvious how much Carrie is suffering. She's had her Negative Image with her longer than either of us, and we completely understand if this is too much for her to consider doing. We just think it's crucial to get our side of the story out there to find out why this is happening so that people will look at us as people again instead of monsters."

Aaron nodded. "I couldn't believe the number of people who told Carrie she got what she deserved. Her friends told her she was doing the right thing by putting her mom in a home. You know, all that talk about how it's not an easy decision and impossible to find a perfect solution. They told her she was doing the best she could. Then, boom!" He clapped his hands together, and I jumped in my seat. "Her mom dies and comes back as a Negative a few weeks later, and everyone turns on her. I mean, everyone! Even the staff at the nursing home who cared for her frickin' mother! Her friends said she chose a bad home. Some of them said they always knew she should have had her mother move in with us or that she should have hired a caregiver—everyone had the right answer, you know? Do you know some people even accused her of elder abuse and matricide? No basis for it at all! But they slandered her name all over the internet! The staff said things like she should have visited more and that she'd broken her mother's heart. It was just awful." He took a deep breath, but his hands remained clenched in fists. "Towards the end of her mother's life, Carrie really trusted these people. She got to know them all very well because she was there to visit her mother three or four times a week. She couldn't go every day, not with the kids. It's vicious, just vicious. She already lost her mother; now she's lost her work, too. She loved volunteering. You know." He pointed to me, probably thinking of the auction. "Her focus was on helping people. But no one liked her meeting with other people or potential benefactors in case they saw *it* and went somewhere else."

NEGATIVE IMAGES

I wondered how safe Joshua and I were in our own jobs. His coworkers had already slandered him. Monica basically ran our business without me. And I doubted I would have anyone requesting to work with me any time soon after Joshua's memorial.

In Carrie's story were all the fears we harbored for ourselves.

The kitchen was quiet. At some point, while Aaron was talking, Carrie's crying stopped. The silence wrapped around me too tightly. It was wrong.

We want to offer people options. And hope. So they don't feel like the only way out is by taking their own lives like Maria Vasquez.

My stomach dropped.

"Carrie?" I ran back to the kitchen. *Please answer. Please answer. Please have snuck upstairs or gone to the bathroom.*

Something smelled. Metallic and tangy and sour all at once. I knew it was blood, and a lot of it, even though I'd never smelled it before.

"Oh my God!" I clapped my hands over my mouth. I needed my phone. I needed to call an ambulance, but I smacked into Joshua, my nose colliding painfully with his chest.

His arms wrapped around me reflexively.

"Joshua! She slit her wrists!

CHAPTER FIFTEEN

I sat on the floor of Carrie's kitchen, my arms weak from scrubbing. It was two in the morning. I thought we would've gone home long ago.

Upstairs was silent, and I hoped that meant Carrie's boys were finally sleeping.

I couldn't shake their little faces from my mind. The way they'd come downstairs to their father shouting on the phone with the 911 dispatcher, Joshua and I standing in shocked silence, and their poor mother on the floor. Joshua had broken away from me, ushering them back upstairs with quiet words, making sure they didn't look behind them.

I remember putting pressure on the top of Carrie's right arm while Aaron did the same on the left to stop the flow of blood.

The thick liquid made the floor slick. It was slimy on Carrie's arms and soaked her white sweater. Aaron's red face mirrored Carrie's blood on the floor as he yelled at her to stay with him.

Once the EMTs came, questions and phrases flew at me like lyrics from a song I couldn't quite remember.

NEGATIVE IMAGES

"What's her blood type?"

"Where were you when this happened?"

"We need more pressure."

"Why was your wife alone?"

"Lift her on my count."

She was hoisted on a stretcher, and as they whisked her away, a drop of blood dangled from her index finger. It finally fell and landed on her entryway floor.

Aaron spoke to someone in the hallway, and I saw him point at me before leaving for the hospital. I guess being a witness to a suicide attempt bonded us enough for him to leave his two boys with us for the time being. I honestly didn't think he had anyone else to turn to.

Police arrived. The scene around me became a series of fragments I couldn't hold on to.

One of them approached me. "I'm Detective Lee. Tell me about your relationship with Carrie Ellsworth, please."

Cameras clicked as crime scene techs took pictures of the kitchen. Someone collected a blood sample.

"What's your relationship to Carrie Ellsworth?" he pressed, his voice sharp and clipped.

"I don't really have one. Well, I handled an event for her a while ago."

"Did you see her harm herself?"

"No. We were in the next room speaking with Aaron."

"Did you hear any noises?"

"It was the silence."

"What do you mean by that?"

"First, we were here in the kitchen, talking. Then her Negative came. When she started to cry, Joshua and I went with her husband to the other room to finish the conversation. I heard Carrie crying in the background, and then suddenly I realized I didn't hear her anymore."

"You and your friend have experience with these Negatives, don't you?" He looked at me like he suspected me of something.

"Yeah."

"Let me ask you, from your own experience, did you think it was wise to leave Carrie Ellsworth in here alone, crying, with her Negative Image tormenting her?"

I felt like I was being cross-examined. Shame filled my whole body, making my hands shake. We should have stayed with her. But it was her husband's idea to leave; how could we suggest differently?

I couldn't look the detective in the eye despite the weight of his stare. "We're different people. I assumed her husband knew her best. I never thought this would happen."

"Were you aware that Carrie was suicidal?"

"No."

He waited, tapping his foot on the floor. I pressed my tongue to the roof of my mouth so I wouldn't be tempted to start talking and found myself studying his hair. Black spikes sprouted from his scalp, as though he had shaved his head and was letting it grow in before he chose a hairstyle.

"What was the purpose of your visit, please?"

I sighed. I had no idea what he would make of it. I quickly summarized our visit and why we'd wanted Carrie's help.

The detective handed me a card as his colleagues came back downstairs. I assumed they'd questioned Joshua and possibly the boys. The officers' shoes clacked on the floor as they strode out of the house.

NEGATIVE IMAGES

The people in the kitchen left a few minutes after the police, informing me that I was free to clean up now. It was clearly the scene of an attempted suicide, but between the crime scene techs and the detectives, I wondered if they might investigate it as something else. Or, maybe they were being this thorough because a Negative Image was involved, and there was still so much unknown about them.

The door shut behind them, and the wails from upstairs grew louder in the silence. I slumped against the island, looking at the pool of blood on the floor.

How would I clean it all? Red stained the floorboards, red distorted the sheen of the tiles, red darkened to brown as it dried on the sides of the wood cabinet.

I couldn't do it. I'd never thought about whose job it might be to clean up a mess like this. I certainly hadn't thought it would fall to me.

This was your fault. You came here.

For a moment, I couldn't breathe. I plugged my hands over my ears and looked around, sure that Dan's lanky frame was just out of sight.

Nothing. Then I realized the voice hadn't been his, but my own, or possibly some blend of the two. Maybe it was my guilty conscience that spurred me onwards, but I thought of Carrie's little boys, and I couldn't just sit around and wait.

I found plenty of old rags and bleach in the laundry room. Sponges and plastic gloves were under the sink. My stomach churned as I began mopping up dark pools of blood. I couldn't get the smell of it out of my nose. I could practically taste it. I used the mat in front of the kitchen sink to absorb some of it, too. It was beyond saving. I could only just make out a pattern of what was possibly roosters.

I couldn't help but feel I was doing hopeless work, a Sisyphean task. Every time I went over an area, scrubbing and wiping, I'd think I must have gotten it all. Then, I would eye the marble countertop or the floorboards and see a hint of red. It was as if the surfaces had swallowed up her blood and were regurgitating it.

A creak of the floorboards upstairs startled me. I prayed it was Joshua and not one of Carrie's boys. I held my breath, then let it out in a whoosh when I saw Joshua on the stairs.

"How's it going? It looks much better and smells a little like a hospital." He gave me a crooked smile. I knew he was just trying to take the edge off, but the thought of a hospital made me think of Carrie.

I cleared my throat. "I think Aaron will need a professional to come back and give this a deep cleaning. I've tried, but whenever I think I'm done, I find something I've missed. If this was my family, I don't think I could ever stand to eat in this kitchen again." I shuddered, just thinking of someone chopping up a bell pepper in the same place Carrie had cut herself open. "How are the boys?"

"Asleep, for now." Joshua had dark shadows under his eyes, and his brows were furrowed. "I've never felt worse for anyone in my entire life. Young boys being comforted by strangers about their mom; it's not right. They're sharing a bed tonight, and who can blame them?"

I sighed.

Neither of us had gotten any update from Aaron.

"What do we do now?"

"Well, I suppose we sleep. Somewhere. They must have a guest room for you."

"No one else is coming? The boys don't have someone to stay with them?"

NEGATIVE IMAGES

Joshua shook his head. "They mentioned an aunt to me but said they hadn't seen her since their grandmother died. Since Carrie got her Negative, basically. I think we're on our own for tonight."

I nodded. "Okay. Where will you sleep?"

"Well, I thought I might stay in the hallway, actually. Just in case the boys get up in the middle of the night."

I imagined the boys sneaking down without us, traumatized all over again by the competing smells of bleach and blood.

"That's a good idea. I hate to think you'll have to sleep on the floor, but ..."

"I don't mind."

We locked up, took the last trash from the kitchen out to the garage, and fumbled with the locks and light switches. I'd texted Aaron to let him know that the boys were okay and that we'd cleaned up as best as we could. He didn't respond.

Upstairs, Joshua claimed a spot on the floor while I found an extra pillow for him in the guest room.

My body was drained, exhausted. But I couldn't get the feeling of the plastic gloves out of my head, the sensation of mopping up all the liquid with thin rags. Even my clothes seemed to have the stench of it.

I cracked open the door. Joshua was snoring. At least he was resting—I wasn't sure if I could. I snuck down the hall to what I assumed was Carrie and Aaron's room. I wanted to wash my clothes, and my options were nakedness or borrowing something of Carrie's. I'd opted for the latter, hoping that everyone would understand. I flipped on the lights and went to the dresser. Carrie had framed photos of her and her husband from their wedding day. I bet she'd never thought "in sickness or health" would include dealing with a Negative Image.

169

"Raiding the dead woman's clothes?" Dan's Negative appeared next to me in the mirror. I froze, bent over still holding the drawer handle. Usually, I fought to dismiss everything he said, but he had said ...

"Dead? Is Carrie dead?"

"Go on about your business," he said slyly. "I'll try not to bother you too much." He sat down on the bed. "It must be awful to know that someone killed themselves just because you showed up at their house. You know, I could have told you that this would all end badly."

My heart hammered against my ribs. He wouldn't give me a clear answer, would he?

The words tumbled out of my mouth anyway. "Is she really dead?"

Dan's Negative ignored my question. He sauntered through the room, looking at photos of the boys on Aaron's nightstand. "I'm sure her kids will love seeing you and Josh in the morning. Especially when they realize you're in mommy's clothes." He winked.

"They won't see me. I just have to wash mine."

"Trying to wash the blood off your hands, Lady Macbeth? 'Out, out damn spot?'" He laughed, enjoying the waves of anger and heartbreak washing over my face. Two years ago, Shakespeare in the Park put on Macbeth, and we went, bringing cups of merlot, which we spilled on our blanket. We washed that thing a few times, laughing at ourselves, saying 'out, out damn spot,' but the stain never came out. Eventually, we gave up and threw the ruined blanket away.

Something in my chest broke into tiny shards that I thought might cut me if I moved the wrong way. I grabbed the first shirt and pants I could find in Carrie's dresser and hastily changed into them.

Dan's Negative stood in the doorway and laughed. I was sick of the control he exerted over me and sick of the helplessness I felt whenever

NEGATIVE IMAGES

I was near him. Tears streaked my vision. I needed space. I needed to get away. I held my breath and walked through him. An unpleasant sensation of pins and needles, coupled with an icy coldness, left me gasping. Dan's Negative continued to laugh, and I sprinted down the hall, unable to be quiet for Joshua or the boys.

Thankfully, the laundry room was next to the guest room. I threw my clothes in the washer with probably too much detergent. Carrie's machine had twice as many settings and cycles as mine. I made sure it was on cold, then went back to the guest room. Once I shut the door behind me, I felt safe, even though I knew it was an illusion. Dan's Negative could come at any time.

My skin was still crawling, so I stripped down and turned on the shower in the ensuite as hot as I could handle it. Carrie and Aaron kept a good supply of soaps and lotions for guests, shampoo and conditioner, too.

The hot water filled the room with steam—droplets bounced off my arms and shoulders and onto the tile. I could finally get this feeling off me. Then Dan's Negative appeared. He leaned against the sink and stared as I worked the shampoo into my hair and built up a good lather. I felt his eyes follow the path of soap as I washed my arms and legs. His stare was a violation. I wanted the muscles in my neck and shoulders to respond to the hot water and relax, but I couldn't get any relief. I sobbed as I rinsed out my hair. A scream rose in my throat, but I had to remember I wasn't alone—in frustration, I pounded the shower wall with my fist. Dan's loud laughter reminded me of a cacophony of trash cans knocked down in an alley.

The soap swirled and went down the drain. I imagined it was blood. My blood.

For a moment, I wanted it to be. It was like a vision, and I had to do what was necessary to make it come true. I studied the glass shower door, pondering the best way to break it.

No. Those weren't my thoughts.

I would not let him win. Dan's Negative wanted me to give up. I wouldn't.

Instead, I turned off the shower, unsure if I still had shampoo in my hair. I grabbed a towel and wrapped myself in it. Dan's Negative still leaned against the sink, watching me, appraising me.

I shuddered and opened the bathroom door. Cold air hit me in the face. I couldn't stay in that small space anymore.

He laughed as I slipped Carrie's shirt over my head. I wanted to scream. I wanted to throw something at him so he felt pain, too. I wanted to clasp my hands around his throat and squeeze. Instead, I took a deep breath and went back to the laundry room to put my clothes in the dryer.

A small face peered at me. Big brown eyes were crowned with a mop of curls.

"That's Mommy's." The boy touched my shoulder with his index finger, his eyes solemn and wide.

"What?" I struggled to sit up and squinted at the sunlight coming in through the blinds. Last night, Dan's Negative had lain next to me. Anytime I drifted off, he poked me, the strange prickly coldness bringing me wide awake again.

NEGATIVE IMAGES

Sometimes, half asleep, I could've sworn I heard Dan talking to me. *My* Dan. I thought I heard him say, "You're stronger than him," and "I'm here, my love." It reminded me of what Carrie had said about her mother's Negative missing a piece. Was this the missing piece of Dan, or something that my imagination conjured?

Of course, it couldn't have been him. But I'd taken some comfort in the kind creation my sleep-deprived brain supplied. Around five in the morning, Dan's Negative finally vanished. And now someone else was poking me.

"Where's Mommy? What did you do to her?"

"I'm sorry..." I fumbled for an explanation. How old was Carrie's son? He could have been in preschool or first grade; I wouldn't have known much difference. What would he understand? What did he already know?

"Ben? Come on. Let her rest."

"But Dad, she's in Mom's clothes! Why did she take Mommy's things?"

I covered my face with my hands so the little boy wouldn't see me start crying, too. But it was all just like Dan's Negative had said. The child had seen me in his mom's clothes.

I heard Aaron shushing Ben and leading him out of the room, the little boy continuing to complain.

"Aaron, wait!" I dragged myself up. "Is she ... how is she?"

Aaron's face was impassive—a muscle clenched in his jaw. Ben hugged him tightly, and Aaron stroked his hair.

"She's at the hospital. She's on a 72-hour hold."

He didn't give more details—as it was, I felt terrible asking in front of Ben, but the words had just come out on their own.

173

Dan's Negative had predicted Ben's reaction to my clothes, but thankfully, he'd been wrong about Carrie.

I fumbled for my phone once they'd gone. It was 7:30. A whopping two and a half hours of sleep. I opened the door a crack. I could hear voices, but I wasn't sure what they were saying. One of them, at least, belonged to Ben. It sounded like they were going to leave the house. The hallway was empty. Where had Joshua gone?

I collected my clothes from the dryer. When I dropped Carrie's clothes into the hamper, I felt another wave of guilt that Dan's Negative had been right.

My head throbbed from the lack of sleep. I needed food and coffee desperately. And I needed to burn my clothes because the blood stains on the knees of my pants hadn't come out in the wash. Of course, I had red droplets on my sleeves, too. I needed to go home.

I could still hear voices downstairs, and the last thing I wanted to do was risk going down so Ben could see I was in my own clothes now and then ask me why they were stained.

I sent a quick text to Joshua. *What's going on? Where'd you go? We should leave.*

I leaned back against the pillows and covered my eyes with my hands.

I couldn't do much besides wait, so I went to our YouTube channel. I hoped that at least some small good had come from posting these videos. The comments section was a mix. It wasn't a viral video by any means, but about 2,000 people had viewed the speeches and Joshua's explanation. I wished we had Destiny's permission to post her interview.

People who'd attended the memorial had posted links to additional videos—all the awful ones where Joshua was blamed for Ainsley's death. Some people shared other tactics that they'd tried to get rid of them.

These included having a home blessed (by a priest, shaman, or psychic), working with a therapist, and visiting the NI's gravesite as Carrie had.

And, of course, some people seemed out to get us. Most of them mentioned Greg Patisis in their comments, as though he had some sort of solution to the problem.

I hadn't heard more from Eduardo, but I sent him links to our videos and encouraged him to share them—the more people who could weigh in on what they'd tried, the better.

A dull thud in the hallway made me spring up like I'd been poked again—I was all stiff and achy from the way I'd been sitting. I leaned over and twisted the knob without actually getting up—a small victory for me.

Joshua had his hands full with coffee cups and a brown paper bag, presumably full of food. He must have been kicking the door with the toe of his shoe.

"Hey," I said quietly as he came in and put the cups on the nightstand.

"Hey." He sounded happy. More than that, though, he was eager and energetic. "I figured you might not have slept well, but we have an appointment."

"Wait, what?"

"Here." Joshua handed me a cup. He smiled. "I convinced Aaron to let us in to see Carrie."

"Really? How? I'm surprised she's allowed to have visitors at all. And what about the kids?"

"Aaron took them to school."

"Seriously? Isn't that a little ..."

Joshua sighed. "I know. It's rotten. But he said he wanted to keep things normal for them. Besides that, he doesn't have anyone. He's an only child. I know Carrie mentioned that she had a poor relationship with her sister, and the boys said they hadn't seen her in a long time, but apparently, she wouldn't even answer the phone. The neighbors have all distanced themselves from the family. The boys hardly have any friends left at school."

"This is terrible. What are they going to do?" I took a sip of the coffee. It was delicious, and the warmth spread through me. "I feel like we should stay and help out somehow."

Joshua shrugged. "I don't know. Aaron is ... hard to read sometimes."

"I have to make a stop at my house before we see Carrie. I can't go over like this."

"Oh, don't worry about that. I've got some clothes for you." Joshua held up the bag that I'd assumed was food.

"What? You went to my house?"

I'd invited him into my life and given him the code to the garage; I just hadn't thought he'd end up using it to pick out clothes for me.

"You look terrified," Joshua said with a laugh. "Don't worry, I didn't go over to your place, actually. I asked Monica if she could swing by and drop some things off."

"Oh. Yeah, okay." I tucked a strand of hair behind my ear, still feeling flustered. "Thank you." I took another sip of coffee.

Joshua was decidedly upbeat, and I couldn't figure out why. We were in a stranger's home. A woman was in the hospital, and I considered us at least partially responsible.

"Wait. Where's Ainsley?"

"You mean where is Ainsley's Negative?" He seemed glad to make the correction, though I'd heard him make the same mix-up himself. "I haven't seen her in almost twenty-four hours."

NEGATIVE IMAGES

"How? Has she ever left you alone for that long?"

"No. I have no idea why this is happening. The last time I remember seeing her was when we got here." He tried to hold back a grin and failed.

I let out a long breath and remembered my last outburst at Joshua. I couldn't let jealousy come between us again.

"Do you think it's because of Carrie?" I suggested.

Joshua shrugged. "You know, I was frustrated that we didn't have our Negatives with us when we first met Carrie and her husband. It would have been easier on us if they were there."

I nodded, remembering my similar thoughts.

"Well, I'm glad you got a reprieve. Dan's Negative has been worse."

"I was incredibly grateful that Ainsley's Negative didn't show up last night. Because of the boys, you know? Although, they probably could have handled it. They saw their mom's all the time. I mean, these things don't discriminate, do they? It's not like they hide whenever children are present."

I bit my lip. If that was the reason his Negative had stayed away, I didn't think I could handle it. Not when I'd been on clean-up duty in the kitchen. I felt like all the hot coffee was boiling in my stomach. "Do you want to swap? I could help them once they're back from school."

Joshua gave me a half grin. "Not that I wouldn't, but I think we'll both be relieved of duty. Aaron's picking up the kids from school."

"Oh." I set the coffee down.

"He said he planned on staying with Carrie during the day and caring for the boys when they finished school."

I wanted to help them, but it seemed like Aaron had it all sorted out. Besides, Carrie was only supposed to be there for 72 hours, and some of that time had already gone by.

177

"I'm glad our appointment is today and not later."
"Think you can be ready in an hour?"
"Definitely."

I wasn't sure why I felt nervous as Joshua and I signed in at the visitor's desk. My palms were slicked with sweat, and I fumbled with my visitor sticker.

"I don't feel right about this," I mumbled as I finally fixed the sticker on my shirt.

"I do. Aaron did say it was okay, and it might help her to know she's helping others."

I still felt uneasy as we went down the hallway. The mood was tense. I couldn't help but think back to my last time in the hospital—sitting with Dan in his room, then being left behind when doctors and nurses flurried in to save him, even though he was already past saving.

I knocked on Carrie's slightly open door.

"Come in," she said, her voice soft.

Her room was dark except for the lights around her bed, which gave her a sort of medicinal halo. Her wrists, which I tried not to stare at, were heavily bandaged. I noticed, too, that restraints hung down from the bed, although she wasn't strapped into them.

Noticing my gaze, she let out a small, pitying laugh and explained, "I guess I'm not *as much* of an imminent danger to myself. They have to release me at some point, so I guess this is the first step, right?"

Carrie grinned up at us, and I smiled back weakly.

NEGATIVE IMAGES

Joshua and I sat in the hard plastic chairs near her bed. I took my time getting comfortable, drawing out the moments before we'd have to begin speaking in earnest.

"How are you?" I finally asked. I could have kicked myself for asking such a ridiculous question.

Carrie gave me a small smile and looked me directly in the eyes. "Well, I'm still here. Although it's proving impossible to get anyone here to believe that I'm not really suicidal, even though I technically tried to kill myself."

"That does seem like an impossible task," Joshua said.

We were silent for a minute, and my guilt kept nagging at me.

"Carrie, I feel responsible for this. I keep thinking that we must have triggered your Negative to act this way. What can we do for you?"

I felt Joshua staring at me, probably a little surprised, but I didn't turn to meet his gaze.

Carrie kept her smile in place, but her eyes were icy. "Help me? I'm past helping. Don't you see?"

Joshua and I exchanged a look.

"What do you mean?" I asked. We both leaned forward as Carrie began speaking.

"My Negative has already gotten me to try to kill myself once. Some doctor is going to put me on an antidepressant and refer me to a psychiatrist, but that isn't going to help unless the psychiatrist knows how to make my Negative Image go away. That's what they want. That's what they ultimately want, is for us to kill ourselves."

I fumbled with my phone. The interview, it seemed, had started. "Carrie, I hate to ask, but could I have your permission to record this conversation?" My finger hovered over the red record button in my voice memos app.

"Go ahead."

I pressed the button, and Carrie resumed speaking.

"I'll repeat what I just said: Our Negative Images are here to get us to kill ourselves."

I cleared my throat. "Why do you say that?"

Carrie raised her eyebrows at me. "You know what happened to the first woman who had one. She's dead. And the Negative is gone. What else could they want?"

I looked at Joshua, knowing that the thread of hope I'd been holding onto was breaking.

Carrie continued, "In my experience, they want us to be afraid and cut off from everyone. At first, it was frightening in the way that you might jump at a scary part in a horror movie. In the beginning, I thought all they really wanted was the easy scare. But now, I think that's when they're learning about us. They're studying what scares us the most and the most effective ways to get to us. As soon as they figure that out, they get much more aggressive." Joshua and I must have looked stricken because Carrie stopped talking. She had been speaking so passionately, so angrily. It was probably a great release for her. "How long have you two had yours?"

"About four weeks," I said woodenly, remembering how Dan's Negative had worked to deprive me of my sleep.

"About six weeks." Joshua sighed.

I couldn't help but look at him and feel utterly flabbergasted. Where was his Negative Image? Why hadn't she upped the ante, so to speak?

NEGATIVE IMAGES

"I'm sure this is a little different for each person," Carrie said, and I recalled my statement to the police officer yesterday. "But ultimately, I think as soon as they figure out what makes us tick, they try to destroy us. For me, that was about a month ago. She started scaring my boys. She'd be with me only when I was with them. Eventually, I couldn't be around them. They didn't want to see me." Carrie blinked rapidly, and her gaze turned towards the light coming through the blinds. She let out a long sigh before continuing.

"I was always the one who took them to school. Of course, that stopped because my Negative Image came with me to drop off and pick up. Imagine walking your preschooler to their classroom and having a Negative Image going with you. Ben always liked me to walk him in, even though the school says we should go through the car line. Kindergarten readiness!" Carrie laughed bitterly. "I can still see the kids' faces. The day they saw her. They all ran from us as we came in the door, clinging to each other and their teacher. They buried their faces and cried. And Ben ... he didn't know what to do. He was so embarrassed. So scared. After that, the school asked me not to come into the building. Even dropping him off in the car line was tough. He was always so scared the closer we got to school, and I could just see this weight on his little shoulders. As he walked away from me, I'd see his back straighten up, and he'd hold his head a little higher." Carrie swallowed and looked down at her blanket. "I guess he mastered that particular Kindergarten skill.

"Of course, after that one day, all the other parents knew about it. They distanced their kids from Ben, and they complained to the school. Eventually, the preschool director called me and politely asked if it would be possible for my husband to drop Ben off in the morning. I was devastated, but what could I do? I let Aaron take him." Carrie paused and glanced at us, probably expecting one of us to say something, but Joshua and I were too overwhelmed by her story. We didn't say a thing.

"My oldest, Jack, is in second grade," Carrie continued, trying to keep her voice level. "He's not welcome at any of his friends' houses anymore. And even though I've asked, and Aaron has asked, none of his friends will come to our house, either. We used to have so many little boys playing in our basement or our yard. We had a lively house. Now it feels too big and quiet. I hate being at home. It doesn't feel like *my* home anymore. And Jack begged me not to take him to school anymore, either. You know, Aaron works late. And I, well, Anita, you know I didn't have a job, per se, just organizations I liked to help. It was always so easy to schedule those meetings and events around our schedules so that I could do all the picking up and dropping off for the afternoon activities. I'm the only one who can take Jack to soccer practice after school, but he makes me park down the street. He doesn't want anyone to know I'm there."

Tears coursed down Carrie's cheeks in a steady stream. She didn't sniffle or wipe them away.

"Now my Negative has taken away my work. Which seems so ... I don't know. Backwards? I know some people just like to serve on boards because they have their own agenda, but I really saw it as a way to give back. Now I can't do that, and I haven't been able to help my children, my husband, or myself, either ..."

Carrie sighed, and her voice cracked when she spoke again. "Now all I have is my home. I sit at home, alone, all day. Aaron has to work. The boys have to go to school. And I have a feeling they all feel more relaxed there than in our home, with me."

NEGATIVE IMAGES

I imagined Carrie alone in her large house. It would be easy to picture her going crazy in its many rooms.

"You mentioned that your home life was wrecked," Joshua began, and I was startled to hear his voice because I'd been so drawn into Carrie's story. "What about your relationship with your husband? Has that changed?"

Carrie's eyes flashed. "Of course it has. I don't like to talk about it, but there's no privacy anymore. In *any* sense of the word. We can't even have a conversation without her joining us. It's been incredibly hard. For him, too."

"I'm sorry," Joshua said. I wasn't sure if he was sorry for them or sorry for asking.

Carrie nodded. She was silent for a moment, making more small folds along the edge of her blanket. "When the two of you showed up and started asking questions, I was afraid. Then I thought that even though it wouldn't benefit me, it might benefit someone else. And I began to feel just a little bit excited that I might be able to make someone else's existence easier or help everyone find a solution. Before you came, I was already waiting for something to happen. For the end to happen, if I'm honest. I couldn't see any way of improving things." She stared at her blanket, at the tiny folds she had made.

My shoulders relaxed; I hadn't realized how tightly I'd been hunching them. It made this more acceptable, knowing that Carrie wanted us here, and it wasn't simply Aaron okaying our visit.

Joshua broke the silence. "Why did you do it?"

Carrie looked up at him, her eyes red but clear. "I think ... she had been getting worse lately. More vile, more hurtful. She spoiled everything. Even my sleep, my food. When you came, I felt a little less desperate.

Then she pounced on me. I think she sensed that spark of hope in me. While you were in the other room, she just ..." Carrie shook her head and looked towards the window again. Joshua and I waited.

"I felt so bad, I can hardly describe it. She made me feel so much guilt over the circumstances around her death and my relationship with my sister. I began questioning everything I'd ever done, looking for how it must have ruined someone else's life. It even became ..." Carrie traced a pattern on the blanket, collecting her thoughts. "You guys hear yours like it's another person talking, right?"

Joshua and I nodded.

"For the past few days, I've heard her *inside my head*. I bought some earplugs a couple of weeks ago, trying to block her out. But then I heard her, just like I hear my own thoughts."

Carrie's eyes were wide with fear as she made this confession as if she expected some instant punishment just for uttering it. My spine tingled, and tears pricked my eyes. Was that what had happened to me last night in the kitchen? Or was it just my guilty conscience piping up? I didn't think I'd survive if I started hearing Dan's Negative inside my head.

"I didn't want to do it. Just so we're clear. Even when I picked up the knife and felt the blood, I regretted it. But I couldn't stop. It was the worst feeling in the world to be in the middle of such a horrific thing. It was almost like my hands were someone else's."

My breath caught in my chest. I thought about lunging at Dan a few nights ago, even though he wasn't there. How would Dan want me to die?

"Did she..." I cleared my throat and hoped my voice was even. "Did she instruct you? Make you do it a certain way?" My hands were clenched in fists, and my nails dug painfully into my palms.

"Um ..." Carrie looked up at the ceiling and stretched out the time before she had to answer. I noticed the veins sticking out on the side of her neck. "I would say so. Yes." She nodded, sure of herself. "I mean, it wasn't like she told me to pick up the knife and slit my wrists." Carrie struggled to get the words out, like her throat hurt just saying them. "She got more excited as I started doing it, and her insults got worse. And I don't know how to say it exactly because I can't remember all of it, but it was like what she was saying ... the memories she brought up influenced me to do it that way. Last Thanksgiving dinner, my sister and I got into an argument." Carrie sighed. "I still feel bad about it, but I think she chose that memory because I was in the kitchen. Only instead of carving a turkey, I carved myself."

Carrie clapped a hand over her mouth, and her eyes grew wide. I couldn't tell if she was about to laugh or cry.

"What are you talking about with my patient?"

A stocky nurse filled the doorway. I hadn't heard her arrive. "You're distressing her at a time when she absolutely should not be upset. You have to go. Now." With her hands on her hips, she took up as much space as Joshua and I together.

"No, please, it's okay," Carrie protested, but her voice was small. She reminded me of a child caught misbehaving by her teacher.

"No, it's not. You're supposed to be resting, not bawling your eyes out."

The nurse turned back to us, her face blotchy with anger. "You need to leave."

I grabbed my phone, still recording, and swung my purse over my shoulder. "I'm sorry, Carrie. Maybe we can finish our talk later."

"I'm putting in a recommendation that you be removed from the visitors list. Whatever conversation you're having needs to happen when she's in a better state," the nurse snapped.

"Shit," Joshua hissed as the doors to the hospital wing closed behind us. I pressed the stop button on my recording, glad that I'd gotten the exchange with the nurse on there as well.

"Do you think that nurse was right? Should we have waited until Carrie was released from the hospital?"

"No. She was glad to see us, I think." The automatic doors opened, and we stepped outside. A sliver of sun peeked out through the clouds. I saw her then, in the parking lot, next to Joshua's car. I grabbed him and made him look at me.

"There's something I wish we'd asked Carrie."

"What?"

"Her Negative Image. I didn't see it there. She didn't mention it, at least not after her suicide attempt."

"So ... what? You think it's gone?" Joshua squinted. I'd turned him into the sun and away from Ainsley's Negative.

"I don't know. Do you think it believes Carrie died? Or maybe it just used a lot of energy getting her to make that attempt on her life."

"Either could be right, I suppose. The only way we would know anything is if it comes back and if Carrie tells us about it."

Joshua started to turn, but I held onto him, feeling bad about what he would see. "You have a visitor, Joshua."

Ainsley's Negative opened her mouth in a smile. Her lips seemed too red, and her teeth too white. I'll never forget the way Joshua's mouth fell open and the way his eyes filled with fear in just a fraction of a second.

CHAPTER SIXTEEN

Joshua's knuckles were white on the steering wheel as he turned onto the street. Ainsley's Negative had been joined by Dan's, and I could see both of them, with their twin sets of black eyes, in the rearview mirror. They smiled at me and vanished as we got on the highway.

"I think we should talk to Aaron."

Joshua nodded. "I actually got a text from him just before we saw Carrie. He wanted us to stop by."

I kept revisiting our conversation with Carrie—the tear tracks on her face and how she held onto her blanket like a small child. What would Aaron think when we told him how we'd left her?

"She can't do anything while she's in the hospital." Joshua covered my hand with his but my mind was so far away that it took me a moment to register the weight and warmth of his touch. After a moment, I relaxed and let myself be comforted.

"I just keep thinking about her. We don't know for sure if she's seen her Negative Image since her attempt. Did you see those restraints hanging down from her bed? To tie down her arms and legs? They've let her out of those. It could come back and get her to try again. She's probably more vulnerable now than she was before."

Joshua shook his head. "I think the farther away she is from the attempt, the stronger she becomes. She seemed determined."

"Still ... she's free to move now, to grab hold of something that might make it easy for her to ..." I left my thoughts unfinished. Images flooded my mind, one worse than the next. Carrie grabbing one of the wires meant to monitor her health and slipping it around her neck. Carrie stumbling into the bathroom, breaking something to make it sharp. Carrie clawing at the bandages on her wrists and biting through her stitches, blood dripping from her mouth. My stomach rolled, and something hot stirred in my bowels.

"Anita, I know it's hard, but this is not your fault or mine. And we have no control over what happens to Carrie next."

I worked my hand out from under his. "I didn't say anything about fault. I just don't want to see Carrie dead." My voice came out harder than I meant.

"I don't want her dead either. I would never have suggested meeting her if I'd known any of this would happen."

"Me either."

Joshua turned onto Carrie's street. My phone vibrated, and I fished it out of my purse. I had an email from Eduardo.

I scanned it and cursed under my breath. "Joshua, this is bad. 'Hi Anita, I appreciate your videos and think it's more important than ever to identify a way to rid ourselves of these Negatives. I imagine the news will break soon if it hasn't already, but my mother has come back to me as a Negative Image. While earlier, I was convinced that we wouldn't have a database here in Argentina, my condition has made everyone more afraid. This NI hasn't been with me long, but she's nothing like my mother. She has my mother's memories, but places blame where my mother would have been more understanding. It makes me worried for the soul of the mother I knew and loved, and I worry about what will happen to us without a solution.'"

"Oh my God," Joshua said.

"This changes everything."

My phone rang in my hand. Monica.

"Have you seen the news?" she snapped.

"I just heard from Eduardo personally. This is bad."

"No shit." Monica let out a loud sigh. "You could be in danger."

I put my phone on speaker.

"What do you mean? Joshua is here, by the way."

"Oh, um, okay. Hi, Josh. People are saying you guys could put everyone in danger, that no one is safe if they know someone with a Negative Image."

Joshua and I exchanged a look. Something clicked into place for both of us. I articulated it first. "They want us to kill ourselves... so we'll come back like them."

"Yes!" Monica practically shouted. "That's what some of the 'experts' are saying!" The sarcasm dripped off the word. "They claim it's some strange force that's working to kill off humankind! Well, okay, the last part about ending humankind is coming from the guy behind the NI database site. He's calling—well, along with his group of fellow nutters, which is actually kind of a lot of people, who are all very, very loud in expressing their beliefs, by the way—but look, they want to basically round you guys up and quarantine you."

Joshua looked at me with his eyebrow raised, and despite how seriously Monica spoke, we both burst out laughing. Joshua let out a single loud bark, and I giggled uncontrollably.

"I'm not joking! People are starting to fucking riot!"

At that, I calmed myself down a little. "Monica," I said smoothly. "I don't think they'll be able to start rounding us up and shooting us or something."

"Just look at the fucking news." Monica hung up.

"Geez, you pissed her off," Joshua said. I couldn't tell if he was serious or if he was just ribbing me, but my face grew hot.

"Maybe we should take a look at it." I pulled out my phone, but Joshua elbowed me.

Aaron was coming out the front door. His hands were clenched, his eyes narrowed.

Joshua and I got out of the car and stood beside it, unsure where to go. As Aaron approached, I realized he wasn't exactly angry. It was something more than that. He seemed ... hurt.

"I tell you that you can visit Carrie, but then I get a call from some nurse telling me that you made her cry? She said you may have set back her progress by making her relive this trauma before she was ready. What happened over there? Why would you do that to her?" His voice softened as he asked the questions, and his eyes were glassy.

"Well, she did cry a little, but she was just telling us her story—" I began.

"I promise," Joshua jumped in. "We didn't provoke her in any way."

Aaron didn't answer right away. He seemed unsure of himself—his hands relaxed and hung loose at his sides, and his shoulders drooped in resignation. He looked defeated.

NEGATIVE IMAGES

Maybe he hadn't expected us to be so forthcoming, or maybe he wasn't sure if he really wanted to listen to our discussion, but eventually, he led us into the house.

For an uncomfortable moment, we lingered in the entryway.

"Would it be okay to put on the news?" Given how upset Aaron had been outside, I felt awkward asking, but I was dying to see if things were really as bad as Monica claimed.

Aaron stared at me for a moment, his gaze darkening. "Sure. Whatever." Aaron refused to look either of us in the eye, perhaps hiding his anger under a veneer of apathy.

Joshua turned on the TV, and its colors swirled over the otherwise dark room, distracting me from my worries for Aaron.

The headline under the news anchor read: *Negative Image Pandemic Spurs New Fears*.

It changed to *NI Database Creator Issues a Call to Action*.

"Shit," I swore under my breath.

"I'm joined now by Greg Patisis, creator of nidatabase.com. Greg, why don't you explain to us what your website is and how you think it could help control this pandemic?"

He sat across from the host, Megan O'Neill, the desk between them large and empty. Greg's mouth quirked upwards as he began to speak. He seemed like the type of person who would enjoy being on TV just for the sake of saying he'd done it.

"Well, Megan, my website started off fairly small. I began by sharing the names and locations of people near me with a Negative Image attached to them."

"And how did you verify this?"

"Well, typically through photo and video evidence."

"Some would argue that that can be manipulated fairly easily."

Greg pursed his lips and nodded in agreement. "It was definitely a concern of mine, too, especially as the website grew. What I began to do was require three people to verify that they had also seen a Negative Image attached to the person in question, as well as add evidence of their own."

That didn't seem like enough independent, verifiable accounts to me, but Megan didn't press the issue.

"Your website tracks people with Negative Images across the United States now. Is that correct?"

"Yes." Patisis looked proud of this fact, even though he was destroying the lives of thousands of people in the process.

"How do you verify the identity of your users? Some of your critics, especially those unfamiliar with the site, have voiced their opinions that few people must actually be using the website and posting photos of their neighbors. They suspect only a handful of people are doing it." I smiled, glad that the newscaster was asking a question I also had.

"You know, I think the people who suggest that are the ones who don't take this situation seriously."

Megan nodded. My stomach rolled. She was going to let him dodge the question.

"They're the same people who claim that Negative Images are not harmful. I think most of them have a Negative Image themselves or have a family member with one. They're so close to the situation that they don't recognize the terrible effects that their Negative Images have on other people."

"Can you elaborate on that?" Megan asked, repositioning herself in her chair.

NEGATIVE IMAGES

Greg leaned across the desk, his arms claiming much of the surface space. "Megan, my daughter, became very disturbed when my next-door neighbor's husband returned as a Negative Image. She couldn't understand why he was back. We had explained his death to her a couple of months ago, and she was understandably very scared to see him again. I think for children especially, it's hard for them to grasp what a Negative Image is and how it's different from the person who died."

"And so because of this, you're proposing a census of all the people in the United States with a Negative Image?"

Patisis nodded. His eyes gleamed. "Actually, I think we need to do more than that. First and foremost, we get information about the people who currently have a Negative Image. Then, we also need a list of their close family and friends since we now know that someone with a Negative can become a Negative themselves. And I think we really do need to consider taking these people who have Negatives and placing them in some kind of quarantine."

Aaron stirred on the sofa behind me, and a guttural moan escaped his throat.

"A quarantine seems a little extreme to some people," Megan commented. "I actually agree with them on this point," she added with a little laugh and a glance towards the camera. "It's not as though these people are sick."

"How else can we stop this? I haven't heard any actionable ideas from anyone else," Patisis answered. Megan opened her mouth, but he pointed at her, effectively shutting her up. "If we prevent the people who have a Negative Image now from becoming too close to anyone else, I think we can drastically cut down on the number of people who are becoming plagued with Negative Images. Think about it. All the Negative Images have come back to a loved one or close friend. We now know that Maria Vasquez has returned to her son as a Negative Image. The only way to stop the cycle is by severing those relationships. That's how we beat this thing. That's how we win."

Patisis had completely taken over the interview. He ended on a note of triumph, and even I had to admit that he looked like someone in charge as Megan O'Connell's smile faltered when she announced the commercial break.

Aaron stood up and turned off the TV.

"What is this about people with Negatives coming back as Negatives too?" His eyes darted back and forth between Joshua and I, almost as though we'd kept this from him deliberately.

I tried to explain, but Aaron cut me off.

"You know what, though? In a weird way, the guy has a point. I mean, you probably don't think about this. You don't have kids. But can you imagine what it's been like for me? I can't protect my sons from this. God only knows how much it's affected them."

Aaron paced in front of the TV, his mouth opening and closing a little like he needed to speak but couldn't find the words. "You know what? I almost agree with that nutter. Maybe it would be better if you were all quarantined."

"How can you say that?" He'd been so protective of Carrie the entire time we were here that I couldn't believe what he was saying.

"What happens if Carrie dies? Huh? Who do you think she'll come back to?" His eyes grew dark—I couldn't tell if he was angry or sad.

Joshua and I were silent.

"Oh, come on! You know her Negative Image would come to me."

"Probably," Joshua admitted.

NEGATIVE IMAGES

"Or one of your children," I said without much thought, only thinking that Carrie's Negative was her mother.

Aaron focused on me with a look of pure hatred. "How dare you?" he spoke quietly. He came closer. Individual beads of sweat were forming on his forehead. "Can you imagine what that would do to a child? And how helpless I would be to do anything for my sons?" His voice rose to a shout, taking up the expanse of the house.

"I'm so sorry. I should never have—"

"Shut up." Aaron turned from me. After a moment, he said, "Thinking of either of my boys afflicted with a Negative is enough. No matter what happens, I can't risk my wife attaching herself to me or one of our boys. What was it he said? That the quarantine could help sever the relationship?"

I held my breath, hoping Aaron wasn't making the leap I thought he was.

"Carrie can't come back here after her hold is up."

I let out the breath I'd been holding. Joshua looked out the window, his jaw clenched.

"You can't tell me that having her come home is in my best interest or my boys' best interest. I want her home," he said as an afterthought. "I really do. I want life to go back to the way it was. But I can't put my boys at risk."

Joshua and I looked at each other for a few moments. I wondered if he was thinking the same thing I was.

"Just because she's not here doesn't mean that her relationship with you isn't the most important one to her," I said. "She could be separated from you, pass away, and still come to you as a Negative Image."

Aaron was quiet, considering.

REBECCA SCHIER-AKAMELU

"That's what everyone says, right? Negatives come back to the person who was most important to them." I couldn't tell if I was having any kind of an impact on Aaron but decided to press on anyway. "When you have a Negative Image, just knowing that you have someone who cares about you is the most important thing in the world because you lose everything else."

Aaron shook his head slowly and gave a small smile. "If that were the case, then Carrie would never have tried to commit suicide. If her relationships with me and our boys were supposed to be as important to her as you say, then the thought of us should have prevented her from going through with it." He walked to the bookshelf and returned with a framed family photo. It was an outdoorsy summer shot with the family in coordinated outfits, and while no one looks posed, you know that they must have been.

"Carrie cared about everything, you know?" Aaron studied Carrie's face in the photo. "She cared about getting stuff like this done, the family photos and all that. She cared about our boys and their school, never missing a game or a recital." He looked up at Joshua and me, his tone softening. "I haven't seen her care that much about any of us in a long time."

"Carrie told us how she couldn't be there anymore for her boys. It's not that she doesn't want to be; it's just that she can't." I swiped at more tears, remembering how upset Carrie was about not walking Ben to school in the mornings.

Aaron didn't respond to me right away, and with his face glued to the photograph, I couldn't read his expression. "It's more than that. If she still felt the same way about us, she would have asked us about the things going on in our lives. But instead, she's just been drawing more and more

NEGATIVE IMAGES

into herself, afraid of everything. I know she can't help that, but it's frustrating to watch. I always thought she'd be stronger, somehow. You know what?" He gave a self-pitying laugh. "When she talked to you guys yesterday, it was the most engaged I've seen her in at least a month. It's the first time she's really taken an interest in someone or something. I wish she'd act that way with me."

"I'm sorry." I apologized, even though it had nothing to do with us but was about his relationship with Carrie.

Aaron waved my words away with his hand, not even bothering to look at me. I didn't like the look on his face. It seemed like he was worlds away. It made me think no one would be able to get through to him.

Silence wrapped around us, but Joshua broke it. "Did you try to talk to her about her Negative Image?"

Aaron blinked a few times and smiled at Joshua, but his eyes were hard. "What kind of a question is that?" He sighed. "I guess you might not understand what it's like being the 'support person' for someone like you. But I did try—of course, I tried—many times, especially in the beginning. At first, she did. Apparently, her Negative was spouting all sorts of crap about me and our marriage. I always thought I had a decent relationship with my mother-in-law while she was alive, but her Negative Image tells a different story. Everything from how I only married my wife for her looks, which her Negative says are dwindling, that I don't think she's an equal partner in our marriage, that she spends too much of the money I make."

Aaron had been talking fast, but then he stopped and caught his breath before continuing. "All of a sudden, my marriage was me, my wife, and my wife's creepy dead mother. Nothing I did or said seemed to get the doubts out of Carrie's head. At first, I could reason with her, remind her that her mother wasn't really her mother, you know?"

Joshua and I nodded. We knew all too well, of course.

"But it just got harder and harder. That thing has a hold on her. It has claws, and I can't get Carrie out of them. Now it turns out Carrie's gonna end her life one way or another." I thought Aaron was going to say more, but instead, he stared off into nothing, that faraway look back on his face.

Joshua looked at me and shrugged. I shrugged back. I didn't know how to deal with a man who acted like he was mourning the dead when his wife was still alive. I thought back to Aaron's comments about the quarantine and wondered if it would be easier for him to believe Carrie was dead if she was removed from the house.

The phone rang, a piercing sound in the quiet. Aaron walked down the hall to take the call.

"Do you think it's Carrie?" I asked quietly, hoping Aaron wouldn't hear me from the hallway.

Joshua shook his head quickly as if dismissing the notion would make it less likely. I hoped he was right. Besides, Aaron had already gotten a call about how we'd upset Carrie during our visit.

Aaron came back in, his footsteps loud and purposeful, his mouth set. "That was the hospital." His eyes were wide and unsettled. "We need to go." He gave me a look. "You and Joshua, too. You're needed, apparently."

Joshua and I followed Aaron out into the hallway as he yelled for Jack and Ben to come down.

We hurried after Aaron, all of us piling into his car. Joshua rode shotgun; I was crammed between the two boys in the back seat. Aaron

NEGATIVE IMAGES

wove in and out of traffic like an artful snake. Being in the back seat made me nauseous. When we finally arrived at the hospital, I jumped out over Jack and nearly kissed the pavement to get some fresh air.

My legs shook, and the back of my throat had a nasty, coppery taste. Joshua grabbed my wrist and pulled. Aaron wasn't waiting for me or anyone. Even his boys were running to keep up with him.

"Come on," Joshua urged.

I groaned and gulped in fresh air. "She couldn't have made another attempt, could she?"

"I can't think of anything else that would warrant us racing down here like this." Joshua's voice was tense.

"She can't be dead."

Joshua started jogging. I forced my legs to run, too.

The staff was quick to point Aaron in the right direction, and there was no filling out visitor forms for any of us. We rounded the corner quickly, and Carrie sat propped up in her bed. She looked drained and pale, but a quick scan of her body showed no new injuries. Only the two policemen stationed outside her door indicated that something had gone seriously wrong.

A detective stood up when we entered Carrie's room, the one who'd interviewed me the night of Carrie's attempt. Detective Lee. He looked out of place in the hospital. I guessed he needed to speak about police business, but Carrie was barely awake. Shouldn't a nurse be here ordering us out of the room?

"I just finished taking your wife's statement," the detective said after we had all shaken hands. "The nurse in question confessed."

Joshua and I exchanged a look.

"Apparently, she overheard part of the conversation you two had with Carrie." The detective sized up Joshua and me with his steely brown eyes. "Then, after hearing the news tonight, she decided to act. She claims she was trying to stop the cycle."

Aaron was silent. The boys looked at the floor. Joshua and I exchanged a look that let me know he was just as confused as I was. Why wasn't Carrie being left alone to rest? Why were Joshua and I also called down here? And the boys. They'd seen so much; did they have to be here for this, too?

Another cop, a young woman, rapped on the door. "Boys? Would you like to pick a snack from the vending machine?" The boys were out the door fast, leaving us alone with Detective Lee.

"Mr. Maguire and Mrs. Walsh," Detective Lee said, looking at Joshua and me, "please tell me why you visited Mrs. Ellsworth today."

"Shouldn't we be letting her rest?" I blurted out.

Detective Lee gave me a half smile. "Ordinarily, yes, but Mrs. Ellsworth insisted that we do this here, and the circumstances are very unusual."

"We all have Negative Images. Joshua and I came to see Carrie about hers and to interview her so that other people could get a more accurate idea of what it's like to have a Negative Image. Then she ended up here."

"Because of her suicide attempt." Detective Lee added bluntly.

"Yes," I said.

"And is that the reason you came to the hospital?"

"We were concerned about her."

"You upset her." Aaron's voice came out in a growl. "I think you just wanted your damn interview."

"It wasn't planned. But we did interview Carrie," Joshua said.

"What did you talk about?"

"Does it really matter?" I asked.

"I just like to make sure everyone's on the same page."

I sighed. It seemed like some kind of a trick, but I wasn't sure what he was getting at. "We talked about why Carrie tried to commit suicide and what life was like for her with her Negative Image."

"Were either of you aware of a nurse monitoring your conversation at any point?"

"Only the nurse that came in to make us stop the interview when Carrie started to cry," Joshua answered. "I felt bad about that. We didn't mean to upset her so much, but Anita and I can tell you that having a Negative makes some parts of life practically impossible."

Detective Lee nodded. "Did either of you talk to any of the nurses after your interview with Mrs. Ellsworth?"

Joshua and I glanced at each other. Detective Lee's watchfulness made me nervous, even though I had nothing to feel guilty about.

"I don't remember saying anything. Maybe we said goodbye to the woman at the desk on the way out, but I'm really not sure," I answered.

"I don't think we did," Joshua said. I shrugged.

"After you left, the nurse who asked you to leave called Mr. Ellsworth and told him you had upset his wife a great deal. She recommended suspending your visiting privileges."

"Aaron told us the hospital had taken us off the list."

"Mr. Ellsworth made the decision," Detective Lee corrected.

"Oh." It seemed like the kind of comment intended to drive a wedge between us. It annoyed me that it was working.

Aaron shifted in his seat and refused to meet my gaze. "It was nothing personal." He kept his shoulders hunched up.

"Of course not," Joshua said, but the way he looked at Aaron suggested otherwise.

I couldn't understand why Aaron hadn't mentioned this when he first spoke to us outside his house.

"I'm assuming you've all heard the latest on the news today," Detective Lee said after a beat.

We murmured that we had.

"Well, that was the other bit that spurred this nurse into action."

"Sorry, what happened exactly?" I asked. Joshua and I looked at the detective intently. I'd pieced together that the nurse had done something to Carrie, but I could only guess at how bad it was.

"A nurse taking care of Mrs. Ellsworth put a lethal dose of morphine in her IV after hearing the news this afternoon. She said she acted based on her belief that Mrs. Ellsworth would cease her suffering if she were deceased, and she feared that Mrs. Ellsworth would be forced to live in what she termed a "concentration camp" type of existence otherwise. Thankfully, another nurse discovered the drug was missing and realized what had happened, stopping the IV shortly after morphine was administered."

Detective Lee looked up from the notes he'd been reading from, and his eyes shifted back and forth between Joshua and me.

"She got the idea that Carrie's existence was pure torture from somewhere. When I pressed her on it, she said she overheard Carrie talking about her condition to some visitors."

"Us," I mumbled. I could feel Aaron's eyes boring a hole in my back.

Detective Lee looked behind me at Aaron and then back again. "Just to be clear," he said, "neither of you are being charged. We don't believe you were responsible for the attack, but obviously, your conversation with Mrs. Ellsworth influenced this nurse."

"What about my wife?" Aaron asked.

Detective Lee turned and acknowledged Carrie. Her body looked limp and smaller than it had earlier that day. Her eyes moved beneath her lids, but she seemed oblivious to what was going on. "She has two officers guarding her door, and we can guarantee that level of safety until she leaves the hospital. The nurse in question has been charged. I've recommended that the nurses who care for Mrs. Ellsworth should come in pairs to discourage another attempt on her life."

Aaron nodded, lost in thought.

"Why did she want to be present for this?" I asked as Detective Lee rose to conclude the interview. "She must have wanted to tell us something."

Detective Lee nodded and shrugged. "I'm not sure what it was. I don't want to wake her. She'll have to call you."

Joshua looked as upset and eager to stay as I was. Aaron moved towards the door and gave us a pointed look to follow. Just as we were about to walk through the doorway, Carrie cleared her throat.

"Wait." Her voice was weak and gravelly. "I wanted to tell you ..." She beckoned us closer. "I heard about the quarantine idea."

Joshua and I stilled. It seemed impossible that she could have heard, but maybe she'd been more alert than we thought.

"I just wanted to let you know, in case you're going to post our interviews. Which, to be clear, you have my permission to do."

"Of course we will," Joshua said. "Now more than ever, it's important."

Carrie gripped Joshua's wrist. Very quietly, so Aaron and the detective wouldn't hear, she said, "I'm going to contact Greg Patisis."

"What? Why?" I asked. I couldn't imagine a worse, more unsympathetic person to talk to.

"Because I agree with him." Carrie's voice was firm. I felt all the energy leave me like a deflating balloon. "And, because no one's tried it yet."

"You can't mean that." My voice was tiny, weaker even than Carrie's.

"I know it's hard to understand, but I do. What would have happened if I hadn't survived my suicide attempt? I know Aaron thinks I would have come to him as a Negative Image." Her eyes flicked over to him, then back to us. "The truth is, I think I would come back to my youngest son. Ben. Lately, things with Aaron ..." She didn't finish her thought. I wondered if their relationship had been much better before her mother came to her as an NI or if it had been struggling anyway. "I just can't bear the thought that Ben might be shackled with me as a Negative Image. It would destroy him."

"Putting yourself under quarantine wouldn't necessarily change your relationship with him, though," Joshua pointed out. "Not if he's still the most important person to you."

"Then I just have to make myself believe that he's not. I have to tell myself that he, Jack, and Aaron are all nothing to me. They're just people I met in another life."

Chapter Seventeen

"You don't think Carrie is really going to contact that nutter about going into quarantine, do you?" I asked when we were back in Joshua's car. The shared car ride back from the hospital had been quiet and tense, and I knew Aaron was glad to see us go.

I kept thinking about Aaron and how he thought it was a foregone conclusion that *he* would get Carrie's Negative Image since he was her husband. I wondered if he'd feel differently about the quarantine proposal if he knew that Carrie thought her Negative would most likely go to Ben.

"I think she will. It's not like Aaron would oppose her. And the boys won't talk to her about it either way. I don't think I've ever met quieter kids. And I mean, shit, you can't argue that it'd be better for her not to since that nurse tried to kill her."

"She's not going to be safe anywhere, is she? She's not safe from herself, not safe from others ..."

"I bet if that quarantine idea gains support, they'll have people there to prevent the suicides."

I shook my head and sat up straighter in my seat. "I think you're wrong. I think the whole goal of that proposition is to get people to break off their attachments to their family and friends and become very close to another person with a Negative. The idea is that once they do that, they can kill themselves without worry of passing their Negative on to someone else. Even if they did, it would be to a person who has a Negative Image already, and who knows if that's even possible?"

At least so far, only Eduardo had his mother attached as a Negative Image. But what if that changed?

"I don't know about you," I continued when Joshua didn't answer, "but I'm starving. Do you want to grab some food and we could eat at my house? We have to decide what we do next."

Joshua sighed. "I'm exhausted, but sure."

I couldn't blame him. It was late, past ten, but I was too keyed up to even consider sleep. One drive-thru stop later, we were at my house, and we had more to discuss than I'd realized.

"I didn't like that cop calling us down," Joshua said as we settled on my sofa. "I know he said we weren't charged with anything, but there was no reason for us to be a part of that interview, was there?"

I took a moment to replay the interaction in my head. "I don't think so, except for when he asked if we'd spoken to any nurses."

Joshua nodded. "Okay, sure. But didn't it feel just a step away from one of those TV shows where we're brought in for questioning?" He laughed a little, but it was forced.

"It's an unusual situation, but it's obvious we didn't commit any crimes."

We ate in silence for a few moments until Joshua brought up the inevitable. "What do you think we should do with the interviews we had with Carrie? She did give us her permission to post them."

I nodded, thinking it over. "I guess ... she's been through a lot. I wish she'd asked us to post them instead of simply giving permission. I can't tell if she really wants it out there or if she's just allowing it."

"She said herself, though, that it made her happy to know she might be helping other people."

I sighed. He was right. "In which case, I almost feel like it's wrong not to post them."

"Exactly. May I?" Joshua gestured to my laptop, and I nodded. He checked our YouTube account, and his eyebrows shot up. "Holy crap. Our views have jumped. Eduardo said he was going to tell people to go to our channel, didn't he?"

I went to Instagram and searched for Eduardo. Sure enough, he had posted a video. I guessed we'd been watching Patisis on the news at the time.

"Many of you are hearing that I have my mother attached to me now as a Negative Image," Eduardo said in the video. "And I wanted to confirm here that this is true. For those of you who've been following me and my family, I want to thank you for your continued support. And I know that for many of you, this is quite scary news to hear. I've become acquainted with an American who's putting together the experiences of those of us with Negatives. She's trying to find out what we've tried to make them go away so that we can hopefully get to the bottom of this. You can find her on YouTube—her channel is Joshua & Anita Take on Negatives. You'll find a link in my bio. Let's support each other. Thank you."

"Well, people listened to him." Joshua turned the laptop my way. We still only had the videos from Joshua's event. "Our views have quadrupled."

I stared at him, a little shell-shocked.

"I think now is the time to post our interviews with Carrie. Even though they're audio only, I think they're good."

"You'll get yourself in trouble."

I jumped. I hated it when Dan's Negative was able to scare me out of the blue.

"Think about it," he said. "You're going to get all sorts of attention. For all the wrong reasons."

I'd been having similar thoughts. All of this was a far cry from the carefully curated Instagram Monica and I maintained for Legendary Events.

"What's he saying?" Joshua asked.

I sighed. "Not to do it." I took a deep breath, only half believing what I needed to say next. "Honestly, I agree with him."

"What? That's crazy!"

"I know, it's just, well, think about it. We interview Destiny, and then she calls me, saying that we can't use it and warning me that Dan's NI will get stronger. Then we interviewed Carrie, and she's now in the hospital. Joshua, what if we're making things worse for the people we're reaching out to?"

Joshua set his laptop aside. "Okay. I mean, I do see your point; it's just ... remember that both Carrie and Aaron said that talking with us really engaged her. Carrie said she felt some hope. Maybe you're right, and we should hold off on finding more people to interview for now. I mean, with all the views we're getting, there's bound to be helpful comments."

NEGATIVE IMAGES

I sighed. "Okay. I guess ... since we already have Carrie's interview and the worst that could happen has already passed ..."

"We should definitely do this, Anita. People are paying attention to us. Now is the perfect time to upload Carrie's interviews."

I felt like I was going to get a headache, but I nodded and let Joshua get to work uploading both parts of our interview.

Joshua had insisted on going home after he finished his food. I couldn't blame him, but a large part of me wanted him to stay. I imagined us curled up on the couch after uploading the interviews, maybe watching a movie. We'd never done anything like that, and I had no real reason to seem like we would. But I wanted to.

My house was empty and dark. It was 1:30 in the morning, and I couldn't sleep. I needed rest, but I needed a drink more. All of this new information from Carrie, the idea that she might willingly lock herself up, and my thoughts about Joshua and the interviews had me on edge. My body was wiped out, but I knew my brain wouldn't shut down. I found some whiskey in the freezer and poured myself a generous splash over ice.

I expected Dan's Negative to be here—it seemed like the perfect time and place to scare me and make me feel like shit—but apparently, he disagreed. Instead, I took my drink upstairs and sat in bed, sipping whiskey and looking for something to watch on my iPad.

What would have happened if Dan hadn't come back? If he'd died and left me behind? It was hard to imagine doing anything else at this moment. But I had always had a faint idea that I would have soldiered on better if his Negative hadn't been haunting me. Perhaps I'd be spending more time with Monica than ever before, throwing myself into the business because nothing else urgently needed my attention.

At least, that was still true. Nothing I did was urgent anymore without Dan. The business was limping along without me. The house had never cared about the updates we'd made for it. The future family had only ever been a wisp of an idea.

I took several more sips of whiskey.

It was only when I laid down, eyes closed and ready for sleep to grab me, that I felt it. I opened my eyes a sliver, but I didn't see him. I closed my eyes again, but my muscles stayed tense.

"Don't you want to know how I got to be this way?" Dan's Negative asked me.

I opened my eyes. His face hovered over mine, one arm on either side of me, trapping me. He leaned closer, his nose practically touching mine.

"How do I get rid of you?" I spewed the words at him. He had me pinned, but I wasn't scared. I was pissed.

"You know I can't tell you that." He smiled slyly, his teeth glinting in the soft light from the bathroom.

"Does that mean there *is* a way?" I challenged.

He hesitated just a fraction of a second, his smile frozen on his face. "Of course not, you hopeful little fool."

"Tell me something else then."

He laughed at me. I should have felt his breath on my face and smelled his mouthwash.

"Can someone have two Negative Images? Eduardo, will he get his father's Negative, too?"

"Wouldn't you like to know? Tell you what. I don't think Joshua is as strong as you are. Let's give Ainsley another week to work on him. Then you might get to find out for yourself firsthand." His eyes were flat, his tone mocking. I hated him.

I reached for Dan's pillow, ignoring the prickling cold sensation when I reached through his Negative. I covered my face with the pillow and cried. And when the pillow was too wet, and I could not catch my breath, I threw it down.

Dan's Negative was gone, the room fully dark.

I laid awake for a long time. Thinking.

He'd hesitated.

He'd froze.

I could believe him and take his words at face value.

He could have hesitated on purpose to mess with me and give me false hope. But as the hours ticked by, I kept remembering his face. And I thought that maybe in his hesitation, I might have my answer.

Sunlight poked through my blinds. It felt like a personal attack on my eyeballs. I rolled over, hoping to ignore it, but then my phone chimed, and I knew I wouldn't get back to sleep. At least I was alone, for now. I curled up in a ball under my blankets and cradled my phone so I could see who was texting me.

Monica.

9:27. *Coming in today? It's Tuesday, just FYI.*

11:03. *We need to talk.*

12:29. I'm worried.

I sighed. Monica was usually more straightforward. These messages were more passive-aggressive, dancing around the fact that I no longer acted like a co-owner of our business.

I started typing out a message and deleted it. I'd rather not have this type of conversation over text. I could barely figure out what to say because I was too busy trying to decipher the subtext.

I typed back a quick response.

Yes. I'll be in soon. We can talk then.

I had lots of other notifications that I had been able to sleep through, apparently. People were tagging me on social media, our YouTube videos had really taken off, and I had emails, too.

What have I done?

I showered and dressed quickly.

My mind wandered to Joshua as I scooped out coffee grounds and added the water to the pot. He was always thoughtful enough to bring me coffee and food. I wished he were here now. And, now that I thought about it, it was odd that he hadn't reached out to talk about the videos.

I dialed him while I waited for the coffee to brew.

"Hello?" His voice was groggy and thick with sleep.

"I woke you. I'm sorry." Coffee started dripping down into the pot, and I couldn't help but feel a little awkward at not being able to offer him any.

"Ainsley was in bed with me. All night. Talking. She said she always hated that the most about our relationship. She said we never communicated well or as much as she would have liked, and if I had only talked with her more and listened to her, she wouldn't have felt like she needed to go out with her friends all the time. She made it sound like if I had just been there for her, we would have been home cuddling and talking, and she wouldn't have gotten killed by me. God, she stressed that last part."

"I'm sorry, Joshua. I bet the real Ainsley would be willing to take some responsibility for her actions if she was here and able to talk to you. No one forced her to go out all the time. She could have met with her friends at home or over coffee. And she definitely could have—"

"Anita," he cut me off, his tone like that of a scolding parent. "I know you're trying to help. But it doesn't make me feel any better. I just need sleep. I'm dying for some rest. And to be honest, it doesn't even matter to me that it wasn't really Ainsley I was talking to. She hit on every single bad thought that I entertained after Ainsley's death. I *did* blame myself for it. I *did* think that I should have done something for her so that she didn't feel the need to go out all the time. I had no idea it was something as simple as talking that she needed."

"But you *don't know* if that's what she needed. That's just what Ainsley's Negative said. It could have been something else. Maybe she was depressed or stressed. Maybe she was just looking for something ... something she didn't know she needed." My voice faded. "Listen." I cleared my throat and stood up straighter. The coffee was finally ready, and I poured myself a cup. Just the smell of it and the warmth of the mug in my hands was fortifying. "I had a weird conversation with Dan's Negative last night."

Joshua didn't say anything. I heard other noises from his end but couldn't tell what he was doing.

"He also tried to keep me awake, like he always does. I said something about getting rid of him. And he said that he couldn't tell me how." I waited for Joshua to say something, but he must not have picked up on the nuance I'd mentioned.

"I asked him, 'Does that mean there *is* a way to get rid of you?' And he paused before he answered."

"What was his answer?" Joshua's voice was flat. Defeated.

"Well, it was no."

"There you go. These things aren't going anywhere."

"But you don't understand! I think they can. What I said, specifically, was, 'Is there a way to get rid of you?' And he said, 'You know I can't tell you that.'"

In the background, I heard what sounded like dishes in the sink.

"It's wishful thinking," Joshua said. "Nothing more."

"If you really thought that, then you wouldn't be trying to get rid of yours; you'd have just given up. And I don't know if you've seen, but I'm pretty sure we've gone viral."

"Really?" Joshua sounded awake and alert now. "What are people saying?"

"Well ... I didn't look too closely at anything," I said as I took a sip of coffee. "I just had a ton of notifications and emails. I can't look at it, honestly."

"What are you doing right now? I'm just skimming through some of these now—there's a lot to process. We should decide what to do going forward."

"What do you mean? Going forward?"

"I mean, how we're going to respond to people."

"Oh."

"Yeah. We need to be on the same page. It looks like a lot of pro-quarantine people aren't too happy with us. I could come over—"

"No, that won't work. I have to go into the office for a little bit. I'll let you know when I'm done."

NEGATIVE IMAGES

I hung up, and when I walked out to the car, Dan was in the passenger seat. No. Dan's *Negative* was. I couldn't afford to start blurring the lines now.

"You look like hell. And your makeup's running," he said with a smile.

I settled my coffee in the cup holder and glared at him. Then, without much thought, I threw my purse into the passenger seat, knowing it would go right through him. I threw it down hard. I wanted to hurt him, even though I knew I couldn't.

"Ouch." His voice dripped with sarcasm. "Right in the balls, Anita. Thankfully, I'm not easily bothered by little things like that."

I ignored him, my mouth pressed shut so I wouldn't take his bait. I just needed to tune him out, pretend he wasn't there. I opened the garage door and started the car. I was reversing out of the garage when I saw him move my purse.

He shifted his hand and seemed to reach inside of himself. He grabbed my bag and placed it in his lap. He played with the zipper, opening the bag slowly.

"Careful." His voice had a sing-song lilt to it, and I caught the ugly smirk on his face as I narrowly avoided hitting another car driving past my house. I didn't blame the other driver for laying on the horn.

I pulled over on the side of the road and stared at him for what felt like forever.

I had walked through this man—this thing. I'd suffered through nights of him poking his finger into my back to give me a chill. When I'd thrown my purse at him, well, through him, at the time, it was out of anger. It was also because I knew I could. I'd wanted him to understand that I wasn't scared of him.

But I was. I was scared more now than I'd ever been. And he—*it*—knew it.

Dan's Negative still stared at me and grinned.

I took a deep breath and focused on getting the car out of the neighborhood.

He fiddled with the zipper. Closing it. Opening it. And drawing out the length of it each time.

"How are you able to do that?" I asked through gritted teeth.

"Do what? This?" He laughed. He picked up my purse by the handles and dangled it in front of his face.

I snatched it out of his hand and threw it behind me. Lipsticks and pens tumbled out as they hit the floor, and I had to slam on the brakes so I wouldn't run a red light.

The lid of my thermos flew off, and coffee sprayed all over the car and me.

"It's uncomfortable, isn't it?" He could have been talking about my bag and his newfound ability to manipulate objects, or the coffee, or both. Regardless, he was right.

He grinned like a devil, mouth too wide and skin stretched tighter. Gaunter. His cheeks were gaunter than they were just last night. He looked ill, like he was wasting away. I imagined something eating him alive from the inside out.

The light turned green, and I accelerated. The sound of everything rolling around in the back seat made me let out a loud sigh.

Dan's Negative scoffed. "I wasn't referring to *that*." He reached behind us and picked up a tube of lipstick from the backseat to make his meaning clear. "I never liked this shade on you."

NEGATIVE IMAGES

He slipped the lid off the cap and rolled the tube up to reveal a matte magenta that I'd never worn very often anyway. I clenched my jaw and gripped the wheel tighter.

"I meant my looks. You noticed; I can tell."

"I was thinking more about all of this new stuff you're doing, but sure," I answered.

"Oh, don't pretend you didn't notice. You have some fight in you—much more than I realized when I was still alive. So, I'll just have to find some other way to get through to you. We'll take a nice trip down memory lane. I'll show you all the pain you put me through, and each change you see in me will be a reflection of that."

It felt like I'd just been dumped in a vat of ice. My chest ached, and I couldn't find the words I needed to solve this problem. Just for a moment, I didn't even know where I was. A moment later, it started coming back to me—little flashes that I put together. The coffee shop was a block ahead of me. Pedestrians breezed through the crosswalk. The light in front of me was still, mercifully, red.

Over the shoulder of Dan's Negative, I saw someone who just couldn't be there. Dan. He was standing in the crowd of early morning commuters who were paying too much to park downtown.

I knew I was crazy, but I couldn't take my eyes off of him, studying every little bit that I could see. He wore the baggy jeans I hated, a white polo, and his hair swooped forward to match his bashfully stooped stance. I'd gotten that outfit back from the hospital in a bag. As the person in front of him moved, the red stain—browning in some places—became more visible. I couldn't quite make out his eyes, but I swear he was staring right at me. It felt almost like he was sending me new energy.

The light turned green, and the SUV behind me tapped its horn.

"No matter what you do, I only have good memories of my time with Dan, and you won't soil them," I said to Dan's Negative as I felt the vibrations of the cobblestones beneath the car.

He laughed loudly, making me jump. "Good memories of the hospital? That's rich."

"No. That was awful. Painful."

"For me."

"No, for my husband. You're not him. No matter how hard you try to convince me, you'll never be him."

"I am, though. And because you're being so difficult, I have to go through all this pain again."

I'd finally reached the parking garage. I eased the car into a spot and let out a low breath. I'd made it. No accidents.

"You don't feel pain. You don't feel anything. Dan did. This isn't reliving anything for you."

I wanted a triumphant moment, but Dan's Negative lingered. I opened the back door of my car to collect everything clattering in the backseat. I couldn't bear the thought of dealing with it when I came back at the end of the day.

"You know, it's really annoying to me when you make comments like this. I might have to do something about that."

In a blink, he vanished and appeared right in front of me, smacking the pens and lipstick out of my hands. They hit the ground of the parking garage, clattering, bouncing, and rolling across the pavement. The sound echoed.

NEGATIVE IMAGES

I froze. He'd hurt me. He'd physically hurt me. My hand stung where he'd slapped me. Dan—my Dan—would never strike me, not even in jest. What else would this thing do to me?

Chapter Eighteen

"Oh, no, he's with you." Monica sounded exasperated and defeated, all in the same breath. She ushered me into her office and shut the door behind me.

Dan's Negative looked Monica up and down like he was appraising her.

Monica crossed her arms over her chest and walked quickly to sit down at her desk while I took one of the opposite chairs. She looked at Dan's Negative for a moment, then swiveled her chair towards me in an effort to dismiss him.

"So ...?" I shrugged and gestured towards her, wanting to get this awkward conversation started so that it could finally be over.

"I thought we should talk. About our business."

I nodded. Our business used to consume my life—the planning, the event promotion, and finding new clients. Being in charge and pulling off something within hours gave me a high.

"We're not doing well, in case you're wondering." I couldn't tell if Monica was being sarcastic to lighten the mood or if it was disdain that I heard now in her voice.

"Okay."

"You don't have any clients."

"Well, there's Joshua."

Monica shot me an 'oh please' look. "Was he planning something else?"

I didn't answer.

Monica bit her lip, and I realized she was trying not to cry. "We have Tricia. There's not enough work for her, though. I knew it—I knew it two weeks ago, but I kept hoping that things would pick up. I feel like even though you're the one with," she gestured towards Dan's Negative, who favored us with a sharp grin, "you're never aware of things, you know? Like, do you realize that more and more people like you are losing their jobs? And there's hardly any repercussions? And then, for our line of work, these Negatives continue to take a toll, and Joshua's event was a big hit to the image we've been building up."

I flushed. She'd been the one who accepted Joshua as a client. It didn't seem fair to put all the blame for his event on me.

"I'm just saying—" Monica sighed and covered her face with her hands. "Okay. Look. I don't want to be harsh. You've been through a ton. But we need to make some serious changes. Can you do that? Can you get some of your old self back?"

I guess I was expecting a rhetorical question, but Monica kept staring me down, trying to force an answer.

"Monica, I—"

"See how upset you've made her?" Dan's Negative chimed in.

I should have expected it. He'd been quiet too long.

"Monica's worked hard her whole life. She thought this company was *it* for her. Look at her face. Do you think she wants you to stay? When your presence threatens everything she's worked so hard for?" Dan's Negative wasn't trying to be sarcastic or insulting now. He sounded almost like *my* Dan. It was the same tone of voice he used when we were arguing over our home budget.

"What's he saying?" Monica shifted her gaze to Dan's Negative.

I sighed. "He's basically saying you don't want me to stay."

An uncomfortable silence enveloped us. Me, looking at Monica, waiting for her to tell me I was wrong. Monica, a faint look of surprise on her face, perhaps because the Negative Image in the room was right. And Dan's Negative, sitting there, grinning at us in his unsettling, devilish way.

"Anita," Monica finally began, taking a deep breath to settle herself. "You know I've always been on your side."

"Sure, Monica's on your side. Have you asked yourself why, Anita?" His grin was too jubilant for my comfort.

"Because she's my friend, of course."

"Oh, Anita." Dan's Negative leaned over to whisper in my ear. "I really think you need to examine this friendship with Monica."

"This is getting too creepy. What the hell is he saying? He keeps saying my name."

Monica's hands shook. This was more than just the general anxiety I'd seen when Dan's Negative was present before.

"Come on! Tell me!" she insisted.

"Monica, don't let him get to you. Let's get back to our discussion."

NEGATIVE IMAGES

Tears glistened in Monica's eyes when she looked at me. And a hint of something else, too. Fear.

"Anita, I can't. I need a minute."

She stood up, grabbed her phone off her desk, and left me alone in her office, shutting the door behind her.

"Don't you want to know why Monica's so upset? I'll give you a hint: it's not all about the business." Dan's Negative sat in her chair and put his feet up on her desk with that idiotic grin on his face. I wanted to punch his teeth in.

"No, I don't want to know." Of course I did, really. But I wasn't going to let him force me into a conversation about it. "Why do you look the way you do? Why is your appearance really changing?"

"I told you. I thought we should relive my pain. All my pain. You probably didn't even notice this—" He lifted his shirt slightly, and I saw a mottled black hole ragged around the edges. "There's the physical pain like that, of course. But then there's the pain that your selfishness caused. *My* pain, *my* suffering, were only ever important in how it affected *you*."

His face twisted in disgust, and I wondered how much of what he was spouting was true. I couldn't let him get in my head, though. I just couldn't. Even if I had made mistakes, even if I had been wrong ...

Focus, Anita. Look at him. Really look at him. It's not real. It's not true. It's wrong.

It was wrong. It was horribly wrong. That wound ... he'd made a point to show it to me. Why would he need to show it to me, if not to find some way of explaining all the other physical changes? His skin was stretched so tightly across his face that it shone. And he expected to explain this as some physical manifestation of his pain? He was hiding something.

I stood up and walked towards the door. Monica was probably still upset, but I needed to figure this out with her.

"Monica?" I opened the door and saw her with Tricia in the reception area. Their backs were towards me, and Monica had propped up her phone as they watched a video. I recognized the voice of Greg Patisis.

"This is huge for us. Carrie Elsworth sent me a message late last night. I have to admit, I was floored. This legitimizes us in a truly awesome way, and I think it shows how what we want for everyone is peace. If the people with Negative Images come here, they can have a space of their own while the rest of us are protected from them. We were prepared for debate, of course, and we've seen a lot of that as well. But getting someone like Carrie on our side, someone who actually has a Negative Image ... I think that really speaks for itself."

"What about the interviews she gave?" another voice asked.

"We're aware of what Carrie said before signing our quarantine petition, and we hope to convince the people who posted her interview to join us. We all want the same thing, and that's safety for people with Negative Images."

While saying that Carrie's gesture spoke for itself, Patisis had undoubtedly added a lot of his own words. He hadn't even relayed what Carrie's correspondence was.

Monica and Tricia turned and looked up at me. They seemed frozen as if I'd just caught them embezzling whatever company funds we had left. None of us spoke, but the video continued in the background.

"This woman who reached out to you, she's been under a great deal of strain, hasn't she?" a woman asked. "In fact, I've heard reports that she was suicidal."

"I certainly don't want to speak on her behalf about her recent mental health struggles," Patisis answered.

My head buzzed at his words. Of course, he would do just that.

"What I can tell you is that I wouldn't share her struggle with you if I didn't think it would help our cause or if I thought that she was incompetent in the decision she was making."

"I thought she reached out in a gesture of support. I suppose it was a little more than that?"

"She came up with a truly brilliant idea. Not only did she give us the names of other people with Negative Images who she thought would support our cause—" Monica turned around and shot me a questioning glance. I shook my head. "She also suggested allowing people with Negative Images to sign up on our website if they would willingly come to one of our quarantine stations if we can find a suitable space for them."

"Can you turn that off? Please?!"

"Anita, you're yelling." Monica came forward and grabbed my arms. Tricia turned away from me. She shook and sniffled. I had an urge to comfort her, but clearly, out of all of us, I was the one who needed comforting, wasn't I? And yet Monica reached out to me from a distance, begging me to settle myself without offering any real support.

Dan's Negative had said I should explore this friendship. Was this why? I couldn't believe that Monica would turn on me after all the help she'd given me after Dan died.

"Isn't this interesting?" Dan's Negative came to stand next to me, causing Monica to back away. He surveyed the scene with his hands in his pockets, not a care in the world. "You know these people. You spent most of your days with them. But look at them now. It's like ... you're barely human anymore." He cocked his head as though he were considering the problem. "See the disdain? The disgust? You might as well be a sewer rat."

I walked towards the door. No one stopped me.

In the hallway, I pushed the button for the elevator, grateful for the space between me and them.

"Don't you wonder how someone who looks at you with so much fear and revulsion could *really* be your friend? Don't you think the reason she's been on your side this whole time is because she thinks she owes you something?"

"Why would you suggest that Monica owes me something?" I turned towards him, but he was gone.

The doors of the elevator slid shut. I saw a man's shape reflected in the metal doors, and the lights flickered as the elevator descended.

Twenty minutes later, I pulled into Joshua's driveway. Ainsley's Negative stood next to him at the door. His eyes were bloodshot; hers, of course, an inky black.

"Ah, I see you're getting a reprieve." He gestured to the empty space beside me.

"He wreaked a lot of havoc this morning, so I think I've earned it. Actually, what he did is one of the things I wanted to talk about."

"Oh?"

I followed Joshua inside, and we sat down on his living room sofa. His house wasn't as disgusting as it had been the first day I'd seen it, but it

NEGATIVE IMAGES

wasn't good. The shades were drawn, the lights were off, and the trash overflowed.

"I don't know if it's wise to bring it up when she's here," I gestured towards Ainsley, "although I'm sure she'll witness it at some point."

"Go ahead."

"Dan's Negative hit me. He did a whole lot of other shit leading up to that—he *picked up* my purse, he *opened it,* and he *threw it* in the back seat—but then when I picked everything up, he hit me. I felt it. It wasn't that prickly sensation. This was real, physical contact."

Joshua leaned back from me. "Anita, are you sure? That doesn't sound right."

"Of course, I'm sure! I was there!"

"But ... how?"

I sighed. "How should I know?! I will say, though, that his appearance has changed, too. I think it's because he used up too much energy interacting with me like that. He claims it's his pain. He even showed me his gunshot wound."

"I don't know, Anita. I've never heard of a Negative Image being able to actually interact with a person or anything else." He stared at me, studying my face until I felt uncomfortable. "You might be the first."

"Has Ainsley done anything like that? Anything at all?"

Joshua looked at me like I was crazy. "That's really scary, Anita. I'm sorry, but no. She hasn't."

"Dan's Negative says it's because I'm being difficult. I think I'm supposed to be more ... damaged by now."

"I didn't know they could do that." Joshua leaned back, his brow furrowed, his gaze far away and unfocused. I wondered if he was thinking of what Ainsley might do to him. "He has the same injury that he did when he died?" Joshua's gaze flicked to Ainsley when he asked me. An image popped into my head of Ainsley, battered and bloody. A massive gash across her cheek and a flap of skin hanging down—something awful enough to drive anyone over the edge.

"Well, I wouldn't have known about the gunshot wound if he hadn't shown me. His face looks waxy and pale, kind of like it did in the hospital. Only, it's not. It's worse than that. It's like ... I don't know how to describe it. His skin looks tight. Uncomfortable. If he gets worse... I can't really imagine it." I thought of Dan in the hospital bed. A pallor was over him like he hardly had enough blood in his system.

"It's hard to think about." Joshua watched me closely.

"He already looks worse than Dan did. What happens when he changes his appearance beyond that? What's supposed to happen at the end? What happens after?"

Joshua rubbed his neck and addressed the floor. "I think what's supposed to happen is that you give up." He looked at me. We both knew what he meant.

"Well, we're not giving up. Not after everything we've been through, not to mention Carrie's interviews—"

"Anita, what else can we do? I thought it was a good idea at first. I thought if we reached enough people that someone somewhere would come up with a way of making the Negatives go away. But I looked at our comments while you were at work, and it seems like everyone is just trying similar things, and nothing is working. What's the point?"

Of the two of us, I'd always been the harder to convince that reaching out to people was a good idea.

"What happened, Joshua? This isn't like you."

NEGATIVE IMAGES

"I heard from Carrie." He walked into the kitchen and poured a glass of water. I hadn't realized how dry my throat had gotten, and I was grateful when he handed me a glass, too.

"Carrie got in touch with you?" I pulled out my phone: no missed calls, no messages.

"That's why I wanted to talk to you—I know Patisis will call me today. She asked me if I would be willing to sign the voluntary quarantine petition."

I bristled. "She didn't ask me." I didn't want to sign the petition, but I hated thinking that she'd reached out to Joshua and not me. "Did she think you could be swayed?"

"No-o. At least, not at first. But, Anita ..." Joshua looked up at me, his eyes watery. He shrugged in what I took to be a gesture of apology.

My heart stuttered in my chest.

"Why?" My voice came out shriller than I meant it to.

"I just ..." He swallowed, and his Adam's apple bobbed. "You know what Carrie did to herself? I ... I think I might be capable of doing that, too. Only no one will find me and take me to a hospital. I'll be alone. I'll die alone."

"No, of course you won't. I'll help you." I hadn't felt this passionate about anything since the day Dan was shot. I remembered how I'd been left alone in his room after he flatlined, how helpless I'd felt as I was pushed aside as doctors and nurses rushed him away. But after that moment of being alone, I'd chased after them. I'd begged and pleaded for them to save him. And when someone finally came to tell me that he was gone, I'd screamed and cried as if any of that could bring him back. I was acting in the same childish way all over again—disbelief over something happening that I hadn't designed and couldn't control. And when reality set in, I'd collapsed in on myself.

"Anita." Joshua placed a hand over mine and squeezed it. His eyes wouldn't meet mine. "You can't be with me all the time. Even Carrie, with her family and us in the house, almost died. It's going to happen." He finally looked at me. "Probably to you, too. I've started to accept it."

"No," I said forcefully. "I won't let anything happen to you. You're ..." I stopped myself. I'd been about to tell him that he was everything to me. He couldn't be, could he? Only a few weeks ago, he'd been an acquaintance. But our circumstances had changed so dramatically. I remembered Monica looking at me with so much fear and suspicion, and that cemented it for me. "I don't know what I would do without you."

"You'd be okay. You're strong."

"I'm only strong because I have you. I know it's crazy, but I can't imagine my life without you."

Joshua didn't say anything for a long time. The moment stretched out, an invisible string pulling between the two of us.

"I'm going to sign it, Anita. Maybe you should, too."

"Please. Don't." I wasn't sure what to say in the face of so much apathy.

Joshua gave me a sad smile. "Last night, I dreamed about it. I could see it happening clearly, and it didn't hurt."

"How?" I didn't want to know and certainly didn't want to encourage him, but the question came automatically.

"I got in my car and sped off a bridge into the water. I had my windows rolled down, and the water was fast."

My eyes welled up. "Oh, Joshua."

"Oh, stop." He was backtracking; his voice said he was kidding, but his eyes were distant. "It probably won't happen that way."

"Of course not."

But it felt like something fundamental had shifted. We'd lost a spark, the one that made me feel like we were on a mission.

"Joshua. Please don't sign it." My mind raced, trying to find the perfect thing to say. If I could find the right words and say them exactly as he needed to hear them, I could change his mind. "Please stay here. I need you. And Patisis is wrong. Deep down, you know he's wrong.

"Besides, Dan's Negative is doing things that typical Negatives just don't do. Don't you want to find out why?"

He sighed and held his face in his hands for a moment. "I don't know how you want me to help you, Anita. I can't help anyone. You should talk to Carrie. She might be able to make you see her point better than I can."

"Fine. I'll call her now and see what she says." My hands shook as I held the phone up to my ear.

"Hello?"

"Hi, Carrie, it's Anita. I saw the news. I was hoping you wouldn't go ahead with signing the petition."

"Listen, I really think you should consider joining me. I know you and Joshua want to find a reason for this and a way to stop it, but I think we can do that safely if we're in quarantine."

Goosebumps broke out across my arms. "After all the bullying that Patisis' fan club has done online, I can't believe you'd say that. They don't have our best interests at heart."

"But it could still be helpful for us—we'd be somewhere safe. We'd be able to live with others just like us."

"They want to hide us away because it's easier, not because it's what's best for us. We have to stay strong. Carrie, have you ever felt like there was another presence? Besides your mother's Negative Image? Like, some version of her that was rooting for you? I know you said before that you felt like part of her was missing."

Carrie was silent for a long time. "I can't tell anymore, Anita. There were a few times, I suppose ... but what does it matter?"

"I just think we're so close to solving this. And I think you're making a huge mistake."

Carrie laughed, and it was a bitter sound like she was completely jaded. "You're the one making the mistake, Anita. Good luck."

She hung up.

I stared at Joshua, who I was sure had heard most of the conversation.

"You're really not going to sign it?" he asked.

"Of course not. I meant what I said—I think there's a way to figure this out."

"And what you said to Carrie, you really think there's some other part of these things out there?"

I nodded. "I'm going to keep looking for answers, Joshua, and I want you to stay and help me."

A corner of Joshua's mouth flicked up momentarily in a smile. "I suppose you want help keeping up with the internet comments and uploads. And you also want me not to sign the petition?"

"Obviously."

Joshua looked up at me—really looked—and then he leaned forward and touched my cheek with his hand. His eyes were sad, almost resigned. "Okay," he said. "I won't. Carrie'll be ticked, though."

"She's going to regret signing that petition."

NEGATIVE IMAGES

His hand lingered on my cheek. His eyes stayed locked on mine. It was hard to feel seen for this long. And what happened next? I realized I had a choice, as small as it was. I leaned towards him, wondering if he would lean away.

Ainsley appeared between us, her eyes level with mine, and I screamed. It was like looking into nothingness, and she'd opened her mouth wide to say something—I imagined it was to tell me that Joshua was hers—and her mouth was cavernous and black, too, framed only by the lurid red of her lipstick.

Joshua's phone rang, making me jump again. I wished I were anywhere else, as Joshua answered.

"Hmmmm. I would say ... yeah, that didn't go too well, did it?" I turned to see Dan's Negative standing behind me. "I shouldn't be surprised, I guess, that you're moving on so quickly—"

"What is that supposed to mean?!"

"Oooh! I touched a nerve there, huh?" Dan's Negative let out a cackle. "Spoiler alert: you're not moving on with him. Uh-uh. You know why?" He leaned over, pressing his face close to my ear. "He's not gonna make it."

"You bastard!"

Something started tapping against my knee, and I swatted away Joshua's hand before I even realized it was him.

"Shhhh! Anita! Patisis called!" Joshua had Patisis on speaker while our end was thankfully on mute.

"Joshua? Are you there?" Patisis' voice was rough; he said each word with force like he wanted to hit you with it. His put-on charm from the interview segments was gone.

"Mr. Patisis, hello. Sorry about that. I had a bad signal."

233

"That's all right." He sounded calmer now, like the person I always heard online. "Listen, your friend Carrie Ellsworth suggested I contact you regarding our petition."

Joshua and I exchanged a glance, and for a moment, I panicked. Would he keep his promise?

"Tell me more about the petition." Joshua kept his eyes on me, but I couldn't read his expression.

"Just you wait. You'd be getting a great deal."

Dan's Negative crouched in front of me, blocking my view of Joshua. "You should encourage Joshua to sign it, Anita. It might be his last shot at survival."

I groaned. He was loud.

Joshua shook his head and put a finger to his lips.

I shrugged. What did he expect me to do? This wasn't like quieting a crying baby.

"I can hear your Negative now." Patisis laughed as though he'd caught Joshua in a trap.

"Well, they do appear from time to time, as I'm sure you know. I'd love to hear some details about the petition, though."

"Sure, Joshua. Well, it's mainly a petition to keep people with a Negative Image, people like you, safe. We're asking you to sign stating that you would go into voluntary quarantine in a safe environment as soon as one becomes available. A place where you wouldn't live in fear of prejudice or feel uncomfortable about the burden you're carrying. Everyone in the unit would understand because they'd all be in your situation. Of course, it would also safeguard the people who live near you now—people who don't have a Negative Image and are worried that they might be at risk of getting one."

NEGATIVE IMAGES

Even I had to admit it sounded good when Patisis put it that way—a commune of like-minded individuals.

"Do you think that might make people, well, forget us? What about a way to educate the public about us so we can find support within our communities?"

I gave Joshua a thumbs up.

Patisis breathed into the phone. When he spoke, it was the gruff man I'd heard at the beginning of the call. "I was under the impression that you were already aware of these details, Mr. Maguire. Carrie assured me you'd be willing to listen to me with an open mind, not set traps. And I'll let you know now that you'll hear from my lawyer if you post this conversation online."

"No, I wouldn't do that. But this concept is still hard for me to wrap my head around. I think hearing more would help."

"Well." I imagined Patisis in an office somewhere, weighing how much to share with Joshua, wondering if he could trust him. "Right now, we have one hundred and twenty-five signatures, which is really fantastic in such a short amount of time. Your friend Carrie was our first signature, and in only twelve hours, you can see the effect that she's managed to have on other people. We've been getting the word out, trying to make sure others like you can hear our message.

"Of course, Carrie has already experienced the lowest point someone with a Negative Image can have."

I thought the lowest point was signing this petition, but I pressed my lips together.

"Because of Carrie's attempt on her life, she sees the wisdom of the quarantine more than someone who's only had a Negative Image for a little while might."

"So, what's the goal of the petition? I didn't think you had a location for people to go to yet."

"We're figuring out the logistics. You know, where all these people can go, how they get there, and who will care for them from a psychological and medical standpoint. But don't worry; we've had help in choosing a secure site."

"Help?"

I mouthed the word *money* at Joshua. He nodded.

"I assume you mean financial help?"

"Oh yes. For something this big, you need investors. You know, this may help create jobs. Residents will need someone to care for them—housekeeping, cooking, surveillance. Not to mention, doctors are still trying to figure all this out, and this way, they'd be able to get a lot of research done quickly, and hopefully, the suffering will end for everyone."

"How much of this do you have lined up? How soon could I move in?"

"We don't have a definite location yet, but a few states are actively lobbying to host you."

I gasped and quickly covered my mouth. How could we possibly combat this? Dan's Negative laughed as if he could read my thoughts, and Ainsley joined in with her own terrible noise.

"Let's say I sign your petition, and you get a place for us to go. What happens?"

"Well, we find a way to get you there," Patisis spoke as if he was explaining something very simple to a child for the tenth time. "I'd have to ask most people to provide their own transportation. Although the CDC is very interested in this idea, they may be willing to help by sending a doctor out to accompany you. I thought of that when Carrie told me that her Negative persuaded her to attempt suicide only after you showed up to try to get her to do an interview. It isn't lost on me that once you make a decision to do something like this, your Negative might try to stop you."

Joshua's mouth hung open—I don't think either of us had expected government involvement, at least not at that level.

"CDC? Wow. So, your investors ... are they mainly government, or is this in the private sector?"

"Nothing is set yet, but I imagine whoever funds us will want access to your medical records, and you'd need to consent to that."

"You know, I thought this was supposed to be a community for us. I'm not really getting that feeling." Joshua sounded stronger—like he had when we were planning to visit with Carrie. "It seems like the restrictions will be, well, very restrictive. Supposing I sign the petition and then decide I'd rather take my chances on my own once I get to your camp?" Joshua gave me a wicked grin. There was no way 'camp' could have a positive connotation.

"Well, we certainly hope that that won't happen. This is, first and foremost, a place where people like you can be yourself and be comfortable. If you're not, I think the first step would be to try to resolve whatever issues you have."

"You would let me leave, though, wouldn't you? I'm not signing over my rights, am I?"

"Well, I think you'd agree that we simply couldn't let you leave without some kind of a plan in place. For your safety, of course."

By now, I was seething. I couldn't imagine Carrie actually signing this thing. Had Patisis gone over all these details with her, too, or had he let her sign it, thinking it would be the solution she was desperately hoping for?

Another thought occurred to me. Carrie had, after all, tried to commit suicide just a few days ago. Possibly another reason Patisis wouldn't care about getting her all the details was that he didn't expect her to survive long enough to actually live in quarantine.

I fished through my purse until I found a pen and an old receipt.

"Does that answer all your questions?" Patisis' impatience was palpable. He probably thought this was too much work for just one signature.

"I have just one more ..." Joshua's voice trailed off as he tried to decipher what I'd written. "Supposing, just for arguments' sake, that Carrie passes away before you're able to build a functioning community. Would her signature count?"

"Yes, of course." Patisis sounded grave, almost reverent. "In a way, it might even carry more weight. She would represent all the people we could have saved if only we'd acted fast enough. Of course, my goal, *our* goal, if you're willing, is for Carrie and everyone who signs up to go on to live in this community until we can find a cure."

"Of course." Joshua's voice was flat and unenthusiastic.

"Will you be signing?" Patisis asked.

Joshua shot me a look and grinned. "No."

Patisis made a noise of protest, but before we could hear what he would have said, Joshua hung up. I tapped the button to stop the recording on my phone.

"I can't believe Carrie signed this," Joshua said as a vein pulsed in his neck.

"I wonder how much she knew when she did."

He shrugged.

NEGATIVE IMAGES

My phone rang, and I groaned in response. It felt like we were caught in an onslaught of incoming communications. I half expected the call to be from Patisis. Maybe he thought I was worth persuading after all. Instead, it was Monica.

"This can't be good," I mumbled before answering. "Hi, Monica."

"Hey." She let out a big sigh. "I'm so glad you picked up. I wanted to apologize for earlier."

"It's okay. That news is kind of close to home for all of us. It's totally understandable that you guys couldn't help staring when I came out of your office with Dan's Negative."

I'd been aiming for compassionate but I was so tired and flat that I realized too late that it might have come across as sarcastic.

"Oh, that wasn't what I meant, although I know that was weird too. I actually wanted to apologize for how I acted when we were in my office."

There was silence while I tried to remember something specific that would warrant an apology.

"Just, you know, asking you to repeat what he was saying. It's just... look, can we talk?"

"Sure. Isn't that what we're doing?" I let out a forced laugh.

"In person."

"I'm at Joshua's."

"Ooooh, tell her to come over," Dan's Negative called from the family room. "This is gonna be good."

"She can stop by," Joshua said, loud enough for her to hear.

"Um ... Okay." I couldn't tell if the awkwardness was because Monica had heard the two of them or if she had just wanted more privacy.

239

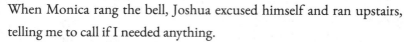

When Monica rang the bell, Joshua excused himself and ran upstairs, telling me to call if I needed anything.

"Hey. Come on in."

"Where's Joshua?"

"He's around. I think he just thought we might want some privacy." Monica relaxed a little, her arms loosening at her sides.

She followed me into Joshua's family room and sat down on the sofa with me.

"Are you okay?" she asked.

I shrugged. Of course, I wasn't. I didn't think I would ever be 'okay,' but Dan's Negative was gone, so I nodded.

"It was just, earlier ... you yelled at us in the office. I've never seen you snap like that."

"I know. But, I mean, I'm assuming you also understand why it would upset me to see you guys huddled over the phone like that."

Monica nodded and decided to move on to whatever she'd come here to discuss. I saw her square her shoulders, a move that always meant that whatever she was about to say was serious.

"I have to tell you something. It's nothing I wanted to tell you. Ever. But ... I keep thinking about the way Dan's Negative has been acting around me, and I can't think of anything else it could be. And it's something you have to hear from me. I can't let him tell it ... he wouldn't even tell it right, anyway, I'm sure."

"What?" One of my biggest annoyances was when someone had bad news and they either built it up to be worse than it really was, or they

NEGATIVE IMAGES

built it up, and it was precisely as bad as I thought it would be. Bad news should be delivered with just the facts, exactly as I had been taught to write a news article in college. It might be dry and boring, but at least it would be the facts.

"First of all, this happened a long time ago."

I picked at my cuticles in irritation.

"Dan and I ... we had a relationship."

CHAPTER NINETEEN

The world didn't stop.

I heard her say the words, and I thought that I should feel angry. But I remembered my confusion the night she and Joshua had both come over to help me when I'd hit my head. She'd found my key—only Dan and I knew where it was.

"When?" I asked, my voice soft.

"Before you were married."

I rolled my eyes. "Was it before he and I started dating? Before I met him? After we were engaged? There's a lot of time there, Monica."

"I knew him before you dated. But when he got serious with you, he broke things off." She looked away, and I was surprised to realize she was trying not to cry. I felt so cold, so detached, and here she was, looking out the window with her bottom lip trembling. Her hands were clasped together tightly, but I didn't give a shit if she cried.

There was more. I waited.

"After you and I started our business, but before you were engaged ... I don't know. I saw him with you after work. Do you remember that?

NEGATIVE IMAGES

When all three of us would grab dinner together sometimes? It started back up again. I felt awful. He'd tell me it couldn't happen again, that you were the one, but then a week later, he'd call me."

I stared at the tears as they made tracks down her face. She made no effort to wipe them away.

"It was wrong, but Anita, he was *my* one. Every time we were together, I knew. He was the one for me. But then you got engaged."

"You were a bridesmaid at my wedding."

Monica nodded without meeting my gaze.

"Your ex-husband was a fucking groomsman!"

"I know."

"How many times did you see Dan after he proposed to me?"

Her eyes glistened. "I don't know."

"A lot? A little?"

"More than I wanted it to happen."

"That's bullshit, and you know it. Was it once a week? Twice? All the times Dan told me he was out with friends, was he at your place fucking you?"

"It was a lot." Monica's voice was barely above a whisper.

"And your ex. Weren't you *his* one?"

"I think so. But now I'm not. He found out, and that's why we got divorced."

I felt no sympathy towards Monica. The fact that this affair had been found out on one side and that Ryan, her ex-husband, hadn't thought to say a word to me only filled me with rage.

"You know what? You're really lucky."

"Lucky? I thought my secret would die with Dan, but it hasn't, and now I know I'm losing you too."

"You haven't bought me out yet. But I'm happy to take a check for my half of the business."

"What? No! Anita, I wasn't talking about our business. I meant our friendship. Please forgive me. I know what I did was shitty."

"Did you see Dan after we were married?"

She was quiet for several moments. "Once or twice."

"Which was it? One time or two? Or does that really mean three or four? Or five or six?"

"I saw him when you got back from your honeymoon. And I saw him once he started helping out more with our business."

Something in me finally fell apart. I thought that, at the very least, Dan and I had had each other at the end. We'd had our dream: remodeling our home, having a baby, and growing my business with Monica while Dan climbed the corporate ladder. Now I knew it was all a lie, and I wondered if he'd ended the affair because he really wanted it to be over or if he would have gone back to her in a month if he hadn't been shot. I would never know the truth.

"I still say you're lucky." My voice was hard. I was barely aware of what I was saying. My heartbeat pounded in my ears.

"Lucky?" Monica's mournful tears were becoming righteous tears of anger. "I've lost everything."

"Oh? What exactly is everything?" She didn't want to enumerate her sorrows, so I did it for her. "You lost Dan, obviously. I can't tell if you wanted to lose him or if he dumped you ... maybe you just lost him to gun violence, the same way that I did. And you've lost me. I would have trusted you with just about anything. But now ... you're just my business partner. We probably won't even have that for much longer.

NEGATIVE IMAGES

You lost your husband, too, I suppose, although since you were busy chasing mine, I'd argue that you didn't really want yours to begin with.

"Now, can we spend some time on me? On what I've lost? I've lost my best friend. I've lost my trust in basically everyone. I've lost my husband twice—to you and to death. I've lost what I thought I had with him while he was alive. And the thing that's torturing me now is that I'm the one who's stuck with his Negative Image. I'll always wonder if he had just left me for you, maybe you'd be the one stuck with this monstrosity, and I'd be able to say that the two of you truly deserve each other."

"But don't you see?" The tears glistening on Monica's cheeks disgusted me. "You're the one who has him. You're the one he really loved all along."

The room felt eerily silent as I worked out what she meant.

"You can't be implying that you're jealous of the fact that I have this Negative Image, can you?" My voice was quiet, almost calm.

"I'm just saying ... well, they're supposed to come back to the person they were closest to, aren't they?"

I was about to yell at her that she was being an idiot, that she had no idea how awful it was to have Dan's Negative trailing me all the time when what she said clicked.

"Shit." I jumped off the sofa and jogged up the stairs, leaving Monica bewildered. "Joshua? Joshua!" For a moment, I was terrified that I'd find him upstairs clutching a bloody razor in his hand or an empty pill bottle, but he met me on the landing, whole.

"What happened? What's wrong?" He grabbed hold of my arms, and his eyes raked over my body rapidly, looking for physical damage.

"The Negatives come back to the people they were close to."

"Yeah ... I know. Everyone knows that."

"No, that's not ... when Dan died, I was holding his hand. Were you touching Ainsley when she died?"

"I ... God, I'm not sure. They finally let me see her when she was out of surgery, and they didn't think she was in immediate danger. I was right next to her until a nurse shoved me away. I didn't even realize what had happened at first."

"I think that they come to us in that moment."

"But it was days before I saw her."

"Yes, but they can choose to stay away. It would be so obvious if they reappeared right when someone dies."

"It's a good theory," Joshua said. I could tell he didn't buy it. "But there's a lot of people with Negatives. They can't all have had the physical contact."

I bristled. "Maybe they did. Maybe it doesn't have to be exact, but just near the time that they died. Maybe someone else thought of this, but nobody believed them. Or maybe their Negative made sure they didn't last long after their discovery."

"Okay, I'm not saying I wouldn't consider it," Joshua conceded. "I wish we could ask more people about it."

"We have to reach out to Carrie, Eduardo, and maybe others on that database."

"Okay. Sure."

"And I can't believe I'm saying this, but we should make a video."

Joshua smiled. "You're right. I can't believe you're suggesting it. I think we should both be in the video this time."

I felt nauseous thinking about being so out in the open, but if we got this theory out there and people came forward, it might help.

"We'll need someone to film us. Unless you've got a stand or something."

Joshua shook his head.

"Maybe Monica. She owes me."

"I'm so sorry about that." Joshua gave me an awkward pat on the back.

"You heard."

"Yeah, I wasn't trying to, but your discussion got kind of heated, and you were both pretty loud."

"I didn't realize."

"Are you sure you trust Monica to do this?"

"I'll film you guys if you need a cameraman," Monica said from the bottom of the stairs. "Whatever you need, I'll do it. Anita is right. I do owe her."

Joshua and I regarded her the way someone would a cockroach in their kitchen. Monica put her hands up and shrugged as if to say that she had nothing else to lose.

I reviewed our video many times before Joshua uploaded it to YouTube and Facebook. Watching it gave me a weird sensation. I couldn't quite identify my voice as my own; my mannerisms were mine, but it was strange to watch myself tuck a strand of hair behind my ear.

"My name is Anita Matthews." I could tell that I was nervous, and I hated it.

"I'm Joshua Maguire. If you've seen our other videos, you know we both have Negative Images. They don't appear to be with us at the moment, but if you're familiar with this phenomenon, then you know that that could change. If you don't believe us, Anita and I are both listed on the database started by Greg Patisis."

"Everyone knows that Negative Images come back to the people they were closest to. I don't think this is incorrect, but I do think there might be another factor. I believe that physical contact is an important part of how Negative Images latch on to people. I was holding my husband's hand when he passed after a gunshot wound in the hospital."

"My fiancée died from injuries she got in a car accident. I was on the scene. I stayed with her in the hospital, and I was with her when she flatlined."

"We know this is just a theory at this point, but if you are someone who has a Negative Image, and you were in physical contact with the person who later went on to become your Negative Image, we'd like to know. Please reach out to us in the comments or send us a DM."

"This information is vital. People like Greg Patisis would like to see all of us with Negative Images living in quarantine for the rest of our lives. If we can learn more about how Negative Images attach themselves, then we might be able to take the necessary measures to keep others safe without putting ourselves in an unlivable situation."

My voice shook during a good portion of that last part, but Monica and Joshua wouldn't let me go back and re-film it anymore. We'd already spent hours filming this short segment. Yet every time we reached the conclusion, my voice shook in anger.

###

NEGATIVE IMAGES

We reached out to Carrie. I wanted to know if she shared a similar experience, but she wouldn't return my calls or Joshua's. I didn't want to "harass" her, as Aaron had put it, so I let it go. Eduardo, thankfully, was more willing to speak about it, and we even recorded a Zoom call that we could all easily share.

"The idea of a quarantine scares me," Eduardo said. "I think community is so important. Of course, people don't like to see my mother's Negative following me around, but my brothers visit often and bring me everything I need."

"Thank you for saying that. I think living in a quarantine would take all my remaining hope," I said.

"Your theory about physical contact is an interesting one." Eduardo looked away at something off-camera, lost in thought. "I know my mother and father were both at home when he passed, but I have no idea if she was physically near him when it happened. As for my mother..." He paused and looked directly at the camera again. "I was the one who found her. And she did have a faint pulse when I arrived. I tried CPR, but she died before she could get medical assistance. So, I think there's at least a chance that your theory is right."

"Thank you so much for sharing that with us, Eduardo," Joshua said.

"Of course. After what happened to my mother—knowing that her heartbreak and confusion were worse because she was alone—I'll do anything I can to help."

"I just wanted to ask you about one other thing," I said. "Have you had any experience with a Negative Image doing more than what they're known for doing? For instance, manipulating electronics, moving objects?"

"Or influencing dreams?" Joshua added.

Eduardo's brow furrowed. "I would have to get back to you on that. I can't think of anything at the moment."

We cut that last question from the recording that we all agreed to share, and I tried to hide my disappointment that Eduardo didn't have anything that came to mind.

Monica shared our videos on Facebook, YouTube, and Instagram. She put her contact list to good use, calling on all the clients we had—reminding them of how I had helped with their daughter's wedding, had pulled an all-nighter to set up a fundraising event, and had found a replacement caterer at the eleventh hour for a high school reunion. She tugged on every heartstring she could, except for my own.

I still wasn't prepared for the barrage of notifications I had waiting for me the next morning—messages on all my social channels, twenty-three voicemails, and my phone pinging with each new notification. I hadn't even gotten out of bed yet.

I was still wading through them when Joshua's name popped up on my screen as he called.

"Anita? Have you seen? We've gone viral!"

"I thought so."

"You don't sound very excited."

I swallowed a lump in my throat. This *was* what I'd wanted—what we wanted. But all the messages, which were still coming, were simply too much.

"I'm on my way over. We need to talk about which opportunities we want to pursue."

"Wait, what?"

I started reviewing my messages, beginning with voicemail. I don't know why I expected it, but I thought maybe people who actually knew me may have reached out either to share their stories or in support. That wasn't what I found.

"You've made yourself an enemy you don't want," a man's voice said. "The quarantine is the safest solution—the only solution—for people like you."

The message had come from a blocked number. I'd known people would be against us. But this felt more personal. My breath came faster; the world felt like it was falling away. Everything on the outskirts of my vision went black, like I was looking at the world through a tiny tube.

"Even when you get what you want, you're unhappy, Anita."

My breathing was shallow and fast. I felt like I would never breathe properly again, and the world was spinning.

I saw Dan's Negative, his face looking more ravaged than it ever had: rotting flesh splitting open along his chin and forehead. But as everything swirled around me, I saw someone else behind him—a man with brown hair and blue eyes. Now, I was sure I was losing my sanity.

"Dan. Help me."

The NI laughed, a maniacal burst of energy that filled the room like a jolt of electricity. I felt like he was taking all my energy. The darkness clouded over the rest of my vision, and I pinched myself, bringing things back into focus.

When I looked up again, it was just the NI—no sign of Dan.

Had this happened to Carrie or anyone else?

I closed my eyes tightly and covered my ears, trying desperately to shut everything out.

It wasn't that I heard the silence as much as I felt it—the whole room had a lighter feeling.

I opened my eyes slowly, just in case Dan's NI was still in the room.

I'd asked Dan to help me.

I groaned, self-disgust filling me with shame.

If I had really seen Dan, if he had really been there, I should have jumped up and tackled him (or not, seeing how well that worked out last time) or at least demanded an explanation. I wasn't sure if I could ever forgive Monica. But wasn't Dan just as much—or more—to blame? I hadn't demanded answers, cussed him out, or even told him that I knew about his stupid affair.

I'd asked for help.

I felt weak. And stupid.

The doorbell rang, and I jumped up to answer it, still in my pajamas.

"Good morning." Joshua looked good—put together, clean-shaven, dressed in a polo, jeans, and Sperry's. In a sense, we'd traded places. Now, I was the slob.

"Come on in. I just need a minute."

I left him standing awkwardly in the kitchen. He seemed unsure of whether to stay there or go to the family room. The last time he'd been here was the morning after I hit my head.

I got dressed and brushed my teeth as quickly as I could. I didn't bother to brush my hair or put in my contacts.

"I brought coffee," Joshua announced as I came downstairs. I gave him a quick smile. "So, what did you think of all the attention we got? It was more than I expected."

"I haven't really looked. To be honest, I was a little overwhelmed. I had a harassing voicemail."

"I'm sorry. I had some, too." He reached out and gave my arm a squeeze before pulling me into a hug. "And it is overwhelming. I think

NEGATIVE IMAGES

I got the brunt of the earlier videos, but this was your first time actually appearing in them. Let's get you caught up."

We scrolled through the responses on my computer. People had chimed in, sharing personal moments of loved ones and strangers who gave my theory credence.

I held my boy in the hospital once they took him off life support. I had no idea he'd come back to me as a Negative Image, but I doubt that I'd do it differently knowing what I know now.

Cared for an old man in hospice. He never had any visitors. He was scared. I stayed with him at the end. Now I wish I hadn't.

There was also related news: Patisis' quarantine had garnered more than enough interest to gain financial support, which worried me more than I could say.

At least now, he had a little resistance. My idea was gaining traction. There was something about it that people agreed with. And if this were a way to get this pandemic under control, then Patisis' whole idea would be rendered unnecessary.

Watching a flustered Patisis on YouTube claim that this new theory had no relevance put a smile on Joshua's face. I was pleased to see Patisis sweaty, gesticulating wildly.

Ainsley tried to join us then, appearing on the other side of the coffee table. She approached us, talking to Joshua and saying what I could only assume were venomous words from the way her lips curled back in a snarl and the volume of the sounds coming out of her.

In a way, it was worse, more terrifying, to hear her and not understand. It was awful to experience the same abuse as another person but still have so much left that wasn't understood.

She smooshed herself onto his lap, not even bothering to do normal human things, like avoiding the coffee table. No, she walked right through it, her hips swaying slightly. I felt the icy cold of her—what should be her—as she sat on his lap and brushed her legs through my own.

"I'm sorry, Anita." Joshua grimaced. I had no idea what she was saying to torture him and no idea how to help.

"It's okay. I'm going to get some water."

I went into the kitchen. The slight distance from Ainsley did nothing to quiet the sound of her garbled shouting. I wondered if she had gotten louder just to annoy me, too, even though I thought her job—the job of all the Negative Images—was to break just one of us.

I opened the fridge, grabbed the water pitcher, and closed it.

"Hello, whore."

I gasped and took a moment to steady myself.

"Bitch." Dan's Negative spat the word at me, his cheeks so hollow that it was painful to watch him move his mouth as he talked. His skin was so thin-looking that I could imagine it ripping if his jaw opened too wide.

"That's a generic insult." It wasn't like anything he'd said before. He'd always been so specific with all the times and occasions he'd used to torture me. Maybe this was more proof that the wasting away part wasn't an act. Maybe he was using up all his energy. But no, he'd manipulated things. My computer screen. The purse he'd flung in the car. He didn't always do it in front of me anymore, either, but he moved things. My car keys had been misplaced. My phone moved to another room. I felt like he was gaslighting me, and I had a hard time understanding the point.

NEGATIVE IMAGES

"I know you like Joshua. You've got a little crush, don't you?" His voice was simpering. "I've only been in the ground for a few weeks. Didn't you love me?"

Instead, I imagined him asking, "Why isn't this working?" and everything made sense. Maybe he was trying everything in desperation. What would happen to him if he didn't achieve his goal? I grabbed a glass out of the cabinet behind me while I tried to decide how to answer him. Monica's confession swirled through my mind, too. He'd obviously wanted me to know about it.

"I did love my husband. Very much." I tried to keep my voice from catching in my throat as I realized that I was telling this thing the truth. "But I don't know if he really loved me." I paused for a moment, not wanting to look up at him. "How much of you *is* my husband? Or are you him at all?"

"Of course I'm him." Dan's Negative snarled, his lips pulled back too wide. "I'm the *real* part. The honest part. I'm all the thoughts that ran through his head before he chose which ones to say."

"Why didn't he tell me? About Monica?" I gritted my teeth. I didn't know why I was asking this Negative and hoping for a real answer, but it was too late to take it back now.

"You've pondered this on your own. Some of it has to be right, doesn't it? Maybe I would have told you if I'd regained consciousness after surgery. Maybe I would have started things up again if I'd survived. But then, as you know, I did try to end it with Monica ... there was a nice long gap during our marriage where she wasn't a factor at all. But then you wonder how long would that have lasted?"

"Dan loved me. Please tell me he loved me. If he'd loved Monica, he would have asked her to be with him at the end when it really mattered, wouldn't he?"

"What makes you think I didn't want her?"

I shook my head. "The nurse told me, when I went back, that you'd said my name."

Dan shook his head and gave me a cruel smile. "Maybe it was Monica who decided to finally end things. Didn't you ever think of that, sweetheart? And in that case, it's better to have you than no one at all. No one wants to die alone and unloved. So, I had you, my sad, little, pathetic wife, who worked for years with my mistress and never knew it."

I swiped the tears from my eyes, and he reached up to stop me. I felt his cold fingers caress my cheek. He wiped a tear with his finger and stared at it as though he were considering something.

"You know, I used to watch the two of you working together, and I always wondered how you could be so held together and professional at work and such a needy little child at home."

I always wore a professional veneer at work—especially at the events. But that's all it was: a false front. According to Dan's Negative, all the other parts that made me human—the stress, the hushed conversations with Monica about whether we were really earning money, the need to vent to him at the end of the day—were disgusting. And weak. Worst of all, I felt it.

"Get out. Get out!" I yelled.

"Maybe the reason you were so needy was because you knew, on some level, that you weren't the only one. I'll tell you this much, not because you want to know, but because I'm feeling generous. Between you and Monica? *I* would've chosen Monica over you anytime. And now that I've

NEGATIVE IMAGES

broken your heart, I'll make you an offer. A one-time offer." He leaned over and whispered in my ear, "I could end this for you. You're supposed to do it, but I think we'd both like this chapter to be over, right? You pick the method, and I'll make it quick and easy for you. Practically painless. You've got plenty of tools all over the house. Knives right here in the kitchen, extension cords in the garage, pills ..."

"Leave me alone!" I screamed and screamed and couldn't stop screaming. His maniacal laughter rang out, and even my own screaming couldn't drown out his noise.

Chapter Twenty

"How did you feel when he said it?" Joshua asked.

The two of us sat on my kitchen floor, our backs up against the cabinets. I'd completely lost it after Dan's Negative's offer; I didn't even register Joshua coming in after Ainsley's NI left.

Eventually, after what seemed like hours, it had stopped. I no longer heard Dan's NI laughing at me, taunting me. My own throat was hoarse and raw from screaming.

I shrugged off Joshua's question. "Terrible, of course. What do you mean?"

"Well, just..." Joshua paused. He seemed to choose his words carefully, and I thought about what Dan's Negative said: he was the honest part of Dan without the filter.

"Were you tempted to take him up on it?" Joshua finally asked.

"No." My voice cracked and came out in a strangled whimper. "Why would you think that?"

He raked a hand through his hair. "The knife. It reminded me of Carrie. And I wondered if she really did it, you know? Or if her Negative offered to do it for her?"

I wrapped my arms around my legs. "I hadn't thought of that. But as far as we know, my Negative is the only one moving things. Nobody else's has."

"True," Joshua said with a sigh. His gaze shifted to the ceiling, and I noticed the red rims around his eyes. I couldn't tell what he was thinking, what he had been hoping for.

"I wonder how Carrie is." It was more of a thought, not something I expected Joshua to answer.

He looked at me with a sad smile. "Oh yeah. We didn't get to finish talking about our posts or what I saw on my newsfeed this morning. She started a mini-quarantine group with Patisis. That's why she wouldn't take our calls."

"What?" I let my legs splay out in front of me on the kitchen floor.

"They're at Leavenworth. They converted just a small part of it into a quarantine unit."

"You don't mean the prison?"

"Exactly."

"Shit."

"I know. Patisis posted all these pictures, you know, showing a cozy little cell for Carrie. It looks like a cross between a hotel and an old folks' home, with, of course, that stern prison structure. She's got pictures up, mostly of her kids. They're framed, but the glass is out. She can't have anything that could be 'dangerous.'" Joshua framed the last words in air quotes. The way his voice vibrated told me he was hiding his anger behind sarcasm.

"They got a great little sound byte from Carrie, too. She talked about those photos and how seeing her family kept her strong and motivated and made it all worth it."

"I thought she wanted to pretend she didn't know them."

"Yeah ... it makes me wonder if our proximity theory makes sense to the people who are pro-quarantine, too."

I remembered the way Carrie's kids had willingly disappeared down the hospital hallway to get snacks, how they'd already begun cutting her out of their lives, one slice at a time. No picking up or dropping off at school, no going to games or practice. And yet she was risking herself in a shitty jail? For what?

"Do you think they miss her at all?"

"Maybe her kids. I kinda doubt it."

"Me too."

We sat there in silence, and I found my mind wandering to all the petty, meaningless details that were making me mad. I'd lost control of my life—my whole life. No business. No spouse. All I had was a too-big house where my Negative could play hide and seek with me all day, leaving me tired, grouchy, and unable to wash my hair or prepare a meal. I thought again of the offer. I thought of what I turned down.

I glanced at Joshua and saw someone who seemed to be in a similar state of mind. He'd built himself up with hope when he first came over today—he had been clean-shaven and had obviously bathed and chosen his outfit with some amount of care. Now his hair was tousled, his clothes rumpled, and I saw how easy it was to prize off that outer armor.

"Joshua?"

"Yeah?"

"What'll they do when someone dies in that prison and comes back to someone else as a Negative? Like Maria Vasquez."

Joshua shrugged and stifled a laugh. "I mean, think about it, Anita. What do you think would happen? I think they picked a prison for a reason. Everyone's in their own cell, not able to touch another person. I don't think the doctors or wardens or caretakers, whatever they call them ... I don't think they'll rush in to save anyone. I don't think they'll do anything at all."

"Everyone there who's supposed to help them will be too afraid of being shackled with a Negative."

"Exactly."

I slumped back against the wall again and drew my knees up to my chest to hide my face. "This is my fault. This was my theory about the physical contact. My stupid idea is going to get someone killed."

"It's not." Joshua patted my back awkwardly, not letting his hand linger. I appreciated his touch, however brief.

"If you hadn't thought of it, they would have figured it out for themselves. After a couple of deaths and a couple of failed interventions leading to caretakers with Negatives? They'd have known. It would be the same."

"Still."

"Yeah. But, maybe what you put out there will stop some people from turning themselves into guinea pigs ..."

I imagined Carrie lying on a prison cot, crying out for help. Boots clomping past her cell on the concrete floor. Would she feel comfort in knowing she wasn't going to come back to someone else? Or regret at choosing to spend her final days locked up?

Joshua and I went to war. Well, figuratively, anyway.

The briefest thought or mention of Carrie made the muscles in my shoulders tense up. We'd gone to her home, unbidden, unwanted. Because of us, her Negative Image ramped up its attacks, leading to everything else and her willing participation in Patisis' experiment. I had to do something to make up for it since making things right didn't seem like it was an option anymore.

We'd scrapped the website idea—our YouTube Chanel had plenty of subscribers to make up for it, and sometimes our Negatives did make appearances, adding some thrill for people who only followed us for the chance to gawk.

Since I'd insisted on avoiding interviews, we'd taken to filming Q&A segments based on the comment sections of our previous videos, and people seemed to engage with them.

"We're concerned about Carrie," Joshua said matter of factly.

We'd set up to film another segment. With a ring light and phone holder, we no longer needed Monica to help us out.

I sat next to Joshua, envious of his ease in front of the camera. He looked relaxed—his posture wasn't too stiff, and he wasn't afraid to move and use his hands often when he was excited. Meanwhile, I still had a hard time convincing my voice not to shake. I clenched my hands together as I prepared myself to speak.

"Once you feel how depressing it is to have a Negative Image ... I mean, it's completely isolating, and I hate to say this, but I understand a little bit why Carrie chose to join Patisis. It must have taken a lot of bravery to share her reasons, and I have no doubt that her family played a huge part in her decision. But she's in danger. If her Negative convinces her to make another attempt on her own life, who will be there to save her? Who will touch her now? These Negatives are nefarious. They know what's going on in someone's life, and they use that. They know your weak spots, and they study you and how you react to stress.

"Carrie, if you happen to hear this, we want you to know that you have support here if you choose to leave."

I cleared my throat. "Okay, time for another question ... Shani wants to know what we think about the medical boycott surrounding people with NIs."

I looked up at Joshua, hopeful that his always up-to-date knowledge of current events would help us out.

"Yes, okay, Shani, so we're starting to see some fear from first responders and in emergency rooms," Joshua said. He settled into his chair more, and I knew to expect a lengthy answer. "Now that the proximity theory has gained some traction, people are wondering how to react around people in life-and-death situations. Of course, things are different depending on where you are in the country—I think in California, some doctors and hospitals have decided not to serve patients who have known NIs. Our addresses are in the database, so that makes it easy to find out who has an NI and who doesn't. Right now, in Omaha, um, I've heard that it may take longer to get an ambulance if you have an NI because different teams of paramedics are willing to accept all passengers, and others, unfortunately, are not.

"So yeah ... I don't know if that really answers your question. I'd love to hear if anyone's experienced any kind of discrimination trying to receive medical treatment. It's really messed up."

"I agree," I said, feeling the need to say something before moving on to the next question. "This is unusual for our channel, but it's always nice to find moments where we can lighten up. Plus, multiple people have asked this over our last few posts." Joshua looked completely confused, and I couldn't blame him. Usually, we decided on which questions to answer ahead of time. But this was a question that I had, too, so I decided to sneak it into the lineup. "And this has nothing to do with our Negative Images, but Joshua, multiple people have asked why you always go by your full name instead of Josh."

He laughed, and I couldn't ignore the butterflies in my stomach when I saw him actually happy. His eyes crinkled at the corners, and he looked unburdened for just a moment. "Yeah, that's kind of a funny story. I used to go by Josh all the time. But when Ainsley introduced me to her parents for the first time, she introduced me as Joshua. And that's what they always called me. Soon, Ainsley called me that, too. So, I just sort of started going by Joshua all the time."

"That's really sweet," I said. His attitude had rubbed off on me, and even I felt a little less stiff.

"We had another question to address, though, right, Anita? Not to bring the mood back down, but—"

"No, no, yeah ... you're right, back to the important issues. Megan wants to know why some Negatives seem to be so over the top while others disappear for long stretches at a time. Joshua, we've talked about this a little bit. Ainsley's Negative seems a little quieter and less active than Dan's Negative."

We exchanged a glance, and for a second, I had a rush, a feeling that we were still talking to just each other even though we were talking for the

NEGATIVE IMAGES

benefit of whoever was watching online. The corner of Joshua's mouth quirked up, and I wondered if the thought had crossed his mind, too.

"I think that these Negatives do only as much as they need to do. They want to get a certain reaction out of us—once they get it, they don't need to do much more. Dan's Negative maybe hasn't seen the reaction that he's looking for yet, so he's still working hard to get that out of you."

"Right."

"He's really been giving you hell lately. But Ainsley, she's been pretty successful in planting some dark thoughts in my head."

"Ainsley's Negative, remember? We always have to think of them as what they are, not confuse them for our actual loved ones."

"You're absolutely right. And that kind of ties into our next question. 'You always say to make this distinction. Does it really help you? I can't look at mine without seeing my best friend, even when I refer to him in my brain as Joe's Negative.' Any thoughts, Anita?"

I cleared my throat. "Yeah, umm, I mean, it wasn't easy for me to remember this myself, at least at the beginning. But I just kept telling myself that Dan, my husband, wouldn't say these things. I had to come up with a way to remember that this thing, this entity, is entirely different. And using the existing language of Negative Images made sense to me."

In my mind, I heard Dan's Negative speak again. *I'm the real part of him, the honest part. I'm all the thoughts that ran through his head before he chose which ones to say.* I'd meant to keep talking, but I paused now, my mouth gaping.

"It's not an overnight process," Joshua jumped in. "And if another phrase or term comes to mind that helps you differentiate this from your loved one, it will also help."

We continued for a few more minutes, answering questions. Joshua did 90 percent of the talking for the next few minutes while my brain kicked back into gear.

Where was Dan? Where was the other part of Dan?

CHAPTER TWENTY-ONE

"**W**hat happened? You looked like you'd seen a ghost—or your Negative Image again." Joshua grinned, making jokes about words that did nothing but inspire fear and hushed tones.

It was obvious to me that he felt like we were winning. Whether this fight was against Patisis and his quarantine ambition or against our Negatives, I wasn't sure. And I hated to deflate his mood.

"Come on. Just tell me." His smile was easy, sincere.

"I'm worried about Dan," I admitted, my eyes not meeting his.

"Excuse me?" Joshua still had a smile on his face, but his eyes were unsure.

"Not my Negative. I always keep that distinction. But he told me today that he was *part* of Dan. And that the other part—the good part, I guess?—is gone. I ... I don't know if I believe him. But I thought about what Carrie said about her mom's Negative and how she felt like it wasn't all of her mother. I mean, if this part of Dan is here, though ... if that part is true, then where is his other half? And I'm being optimistic here, but what will happen to my husband when my Negative Image is finally gone?"

"What are you talking about? His soul or something? The afterlife?"

"Well, yeah, I guess. I mean, what if there is an afterlife, and in getting rid of my Negative, Dan doesn't get to go where he's supposed to?"

Joshua shrugged and packed up the ring light while he spoke. I couldn't tell if he was taking this as seriously as I was.

"I haven't told you this, and it'll probably sound crazy. But sometimes I see him. My Dan. Sometimes I hear his voice." I was very still, practically holding my breath until Joshua responded.

He looked up at me, and I could relax a little when I didn't see judgment in his eyes. "Honestly? Yeah, it does sound crazy."

We both laughed a little, and it was easier to breathe as he kept talking.

"But, on the other hand, you've had a lot of experiences with your Negative that I haven't." He sighed. "I guess it kind of depends on what you believe in, right? Personally, I believe that most of us end up in purgatory. I don't think many of us are good enough for heaven. But I don't think we're necessarily bad enough to deserve hell, either." He grew quiet and frowned slightly. "You know, I literally spent years working to be better. To be good enough for Ainsley. I did it because of how she was raised and everything I knew she would expect out of life. I chose my career path based on what I thought would make the most money so that it would be easy for her to be happy.

"The truth was, we were probably never a good match. I thought we were; I thought we'd get through anything. But the truth is, we'd started to grow apart even before we were engaged." He cleared his throat and shook his head as if to clear it. "I'm not sure how I got on that tangent. I guess I was just thinking about what you'd said about the parts of us.

NEGATIVE IMAGES

I hope that there's a part of her that knew how to be happy. I hope that part of her is happy now, somewhere."

"I think you're right, though. About purgatory. Nobody's perfect. I can almost imagine that purgatory is gone, and instead of everyone being sent to one place or the other, they're being split. Their bad half comes here to mess with us, just like a little devil, and the other half gets to go..." I sighed. "Somewhere better," I finished. It was a stupid theory.

"I mean, I don't have any answers, Anita. I trust that people will end up where they're supposed to be. And no matter whether this Negative is part of your husband or just some fabrication that knows all the details of your life with him, you can't let him win. If some part of Dan is out there, he'll be all right. You'll just have to trust that wherever he really is, he'll take care of himself."

"I guess you're right. I just wish I could be sure. I mean, he's not the husband that I thought he was. Lately, I wonder if I knew him at all. It was so hard answering that question today. I completely lied—there was so much I didn't know about him. And I'm angry—he made me the biggest fool! But I still don't want anything bad to happen to him."

"You know, maybe that's the other half of all this."

"What do you mean?"

Joshua sat down, and I joined him, sitting across from him to study his face.

"I mean, the people who come back as Negative Images. I think they must be troubled, almost like they lived two different lives. Obviously, Dan was cheating on you the whole time."

I flinched.

"Sorry to be blunt."

"It's okay," I lied. It was terrible.

"I don't believe Ainsley was ever happy with me. I think she wanted to be because she thought she should be. On paper, we were a good couple. But obviously, she had lots of other interests that didn't involve me. I don't know exactly what—or who—they might have been, but she was trying to live the life she thought she was supposed to live, not the one she wanted to live."

"I wonder if you're right. But I suppose that would be a hard one to find out. You know, to get people to speak about their loved one's flaws while that person's Negative Image spouts off everything bad about them the moment they so much as think it."

My house had felt overwhelmingly large in the days after Dan's death. Then it became frightening in its many empty rooms because I couldn't tell which of them might hold Dan's Negative.

So, I was surprised but cautiously happy when Joshua suggested staying at my house for a little while. I didn't understand why uploading YouTube and FacebookLive sessions exhilarated him, but the energy and shift in his mood were palpable. I hadn't even seen Ainsley's NI as often since we started our video sessions, making me wonder if engaging in something that brought its own positive energy might be enough to suppress these Negatives.

It was only when Joshua explained that I understood what was really going on.

NEGATIVE IMAGES

"She's not here as much during the day because she torments me every night," he said as he took a sip of coffee—he'd been drinking more of it, which I hadn't noticed until he mentioned his evening struggles.

"Sometimes, I can't sleep. Other times, I do, and it's worse. Anita, I think she's manipulating my dreams. I would say it was a crazy idea, but if yours can manipulate objects, maybe each one has their own ..."

"Superpower?" I raised my eyebrow, going for levity.

"Well, the villain equivalent, yeah. Whatever that would be called."

"It could be." I'd shrugged, casting my mind toward all the news that we had on Negative Images and how they worked, feeling bad when I realized I was doubting Joshua. "Maybe people don't share this information because it doesn't align with what we know. Or maybe they just think they're going crazy."

"I feel like I'm going crazy, "Joshua confessed. "So, can I stay here? Just for a little while? I want to see if she keeps up her tactics in a new environment."

I almost said no. I remembered all too well how Dan's Negative had ramped up his evening attacks at Carrie's house. But Joshua's NI had always been different. And I couldn't say no to him. Besides, it meant a little less empty space to deal with, even though I'd also gain a second Negative Image. The house might even feel crowded.

For three days, everything went smoothly. Joshua was sleeping in late, but I expected it.

I sat at my laptop in the kitchen, morning sunlight splashing across the table. I took a sip of my coffee, and my fingers hovered over the keyboard. I was gearing myself up to look at our latest comments, but then a large crash erupted upstairs. It sounded like breaking glass.

REBECCA SCHIER-AKAMELU

I took the steps two at a time and ran into the guest room to see Ainsley's Negative looking at me. Whining sounds came out of her mouth, but of course, I couldn't understand her. I tried to open the door to the en suite bathroom, but it rattled in the frame. Joshua must have locked it.

My heart pounded in my chest.

"Joshua!" I shouted as I tried again to turn the knob. "Open up! Answer me!"

Silence, except for the sound of me panting for air. My mind filled itself with terrible images, one worse than the next. I saw Joshua with a bloody fist, the mirror above the sink now a web of deadly shards on the floor. I saw him cutting the palm of his hand on the mirror as he prepared to dig it into his throat. I imagined him in the tub, filled with warm water that was slowly turning pink and then red with blood.

"Joshua?!" I screamed at the top of my lungs and banged on the door. Nothing.

The silence was eerie, so much worse than the sound the glass made when it broke. It was so quiet I could almost imagine the room was empty.

I ran my finger along the door frame, looking for the key. It was gone. "Shit." I rushed back to the hallway, sliding my hands along the doorframes until I finally found a key on top of the laundry room door. Dan again? Dan's Negative, I meant. The laundry room didn't lock—I would never have left a key there.

I rushed back, slipping the key into the hole, catching the lock quickly, and opening it. My sweaty palms slid off the knob as soon as it turned. The door hit the wall and bounced back. I frantically scanned the room only to find it was empty. The mirror was broken. A few larger, stubborn pieces stuck in place, reflecting bits of me back at myself. My worried eyes stared back at me from a shard on the floor. But Joshua wasn't here. "Ah, Anita. I thought I might be able to get you up here this way." Dan's Negative was reflected in the mirror now, too. He grinned at me, a confident, tricky-looking smirk made more terrible by his deformed mouth. Ainsley stood behind him in the hallway, smiling at me, her black eyes unreadable. I imagined she felt gleeful—victorious, even.

"Where's Joshua?" I whirled around, wanting to deal with him directly.

"Out of the way," Dan's Negative answered. The smile left his face. He stepped towards me, and I took a step back, my sneaker grinding up a small piece of glass into the tile.

"What are you doing?" My voice sounded too breathy, almost like I had the wind knocked out of me.

"Bringing Joshua here was a terrible idea. Ainsley's losing her hold on him. Once we get rid of you, she'll break Joshua. He'll go ahead with the plan she's given him. Do you know what it is? Has Joshua told you?"

My breath came in shallow gasps, my mouth too frozen to speak.

"She's gotten him to dream in more and more detail about how his story ends. He's going to drive his car into a lake and sit there, seatbelt on and everything, waiting for the water to come in so he can drown."

"No," I managed to say, even though it was exactly what Joshua had described to me.

"Eventually, yes." Dan's NI grinned, the skin on his face pulling so tight that his eyes looked like they might pop out of his skull.

I tried to move past him, to leave the bathroom. I thought he couldn't possibly hurt me. Wouldn't it have taken all of his energy reserves just to break the mirror?

I walked towards him; he lifted an arm to block me, but I didn't slow down. I thought I'd walk through it, but instead, his bony forearm cut into my ribs. I grabbed his wrist, and the skin slipped in my grasp like it had detached from the muscle and bone during decay.

"You think I'd make this easy for you?" he hissed in my ear.

My heart leaped into my throat. "Joshua! Joshua! Help!"

The Negatives stared at each other, one set of black eyes studying the other. They didn't speak, but the energy shifted between them. Dan's Negative nodded, and Ainsley vanished.

"No!" I howled. "Joshua!"

"He has his own problems to deal with," Dan whispered. He took a step towards me, and I took another step back, putting myself farther away from the door. Now I was wedged between the countertop and the shower, the toilet behind me.

My foot slipped on a large piece of glass, and I nearly fell into the tub. Dan's Negative laughed at me as I scrambled to regain my footing. I had to put my hand down to catch myself, and I nicked it on a large shard of glass.

He laughed, and when he let loose that terrible sound, it split open the side of his mouth. It reminded me of someone pulling a rotisserie leg off a chicken.

I grabbed the glass shard, ignoring the cut in my palm. As I gripped it tighter, blood gushed around the sides of it.

"Yes," Dan's NI breathed loudly. "That's only the beginning, Anita. Let's keep going!"

I think he expected me to kill myself, to end this long bout of torture. Instead, I lunged towards him, slashing at his face. He stepped back much quicker than I thought he could, but I managed to catch the glass

NEGATIVE IMAGES

on his split cheek. He was against the wall now, giving me just enough time to lunge at him. I aimed for his chest. I wanted this over and done with.

Just as the glass met him—I swear I felt it sink into his rotten flesh—he vanished. My momentum carried me into the wall, and the glass worked itself farther into my palm before I stumbled backward.

"Damn it!" I threw the glass down on the floor behind me. My hand pulsed in time with my heartbeat. "Joshua!" I yelled down the steps. "Joshua!" I picked up my pace, nearly tripping down the stairs. Noxious fumes wafted towards me as I opened the door to the garage.

Joshua was in the driver's seat of the car with the window rolled down. His head was tilted back, and he said nothing when I opened the door and slapped him across the face with my bloody hand.

Chapter Twenty-Two

Thankfully my phone was in my back pocket, so I dialed 911. Joshua had a pulse, but I had to drag him outside for fresh air. He fell out of the car with a slight tug, but getting him to the driveway was almost impossible. I grabbed him under the shoulders and practically fell over as I strained to lift him. I tried again, this time sitting behind him, letting his head rest against my stomach as I scooted us backward on my butt until we reached the driveway. I lay panting on the ground—Joshua didn't make a sound. I prayed he hadn't been unconscious too long. After all of this—our work, our mission, our friendship—this couldn't be how things ended for him.

I breathed a sigh of relief as Joshua exhaled audibly. Was it a sign that he might pull through now that he was getting the oxygen he needed?

My mind replayed my encounter with Dan's and Ainsley's Negatives. It had sounded like she wasn't ready to get Joshua to do this—at least not yet—but that must have been a ploy. Presumably, she was in such a hurry to see Joshua dead that she'd settled on carbon monoxide poi-

NEGATIVE IMAGES

soning instead of drowning. I couldn't get over the way Dan's body had felt—solid and disgusting and unreal all at once.

Had Ainsley's Negative messed with Joshua's mind? He'd mentioned his dreams—but was he sleepwalking? Had he really started the car? Had he rolled down his window to let the fumes in faster? I couldn't picture him doing any of that willingly.

I shivered, the early March sunlight doing little to keep me warm. I couldn't tell what Ainsley's Negative was capable of. If she had moved anything or touched Joshua, he hadn't told me. I had to assume, for now, that she couldn't take on a corporeal shape.

I thought that realization might make me happier, but instead, a wave of loneliness swept over me. As far as I knew, my Negative was the only one who had offered to kill me. He could do it, too.

"Shit." My breath came in ragged gasps as tears streamed down my face. Three thoughts came to me simultaneously, none of them helpful. The first was that I could hear the sirens coming. The second was that I couldn't remember much about how paramedics might respond to us—but I remembered from our last video session that we might have a tough time. Joshua's face had been all over the internet lately, along with mine. Our YouTube clips had even aired on several news networks while the talking heads debated the merits of our theory. Thirdly, my hand was bleeding profusely—I'd stained Joshua's shirt and my own, and red streaked the driveway.

Tires crunched over the pavement as the ambulance pulled up in front of my house. Two EMTs got down while a third stayed behind the wheel. They walked cautiously, not rushing to help but instead assessing the situation.

"We got a 911 call from this location," said a bulky EMT. His voice had a drawl to it—just enough to suggest Southern roots and all the time in the world. "Ma'am, can you confirm who you are and whether you have a Negative Image attached to you?"

They could clearly see Joshua splayed out on the driveway, but they'd both come to a stop several feet in front of me. My whole body itched to jump up and scream at them to move faster. I could hardly answer without shaking.

"Yes, I'm Anita Walsh. I called for my friend Joshua Maguire, and we both have NIs." I wanted to lie, but I didn't think there was much point—the second man had his phone out, and I could guess what he was looking at. After a long moment, he looked up from his phone and gave his partner a nod.

The larger man jogged over to Joshua, and the driver hopped down to help him. *Finally, some urgency,* I thought.

"What happened?" the second EMT asked me. His beard and sunglasses made him hard to read.

I swallowed and tried to explain everything that was important while leaving out as much as possible.

"I heard the car running in the garage. I just got a bad feeling."

"And what happened to you?" he asked. I'd pressed my hand into my shirt, but drops of blood hit the cement.

"Nothing really."

"Let me take a look at that." The bearded EMT put on gloves and approached me.

"It's just a cut," I protested and turned away from him. "Joshua is the one who needs help!"

"He's breathing; he's got a pulse," the large EMT called out.

NEGATIVE IMAGES

Joshua's white face became obscured by an oxygen mask. The driver prepared the gurney. They hoisted him on expertly, unlike how I'd dragged him from the garage.

"Thank God." I let out a sigh of relief—he'd be fine once they got him to the hospital.

I trailed behind them as they wheeled the gurney to the back of the ambulance.

"We have a hands-off situation coming in. ETA eight minutes," the bearded EMT said into his radio.

"Hands off?" I hated the way he came up with that phrase so easily. It was a term. "What does that mean, exactly?"

The EMT lowered his sunglasses to look me clearly in the eye. "Nobody wants to collect a Negative Image of their own. Obviously, you guys have NIs. It just means there might be a longer wait for him to get treatment. But if he starts to head south, then he'll be in a 'hands-off' situation."

"He might not get help?"

Joshua looked so small, suddenly, under the oxygen mask as the other two hopped down and walked to the front.

The bearded EMT gave me a noncommittal shrug. He wouldn't meet my gaze.

"I'm coming with you." I climbed into the back and squeezed in next to Joshua. "I'll do anything that needs to be done to him, okay?"

"Let's go!" the driver called out from the ambulance. I grabbed Joshua's hand with my uninjured one, and the ambulance took off, sirens wailing.

"You're going to need to go the ER when we arrive. That hand needs stitches," the bearded EMT pointed out as he hooked Joshua up to a heart monitor.

"No. I have to stay with him."

"I'm trained for this, you know? Years of my life dedicated to saving others and dealing with gruesome injuries. Deaths. I'm sitting here, trying to help this guy but touching him as little as possible. If he dies, I'm screwed. I have a wife and three kids at home who depend on me. You think I could go back home to them with a chance that this bastard was attached to me?"

I could feel how tense the air was in the small metal box. We went over a bump, and I lurched to the side.

"And you—you think you can just come with us and what? Take direction? Be our hands? You think you're gonna save him?" He pointed at Joshua as though he were worthless.

"Please. I don't think he's going to die. He's strong. And, I promise, I'll do anything that needs to be done to him so you don't have to touch him."

For a moment, he didn't say anything. "You can't drip blood all over him."

"Then fix my hand for me. Or if you can't, at least radio ahead that I need to be treated alongside Joshua so that I can be there to take care of him. Please."

He sighed. "I really shouldn't do this."

"Okay." I stretched out my shirt, wrapping the bottom of it around my hand.

"Wait." He glanced at Joshua, then at me, and cursed a little under his breath. "Just so you know," he said as he pulled some disinfectants out from a cabinet, "I'm in favor of the quarantine for people like you. You put people like me at risk. I can't imagine living with one of those things attached to you. It's gotta be an absolute hell. But it's just like any other highly contagious disease like Ebola or COVID or something. You've gotta think of other people first. Would you wish this on your worst enemy?"

I thought of Monica and the affair. How she was somehow still ignorant enough of NIs to be jealous of the fact that Dan's Negative had latched itself onto me instead of her. "No. I don't think I would."

"So, why won't you do it? Why not go into quarantine with the others so people can handle you better when you need medical care instead of placing me in this awkward position where I don't wanna risk touching your friend? People like me—nurses and doctors—we don't always get a heads-up. Some people do their best to hide it."

I swallowed hard. He wouldn't change my mind—he hadn't lived through what I had, dealt with all the violence, the abuse, the threats. But he was right, too. I'd never considered things from his point of view.

"No one would touch him if he was like this in quarantine either," I countered.

He raised his eyebrow at me, then turned his focus to the machines hooked up to Joshua. "Oh, I know it'd be hard to find someone who'd wanna do it, but there are better people out there than me who would. Trust me."

"Like who? Even someone who's practically a saint would probably avoid doing it."

He shrugged. "Who knows? Maybe someone with a Negative happens to be a surgeon or something? And they could go into quarantine, too. Of course, there's always the money. I've heard rumors that positions at Leavenworth will be high paying just because of that risk."

"I suppose it's possible," I said grudgingly. "We might be able to get care. But I really don't think that's what's going to happen. I think people want us in quarantine because they don't know how to integrate us into society. And if we could just keep our jobs and as much normalcy in our lives as possible, then we'd be able to fight these Negatives. We'd have more to live for."

I expected my words to reach this man, maybe even make him reconsider his opinion. Most people with strong opinions never take the time to speak to someone with an opposite view.

But all he did was shake his head as if I was the one missing the point.

"This is going to sting." He dabbed the palm of my hand with disinfectant.

My eyes watered, and my other hand started shaking.

"I really can't stitch you up in here. It's a moving vehicle. But I can radio ahead for you, and I think under the circumstances, they can stitch up your hand for you while you're in with him."

I nodded a little. With the vast difference in our opinions and experiences, I'd expected him to make life even more difficult for me. "Thank you. I really appreciate it."

"Consider the quarantine, though," he said, pointing a finger at me before he reached for his radio.

I listened as he radioed the hospital, again mentioning that we were a 'hands-off' case and advising that I needed stitches and to stay with Joshua. It didn't make up for his other comments, but at least I know he did what he said he would.

NEGATIVE IMAGES

I shouldn't have left Joshua alone, even for a minute. We should have developed some sort of protocol for how long we could be apart from each other. Taking him to my house had loosened Ainsley's hold on him, but I should have guessed that that loss would have pushed her to work with my own Negative to regain her footing. I knew it wasn't totally my fault, but laying the blame at my feet was soothing in its own weird way. The situation called for blame to be apportioned to someone. If it was me, that was fine. I was happy to be the guilty party if Joshua survived.

As I took one of his hands in my good one, I realized how much I cared about him. This wasn't that different from the time I'd sat next to Dan in the hospital. I began bargaining with an unseen God to keep Joshua alive, blaming myself and promising to do better. Thinking of those last days with Dan struck me differently now. I couldn't tell if it was finding out about Monica or seeing his face on my Negative Image, but for the first time, it occurred to me that I didn't miss Dan.

The realization made me feel empty and hollow like someone took away an ache and left a pit in the middle of my chest.

How am I supposed to love someone who is gone? Who I now know was unfaithful to me, not just once, but countless times? If I had found out about his affair in any other way, I would have filed for divorce. I would have gone out with Tricia, who was not even close to a real friend, just so I wouldn't have to go home and be alone. I would rag on every little habit he had, from leaving his clothes on the floor to calling me Ann as a terrible attempt at a nickname to his irritating use of sarcasm and his inability to buy color-safe bleach.

I would have shed him and our marriage like skin and then started over, eventually, with someone new.

But death changes things. I'm a widow. Not a divorcee.

"Hey. We're here," the EMT said to me. I released Joshua's hand so they could wheel his gurney into the hospital. I followed behind them, alternating between walking quickly and jogging to keep up.

"You're not to touch him, understand?" a doctor said to me before she even introduced herself. "We've got to assess him, and we've got to take care of that." She pointed to my hand as if it were something I should just cut off to be more hygienic. "I know you're concerned about him." She placed a hand on my shoulder. "But please take a seat."

She turned her focus to Joshua. A nurse joined her to hover over him, attaching him to machines to monitor his vital signs. He still wore an oxygen mask, which resembled a sea creature from my viewpoint.

Another nurse arrived and planted herself in front of me, blocking my view of Joshua.

"I'm going to give you a local anesthetic," she said, swiping my hand down with more disinfectant. I looked away and listened to the steady *beep beep* coming from the heart rate monitor. Four pricks and tingling sensations later, the nurse announced that she was done.

"How long was he in the garage before you found him?" Joshua's doctor asked.

"I'm really not sure."

"A window of time, maybe?"

"Um ... five or ten minutes?"

"Okay. That's hopeful. We're going to put him in a hyperbaric chamber since he's still unconscious. It will get more oxygen into his system quickly."

"Can I be with him?"

The doctor paused, and my heart clenched. "He'll be back—probably by the time your hand is done getting stitched up."

NEGATIVE IMAGES

They wheeled him out, and for a few minutes, I was entirely alone, listening to other doctors and patients outside.

Another doctor rapped on the open door before coming in the room. "Okay, that should be pretty well numb by now. Can you feel this?" He poked my hand with the edge of an instrument.

"No, just pressure."

"Good."

I looked away, feeling quick pulls and tugs on my hand.

I sighed. "If you were me, and you had a Negative, what would you do?"

He looked up at me in surprise, his blue eyes piercing mine as if I'd just asked him the dumbest question. "I'd go into quarantine. I think that's the safest place for you."

"Do you know anyone who has a Negative?" I asked.

"No. Thankfully, I don't."

We sat in silence as he stitched. For the first time, I felt unsure. Was I jumping to conclusions, thinking that people living in quarantine wouldn't get the care they needed? They'd at least have a chance to build the same kind of relationship that I had with Joshua. Were we wrong?

"Ouch!" I cried out as the needle went into a fleshy part of my palm that the anesthetic hadn't numbed.

"Sorry," the doctor said. He pointed with one gloved hand to a space behind me, and I knew that Dan's Negative had come to join me.

"No worries." I grimaced as the doctor pulled the needle out of my palm. A pinprick of red showed there, and he went back to stitching me up.

"You know, I don't think Joshua is looking too good," Dan's Negative said. He took a seat on a wheeled stool next to me, observing my stitches with interest.

"You can't get that—thing—to move, can you?"

"He usually doesn't do what I want him to do. If he did, I would have asked him to leave a long time ago," I said dryly.

The doctor grunted and went back to my stitches.

"I think you're just prolonging Joshua's pain," Dan's Negative continued. He focused those black eyes on me, and I very determinedly stared at the floor, not wanting to mess up all the work the doctor had done.

"It would have been much kinder of you to let him go through with it. If he lives, he'll be a vegetable." Dan's Negative smiled as he spoke as if he were giving me the best news of my life.

The sound of something rolling by in the hallway caught my attention. A moment later, nurses wheeled Joshua's bed back into the room, followed by the doctor.

"Are you family?" Joshua's doctor asked me.

"Well, not exactly. But I don't know what family he does have, or where they are." There was still so much I didn't know about Joshua. I had no idea if he had siblings or where his parents might be. At this point, I knew more about Ainsley's family than his.

The doctor glanced back at Joshua, then at me.

"Look, it's pretty unlikely that anyone else will come forward for him just because of who we are. I think for right now, I'm all he's got."

The doctor considered me, then nodded. "It looks like there's a good chance that he has no lasting brain damage. But we'd like to get him conscious, and for some reason, he's just not coming around."

NEGATIVE IMAGES

"He's lost the will to live," Dan's Negative interjected. The doctor glared at him for a moment before continuing.

"We're unclear as to why he's not regaining consciousness. It might have something to do with the nature of his trauma and how it was inflicted on him. Is there anything you can think of that might help him?"

I shook my head. It was hard to see Joshua lying there, looking so pale.

"You're all set." The doctor who had worked on my hand gave my wrist a pat to let me know he was done.

"Thank you." I turned my attention back to Joshua's doctor. "Can I sit with him? Maybe it would help. We've been through a lot together, especially these last few weeks—"

"It can't hurt. Someone will be back to check on him." She went out of the room, her back ramrod-straight.

I sat with him, angling the chair so that I was staring at the length of Joshua's body instead of sitting next to him with the chair pointing at his feet.

I didn't know what to say. I felt stupid and clumsy, putting my left hand over his when my impulse was to use my right. I gave his hand a squeeze and watched his vital signs as though something might change with just my touch.

Nothing did.

Chapter Twenty-Three

*B*eep. At first, I expected the sound to continue. I must have fallen asleep. It was just a dream. A bad dream. But it had transported me back to the day Dan died. I expected to see that shell of Dan's face when I sat up, but instead, I saw Joshua—still breathing, still with a little color in his cheeks.

"We have a lot left to do, Joshua." I studied his wan face, wondering what he would say. He turned his head slightly on the pillow but made no indication that he heard me.

My mind turned to Carrie, and I thought of calling her. Maybe she could tell me more about that night and whether her Negative Image had ever behaved oddly. It bothered me that Eduardo hadn't seen anything like what I was experiencing, despite having the longest history with Negative Images. I debated emailing him to see if anything had come to mind since we'd last spoken.

Or, maybe Carrie could give me details about the care she was receiving in quarantine. Maybe then I would think differently of it, and she would convince Joshua and me to go. After all, what was left for us here?

NEGATIVE IMAGES

I'd decided not to be swayed by the paramedic, but after spending time in the hospital, watching Joshua breathe, I wasn't sure anymore.

I pulled out my phone. "I wish you were awake," I told Joshua. "I'm going to call Carrie. Hopefully, she'll talk to me. I wish you could tell me what to say."

It rang four times, and then I got a message.

"Carrie Ellsworth," Carrie said her name in a stilted, formal way. "Is no longer accepting calls at this number," a cheerfully robotic voice said. "Please hang up and call the Negative Image quarantine center at 888-555-5555."

"They took her phone!" I said, forgetting that Joshua wouldn't answer.

I called Carrie's number one more time so that I could write down the number to the service. But instead of dialing it, I called Aaron Ellsworth.

"Hello?" Aaron's voice sounded gruff. I couldn't tell if he was upset or maybe just tired. I wondered if he realized who was calling and if he had saved our numbers from the time we watched his sons.

"Hi. This is Anita. I know that Carrie is at the quarantine center. I just … I needed to talk to her. Joshua made an attempt on his life today. But when I called her cell phone, I got an automated message."

"Yeah, she doesn't have her cell anymore."

"Doesn't that seem a bit strange to you? I mean, people are so glued to their phones now … it's hard to think that she was okay giving it up."

I couldn't imagine Carrie—the confident woman I'd wanted so badly to emulate—willingly handing over what was essentially her remaining autonomy to someone else. Carrie made the shots instead of simply accepting other people's decisions. I remembered her calm control during the planning sessions we'd had for the auction. She was never rude but wasn't shy about asking for changes if one of my ideas didn't suit her vision.

"She lost her phone privileges," Aaron said, his tone matter of fact. "They took it from her after they realized that she was posting on social media without permission."

My insides went cold. "I ... I didn't see any posts of hers."

"They took them all down."

"She should be allowed to post whatever and whenever she wants. It's a voluntary quarantine."

"Yeah, but they don't want any negative press."

"Is Carrie okay?"

There was a long pause before Aaron answered. "I'm sure she's fine. As fine as she'll ever be. You know, I thought bringing her home wasn't a good situation, and I was glad she felt the same way. This is what's safest."

"Don't you speak to her?"

"Not often. I find it's easier that way, especially for the boys."

I hung up. I didn't mean to. I had more questions, and I wanted more answers, but Aaron seemed like he hardly cared. Not about Carrie, not about his family, and certainly not Joshua or me.

Feeling resigned and wishing more than ever that I could talk to Joshua, I dialed the number for the quarantine center.

It rang once, twice, and a third time. Would they even let me speak to Carrie?

"National Negative Image Quarantine Center. Can I help you?"

"Hi, I'm trying to reach Carrie Ellsworth."

"Oh." Her voice went up in surprise and down again in some mixture of awkward disappointment. Kind of like when you're asked about a mutual acquaintance that you don't like. "One moment, please."

NEGATIVE IMAGES

I waited on hold—no music, just a periodic clicking noise to let me know I hadn't been disconnected.

Finally, the woman came back on the line.

"Carrie isn't available at this time."

"Please, it's about my ... cousin," I said, deciding on the spot that I should pretend to be someone else. I didn't know if the receptionist knew who I was, but I didn't want to take the chance that she did.

"I wanted to know what she thought of the quarantine program because he also has a Negative, and I'm trying to persuade him to go."

"Oh." This time, her tone was more pleasant.

"You see, he knows Carrie, and I don't know anyone else who could convince him."

There was a moment's pause. "Let me see what I can do."

This time, the hold was longer, and the periodic clicks became routine.

"Hello?" I recognized Carrie's voice. She sounded unsure of herself—nervous, even.

"Hi. Carrie?"

"This is Carrie." She paused briefly, and when she spoke again, her voice was stilted, almost as though she were reading from a script. "I understand you wanted some information for a relative about the quarantine program."

"Yes. It's my cousin, Joe." I licked my lips. My brow started to sweat. I felt certain that someone else was listening in.

"Can I speak to Joe?" Carrie asked.

"He actually ... well, he's in the hospital. He's not conscious. I'm just worried that something will happen to him when he's released."

"Sure. I understand that. And what's your name? I don't think I caught it."

Carrie had thrown me. I thought back to the last time I saw her in the hospital. She had tearfully and passionately told us about her NI experience, and she seemed at peace—almost happy—about her decision to go into quarantine. Now, she didn't sound like herself at all. She didn't sound upset. She didn't sound happy. Or bored. She sounded wrong.

"My name is An ... drea. Andrea Charles." The phony name was slippery and awkward—I wasn't even sure I could remember what I just came up with. I wondered if Carrie had heard me stumble over the unfamiliarity.

"Well, Andrea, this program and this facility are wonderful. I feel very comfortable and safe here, but honestly, the best part of this whole experience is knowing that I'm not alone. It's very comforting to have people near me who are experiencing the same problem. We really lift each other up."

"But you've had your phone taken away."

There was a slight pause.

"No. I gave it up voluntarily."

"But why? You see, I only ask because Joe was trying to reach you. He couldn't get your cell, and he tried calling your husband at home to see if you had a different number. Aaron said he barely speaks to you."

"Well, I just ... I found it easier to cut ties with my old life. It keeps me from feeling so hopeless—I pretend that I'm starting all over."

"But, Carrie, the whole reason you went into quarantine was for your family's sake. Surely you want to keep a relationship with them open? Especially with this information, that proximity can affect who gets a Negative Image."

NEGATIVE IMAGES

"In due time. Once I start to feel better, I'll reach out to them again."

"Is that what everyone does? Give up their phones and their relationships outside the quarantine?"

"Most of us do, I think. I can't speak for everyone."

"Of course not." Anger flooded my brain, and I couldn't think of anything else to say.

Carrie cleared her throat. "Was there anything else you wanted to ask?"

"Yes," I said, deciding to be aggressive. "You're in a prison, correct?"

Carrie let out a forced laugh. "Yes, but only technically. It really doesn't feel anything like that."

"Do you get locked in at night?"

"Yes, but only for our own safety. We're more likely to hurt ourselves in the evening."

"I see. Do you get time outside?" I wanted to add in the yard, but I held myself back.

"Of course. Twice a day."

"Visitors?"

"That depends. They have to be understanding of why we're here. You know, it's a tough decision to make. We really don't want to see anyone who's not supportive of it."

"Oh, in case they ask you to leave?"

Silence.

"Can you leave, Carrie?"

"Uh, yes, but we are assessed frequently by a doctor and a psychiatrist, and they've never recommended that anyone leave."

I wished Joshua were hearing this. His heart rate monitor beeped steadily. He would have recorded the whole thing. I grabbed his phone and hit the camera icon, and quickly toggled to video. I put my phone on speaker. It was the best I could do.

"Would you need the doctors to give their approval before you leave?"

"Yes. Well, technically, no. But that would be very unwise, and I've never seen anyone leave here without their approval."

"Has anyone left?"

"No, actually." Carrie sounded mildly more relaxed.

"Has anyone tried to leave?"

"I ... I don't know." I took that as a maybe, probably.

"Has anyone in the quarantine program attempted to take their own life?"

"That's a good question. I don't think I have information on that for you, though."

"Has anyone killed themselves?"

"Oh." Carrie's voice sounded sad. "No," she added quickly.

"What are the medical procedures like there?"

"Medical procedures?"

"I only ask because Joe found himself in a 'hands-off' situation here. Basically, the doctors want to limit physical contact, in case he died and came to them as a Negative Image."

"Wow. You know, we don't have that problem here, and I am so ... grateful for that." The pauses in Carrie's speech made me worry that she really was being fed these answers. Maybe someone was whispering in her ear, or maybe they were simply sliding notes across the table. "Do you think this sounds like the right opportunity for your cousin?"

"Opportunity?!" I cleared my throat. What was she doing? Trying to offer me a share in a stupid MLM scheme? "Sorry. Um, I mean, he's unconscious. He can't make that decision right now."

NEGATIVE IMAGES

"Oh, he doesn't have to. We're transitioning, I think, and now people can recommend their family, friends, probably even coworkers and neighbors for the quarantine."

"What are you saying? You have people there against their will?"

"It's for the best. For everyone."

"I see. So, it won't be strictly voluntary anymore?"

"No. It won't. Be care—" Carrie's voice was full of steel, and just as I thought she was about to warn me, the line dropped.

My mind reeled. The thought of Carrie being fed all the responses seemed more plausible now. That's why she sounded so stilted and apathetic. That explained all the long pauses in her speech because she was waiting to be told what to say. I couldn't be sure if she knew she was talking to me. Andrea and Anita are close enough names that she probably did. She tried to warn me. I imagined poor Carrie being led back to her jail cell. She probably didn't have any relationships with the others if they were only let out twice a day.

I wanted to ask Joshua what I should do, but of course, he was still unconscious. I became more aware of how cold and sterile the room was, and the beeps coming from Joshua's machines were so loud. Any second, someone—a nurse or the doctor caring for Joshua—might pop in to tell me we were being transferred to the quarantine in Leavenworth. Had it started happening already?

"Okay." I studied Joshua, his wan face, the oxygen tubes coming out of his nose. "Since you can't chime in ..."

I typed in his password and uploaded the audio file to our shared YouTube account. In the description, I wrote: *If you have a Negative Image, you might be in danger. If you're against a mandatory quarantine in Leavenworth prison, gather your allies NOW.*

295

A half-hour passed.

My phone rang. My palms started sweating when I saw her name on the screen. Monica.

I still wasn't ready to talk to her. I might never be.

I answered anyway.

"Hello?"

"I just saw your post. What can I do to help?"

I sighed. At least she was direct and, hopefully, on our side.

"I'm not sure. Joshua and I are at the hospital. He nearly killed himself." Tears pricked my eyes. "I was just a few rooms away ..."

The urge to break down into tears and tell Monica everything that I wanted to tell my best friend—how the NIs were getting stronger, how I'd been attacked—overwhelmed me. I reined in the impulse.

"I'm so sorry. That must have been horrible. Will he be okay?"

"I think so. I hope so. His scans were promising. He just needs to wake up."

"Do you want me to stop by?"

I sighed. Having a friend here would take so much stress off my plate. Monica had been such a comfort after Dan passed. But the morning of the funeral, when she had come by to help me get ready, held such a different meaning now.

"I don't know. I'm not even sure if they'll let you. I think the number of people that can be in here is restricted. Can you keep an eye on things while we're here? Watch the news, maybe check out the house? I'll call you when Joshua wakes up."

"If you haven't seen any comments, don't look now. People are pissed. I mean, you've got supporters, too, but ..."

NEGATIVE IMAGES

I closed my eyes as Monica spoke. It killed me to think of all the negativity swirling around me. What a mess I'd made.

"Maybe I shouldn't have posted it, but Carrie ... she didn't sound like herself. And if what she said is true, I probably made some enemies."

"I think you already had enemies before this latest post." Monica gave a little laugh, the kind you do to alleviate tension when something really isn't funny. "I'll drive by both of your houses. Are you staying together when you get out?"

"What? Um, yeah, I mean ... probably. Then I can watch him. Probably his place." I didn't want to set foot in mine right now—just thinking of walking through my garage made me nauseous.

"Okay. I'll go by his place more often then."

I didn't know what to say. Apparently, neither did Monica. I heard footsteps echoing on the tile floor. I cleared my throat and sat down, dying for the silence to end.

"How are you?" she finally asked.

"I'll be fine. I'm strong."

I doubted it, but it seemed like something I *should* say in this kind of situation. I cut the call.

Chapter Twenty-Four

Twelve hours passed.

Notifications chimed so often that I silenced my phone.

I'd looked at some of them, and it was worse than I could have imagined. People I'd never met before were wishing for me to die. It made me sick to my stomach any time I heard a chime. Not hearing them was better, but any time I picked up my phone to see if there was news from Monica, I had a stream of notifications to clear. I wished I could just turn them off, but part of me wanted to keep an idea of what was happening. Besides, I knew Joshua would want to know when he woke up.

Joshua still lay in bed, pale and unconscious.

I spent a restless night in the chair next to his bed. Drifting off only led to thoughts of Dan.

I tried not to linger in those memories because all that they were, even more obvious and painful now, was another lie.

They sucked me in anyway.

I kept thinking back to the day he'd been shot. If I hadn't asked him to pick up the flowers, Monica might have. Whenever he'd helped out with one of our events, I thought he was doing it to help me. My vision of the perfect business, the perfect marriage, had all been a lie. He might have been helping for Monica's sake, not mine. Or, maybe it didn't matter to him. Maybe he wanted to help because of us both.

I wished it had been Monica who'd made the call and asked him to get the flowers. Then, the guilt would have been placed on her head. Would she have confessed everything after he'd died? Or would she have let that secret be buried with Dan?

I checked my phone again to see if Monica had sent any updates when an email came in from Eduardo.

Anita,

I don't know if you saw the message I sent earlier. But I spoke to my brother—he had a friend with a Negative that acted similarly to yours. It could touch him, I think.

Unfortunately, he's passed away now, too, and his death couldn't possibly have been a suicide.

Please, be careful, Anita.

Eduardo

I hit reply, hoping that if I sent something off quickly, he'd see it as soon as it went through.

Eduardo,

Thank you so much for letting me know. Do you have any other details? How was the relationship between the NI and your brother's friend? Was it strained in any way? I don't want to go into great detail, but my husband was unfaithful to me. Was there some type of betrayal involved here?

Thank you for your help,
Anita

I hit send.

"You look worried about something."

I glanced up. Joshua was looking up at me from the bed.

"Joshua! You're awake!" I didn't think—I leaped out of my chair, leaned over the hospital bed, and kissed him.

He kissed me back, his hand cupping the back of my head to pull me closer.

"What in the world!"

I straightened up and turned to see a nurse with a wide-set stance standing in the doorway with his hands on his hips.

"You've disconnected something. I rushed in here thinking he was dying." He glared at me as he approached the bed. Rather than reconnect whatever was causing the trouble, he gave a long sigh and turned to study Joshua. "You're awake, I see."

"Yes. I'm fine. Never better."

Joshua winked at me. I couldn't believe what I'd just done, and for just a minute, I was giddy, the burden lifted.

"That's a relief. You can get dressed. I'll tell the doctor you're awake, but it's safe to say you'll be discharged soon."

He lifted Joshua's hand and disconnected the IV. "I shouldn't tell you this—especially you, just waking up. But you don't seem too concerned, either..." the nurse said with a quick sideways glance at me. "You're trending. I don't know if you considered that before posting—" he gave me a stern look—"but people are speaking out against you, and people are speaking out for you, and it's a lot. I hope you're prepared to leave

NEGATIVE IMAGES

here because if you dawdle, it will get ugly. Even in the lobby, people are arguing. Somehow, people pieced together where you were." he said before striding out of the room.

Joshua sat up and gave me a look that was part amused and part concerned. "I obviously missed something."

I nodded. "Many things. What's the last thing you remember?"

His brow furrowed, and his eyes grew dark. "I know I went to the garage. I have this image of my finger holding down the button to lower the car window. But that's it. I ... I don't know what I'd do without you, Anita. Hell, without you, I wouldn't be here. I can't believe she controlled me like that, just like a puppet. I have no idea what happened after."

I'd planned to fill him in, but now that he was staring at me, trying to put on a brave face, I couldn't say any of it—how panicked I was when I saw him in that car, how close it had been.

"I can guess the rest," he said quickly. He stood up, surprisingly strong after his ordeal.

I turned away, realizing he was wearing only a hospital gown that opened in the back.

"I'm so sorry all of this happened. They asked if you had family, and I didn't know who to put them in touch with."

"That's okay. There's no one."

He said it easily, as if it was no big deal, but it broke my heart. I heard Joshua's hospital gown hit the floor and the sounds of him going through his things.

"You don't have any family at all?"

He sighed. "I mean, technically, yes. But they haven't been in my life in over 15 years."

"Wow. Joshua, I had no idea. That must have been so hard."

I risked a quick glance over my shoulder and saw him buttoning his shirt. One side of his mouth quirked up in a smile. "I won't disagree with you. But it was all for the best. My dad was never around to begin with. My mom has her own issues."

"I'm so sorry. I never realized that you didn't have anyone else to lean on."

"It's okay. I'm used to it. Tell me about the other stuff I missed. What exactly did you post? And have you kept up with the comments, I hope?"

He knew me and my relationship to the internet too well. "I haven't."

Joshua let out a guttural laugh. "I knew it. Okay. So, what was it?"

I quickly relayed everything he'd missed out on: my conversations with Aaron and Carrie, how I'd suspected she was being told what to say, and how I knew it needed to be shared.

"I hope I did all right. I really, really could have used your input."

Joshua gave me a half smile. "Honestly, I'm impressed that you did all of that. It was a pretty ballsy move. My only input is to see what the hell is going on now because, apparently, it's something."

We hadn't gotten the discharge papers yet, so we huddled over my phone together, looking at the YouTube comments and what the news was reporting about us. And, in connection with us, Greg Patisis.

"We know that Carrie is happy and safe in her new home," Patisis said in a video response. "Carrie has graciously let people see where she's staying, and she says it's good for her and her loved ones. That's who we have to believe right now—the woman who is here, living here." Patisis leaned forward, and although his voice remained steady, a vein stuck out on his forehead. "People like Anita Matthews and Joshua Maguire

NEGATIVE IMAGES

are not only terribly disillusioned and misguided, they're dangerous. Spreading false information can lead to others making bad decisions.

"Now, I know I've gotten a lot of mail and questions." Patisis licked his lips and clasped his hands on the table in front of him. "People want to know about something that happened in the call. About the quarantine becoming compulsory instead of voluntary. While Carrie was correct in saying that we were opening up the process to relatives and friends, she didn't mean that anyone was losing their rights. We're simply allowing friends and loved ones of an individual afflicted with a Negative Image to recommend this lifestyle."

I gasped. "Lifestyle?!"

Joshua elbowed me to pay attention.

"It would, of course, be illegal and against a person's individual rights to place them here against their will. While we do have the capability to commit someone here for a short time should they be dangerous, no one will be forced to move here."

"But Carrie said she didn't know of anyone leaving."

"Exactly."

"I see you two have been catching up." The nurse was back, a stack of paperwork in his hands. He went over the discharge instructions as quickly as possible. "Do you have a plan?"

Joshua and I exchanged a glance.

The nurse reached out to me, putting a heavy hand on my shoulder. "My brother has one," he said, his voice a husky whisper. "I try not to bring it up here because of how divisive the topic is."

I nodded, thinking back to the conversation I had with the EMT in the ambulance.

"You've had someone here asking about you—a man. Your records are all still confidential, but he's been pretty loud about it. Most of the waiting room knows you're here."

I hated the idea of calling Monica, but it was probably safer than an Uber. "I came with you in the ambulance, so I'm hoping she'll pick us up," I explained to Joshua.

"Anita?" Monica asked upon answering, her tone worried.

"Joshua woke up. He's being discharged."

"That's great news!"

"Could you pick us up?"

"Um. I don't know."

"What do you mean?" I tried to keep the concern out of my voice, but I didn't like the way Monica sounded.

"You asked me to check out your houses. There are cars lined up on both of your streets. No one's even trying to be discreet—it's a bunch of people looking for you guys."

"Shit."

"Yes. Shit."

"Where are you now?"

"I'm driving around midtown. I don't want to go back to my house, either. When I left, I noticed a black car following me. I haven't seen it in a while, and maybe I'm just being paranoid, but ... I'm on that website, too. I don't know if it's a good idea for me to pick you up anymore."

"Fuck." I ran my hand through my hair and let out a yelp of pain. I'd forgotten the stitches.

"Are you all right?" Monica asked.

I examined my hand, but it looked like all the stitches were still in place when I peeked under the dressing. "I'm fine. Can I talk to Joshua about this and call you right back?"

"Of course."

"What happened?" He grabbed my injured hand, looking at the bandages.

"Dan's and Ainsley's NIs teamed up. They thought they could get both of us. Ainsley's NI planted some idea in your head that got you out to the garage. They tricked me into thinking you were in the guest bathroom. Dan's NI broke a mirror. And once I got in there, I couldn't get out. He was just so strong."

"He did that? He hurt you?" Joshua held my hand in his, staring at it as though it were a rare artifact.

"Yeah. Well, it was the mirror. But we have an issue." I quickly relayed Monica's information to him.

"Should we still ask her to pick us up?" Joshua asked.

I shrugged. "I can't think of anything better. I don't have any cash, do you?"

He shook his head. "Not unless you have my wallet."

My phone rang. Monica again. I frowned. It wasn't like her to be so impatient.

"Hello?"

"Anita, I have to pick you up." There was something wrong. Her voice was shaky and timid—all the confidence I associated with her was gone.

"What's wrong?"

"I'm so sorry. I was at a stoplight and ..." She inhaled sharply, like she was in pain. "I just don't have a choice ... please, meet me outside the hospital." Monica cried out as if in pain, but the call cut off.

I nearly dropped the phone; Joshua's mouth opened in shock.

"Is she ... do you think she's okay?" I asked. I knew what I'd heard. I knew, in my gut, what this meant. Monica, my friend, the girl who'd given me so many safety pointers in college—always have your keys in hand so you're not fumbling with them at the side of your car, always check your backseat, always lock your car as soon as you get in—was taken.

Joshua put a hand on my shoulder. "No. She's not. Anita, I'm so sorry."

I sat down in a chair. I was shaking all over, and everything started to look blurry as tears filled my vision. "This is my fault. I got her involved. I asked her to keep an eye on things while we were here."

Joshua knelt down in front of me, and I practically knocked him over when I leaned in for a hug.

"We have to get up, Anita. Do you know where or when we're supposed to meet her?"

I shook my head. "She mentioned that she was in midtown earlier, and that's not too far from here. She might be here already."

We were walking to the door when my phone chimed again. An email.

"Wait. Just a sec."

"But Monica—"

"It might be Eduardo." I was looking for a lifeline and praying that this was it.

NEGATIVE IMAGES

Anita,

I'm sorry, I really don't have any more information about him or his father. He died of old age. I don't know very much about any betrayal, either, but I believe it might make them more desperate. I don't know your beliefs, but for myself, I think betrayals and other actions damage us. There's a consequence to them. Here or in the hereafter.

I saw your latest video. Please be careful; if I can help, please let me know.

Eduardo

I felt foolish. I'd thought—hoped—that Eduardo might have some information that might help us. At least he'd offered to help.

Eduardo,

I know this is a lot to ask of you. But I think something bad is going to happen to us. I think someone might take us.

Please, if you see anything about us, especially if we go into quarantine—I need you to know that this is all happening against our will. Please reach out to any media contacts you may have to spread the news. Thank you for everything,

Anita

I hit send, and not a moment later, my phone rang again. Monica.

"Are you coming?" She was crying—a sound I'd never associated with her before.

"Yes. We had to sign discharge papers."

She—or whoever was with her—cut the call.

Joshua and I peered into the hallway—it looked like a typical hospital. I'd expected some sort of panic. Hadn't the nurse mentioned that the waiting room was full of people arguing?

I turned and saw the nurse who'd scolded us for kissing, motioning to us from the other side of the hall. He gave us a friendly wave.

Out of all the people in the hospital, he was the only person who hadn't recommended that we go into quarantine. I jogged towards him. Maybe we could avoid being kidnapped after all.

I jogged up to him. "Please, we need to speak to security. Our friend was supposed to pick us up, but I think someone hijacked her car. She's in danger. She's probably at the entrance."

The man's eyes grew wide. "Oh wow. Okay. Um... come with me. We need to put you somewhere safe while we get this under control."

We followed him through several hallways—I lost track of all the turns we were making. We only slowed down when he needed a badge to enter a different wing. In fact, we'd been walking so long with no clear destination in sight that I started to worry that we'd made a horrible, costly mistake. Glancing at Joshua, I could see the concern on his face, too.

The hospital was quieter the further we walked. Someone laughed at a TV show, and other nurses looked up at us as we walked past their stations, but no one was moving urgently or panicking.

Then the air changed.

My skin broke out in goosebumps as Ainsley's NI spoke in garbled static.

"Who is this guy, Anita? Why are you letting him lead you around the hospital while Monica is sitting out front with a black eye, having all her fingers broken one by one?" Dan's NI was merciless. It felt like he might as well have plucked those fears straight from my brain.

The nurse turned around at the sudden noise, and he wasn't the only one. I caught fearful glances from the patients and visiting friends in the rooms, and the nurses in the hallways gave us a wide berth as we stepped forward.

"I'm so sorry," I said to the nurse leading us.

"We're almost there." He sounded reassuring, but the back of his neck was sweating.

As we walked, people stared. An older nurse lifted her phone as we passed. Was she reporting us or warning others ahead that we were coming through? The hallway began to feel narrower, and the ceiling seemed to be coming down on me. I couldn't quite catch my breath.

"Okay." The nurse pressed his badge against a keypad, and it unlocked. "This is security. Hi Charlie." The nurse greeted a slender guard with inky black hair.

"Paul. Who're these people?" His eyes raked over us, narrowing as he took in our NIs.

"They need some help. Can you let them look at the security feeds?"

Charlie let out a loud sigh. "What for?"

I glanced at Joshua. It was hard to tell whether he was asking what he should be looking for or why he should bother to let us look.

"My friend's car ... I think she's been hijacked. She drives a black Honda Civic and is probably at one of the entrances."

"Probably bleeding profusely or slumped against one of the windows, unconscious," Dan's NI whispered to me. "She'd be in much better shape if you'd just gone the first time she called. But no, you're here, trying to save yourself instead of worrying about her."

"Tell that thing to shut up," Charlie growled. "Okay. Black Honda Civic near the emergency entrance."

I leaned forward. It was Monica's car. I saw two shapes. "That's it. That's her. Can you send someone down?"

"One second." Charlie grabbed his walkie off his belt. "J.C., we've got an issue at the west ER entrance."

A response came through immediately. "Copy that."

"Paul, I'll take it from here," Charlie said.

"Thank you for all your help, Paul. We really appreciate it." I could have hugged him, but I held myself back.

"Of course. Stay safe." He left. I had my eye on the door, watching it shut after Paul left. A grunt came from behind me, and when I turned, Joshua was curled up into a ball on the floor. Charlie brandished a gun, which he swung to point at me.

"On your knees. Hands behind your back."

Charlie barely waited for me to move before grabbing my wrists, forcing them behind me, and tightening a zip tie around them. Then, he did the same to Joshua, taking advantage of his pain. He worked quickly, as though he'd done this to countless people during his line of work.

"J.C., I have Maguire and Mathews en route. Pull around."

"Copy that."

Dan's Negative grinned from his place by the monitors.

"I told you so." He gloated. The TV screens were reflected in his large, black eyes. "She's slumped over. Out."

"Shut. Up. You lying, sick—"

Charlie cut me off with a quick slap to the face. A ring's band clipped my cheek, and my head rocked to the side.

"Silence. We have a short walk. It doesn't have to be grisly. But it could be. Do you understand?"

I nodded and focused my eyes on the ground.

"If you'd like to stay alive, then don't try anything. I am armed. Don't look at anyone. Don't try to get anyone's attention. Look straight ahead."

Charlie opened the door and pushed Joshua and I out ahead of him.

I risked a glance back at the TV screens. Dan's NI stood in front of them. His wide mouth split open as he laughed.

The security room was next to a flight of stairs, giving us no chance to look at anyone, even if we wanted to. We saw no one on our descent. Charlie got in front of us and opened the door at the bottom of the stairs.

Monica's car idled at the curb. She sat in the passenger seat and remained completely still as Charlie opened the back door. Joshua slid across, and I was pushed in behind him. Charlie shut the door and patted the roof of the car. The driver locked the doors and took off. Dark glasses and a cap made it difficult to gauge what he looked like.

"Cut it out. I see you back there, trying to get a good look at me. Didn't you hear what Charlie told you? Shut the fuck up, don't try to get anyone's attention, don't try to distract me, and don't try to wake up your friend, got it?"

Joshua and I nodded.

The man drove down Dodge straight until we got to the highway. I-29 South. We were going to Leavenworth.

CHAPTER TWENTY-FIVE

Two and a half hours later, we arrived.

Monica had woken up about a half hour before we got there. She'd immediately screamed. The driver had swiftly struck out with his fist, catching her in the stomach and causing the car to swerve. Earlier, Joshua had tried to catch my eye, thinking we could do something to derail the driver. But from my point of view, I could see that he had a gun, too. I'd given Joshua a forceful shake of the head. I wasn't interested in getting shot like Dan or in a car accident like Ainsley.

The car ride had been silent, giving me time to be alone with my thoughts. I was dying to talk to Monica, to apologize. I'd done my best—what I'd thought was my best—but I kept thinking about what Dan's NI had said and wondered if I'd just made this worse for her.

I was so lost in my own thoughts, trying to find a way out, that I didn't realize how close we were. I hadn't expected the prison to look so ... official. The dome at the center of the rectangular structure made me think of the Capitol Building, of democratic processes, as well as lobbying and wasted tax dollars. But it was a prison. United States Penitentiary

312

NEGATIVE IMAGES

Leavenworth. Although it had lost its designation as a maximum-security prison and was now medium-security, it looked imposing.

"One-fourth of it is for you guys. For now." The driver sounded pleased, and I wondered if he thought we would eventually take up more space in the prison. He slowed down to identify himself to an officer at the gate, and we were allowed through, the building casting a long shadow in the evening sun. My heart started racing as the man let the car come to a stop and shut off the engine.

No one said a word. Then he leaned across Monica and opened her car door.

"Get out of the car, Monica," he ordered.

Monica swiped her cheeks against her shoulder in an effort to wipe away her tears. With her hands behind her, she struggled to turn herself towards the door. The driver grunted in disgust and pushed her out.

Dan's Negative popped up, situated on the center console. It was the only time I was grateful to see him.

"So, this place. This is where you're going to kill yourself. I'll be honest. I would have preferred to watch you die at home, where we shared so many memories."

"Why does it matter?"

"Here's the thing, Anita, and I'm kind of ashamed to point this out to you. But you had a theory. And it turns out it was right."

I laughed. It was such a typical villain moment—that when I was at the lowest point, close to the end, he would come in and explain why everything had happened the way it had.

I calmed myself. "Which theory? The physical contact?"

REBECCA SCHIER-AKAMELU

Now it was Dan's Negative's turn to laugh, his jaw hinging back, exposing his molars. "Cut the crap. That was bullshit. Proximity is a much smaller component."

"God, I hate these fucking things," the hijacker complained.

I noticed Ainsley's NI stationed between Joshua and the door—the car was getting crowded. She made rasping, staticky sounds, and I wondered if she was having a similar conversation with Joshua.

"Okay. So, which one was it?" Dan's Negative was screwing with me again, and this time, I couldn't be bothered. Now I was here—the quarantine was right in front of me, and for once, I was scared of something that wasn't him.

"You noticed my strength. You noticed my appearance change. You were right—I'm not around you when I've exhausted myself. And now I'm literally falling apart in front of you."

I faced him head-on, wanting to be able to read him because his voice had lost the taunting tone, although the gravelly notes had grown more pronounced. But his eyes were just flat pools of black.

"I'm not the only one. The only one who's gotten stronger. Your new friend in Argentina told you that. You see, it's just a matter of time. Most people cave before it gets to the point we're at now. I need to get rid of you. One way or another, I *will* get rid of you."

I sighed. Men in camo—soldiers—milled about on the grounds, even though this wasn't the military prison. "We don't have time for this."

"That's right, we don't have time—you're about to meet a celebrity," the hijacker said as Greg Patisis stepped out of the building.

"There was something else that was right," Dan's Negative continued.

314

NEGATIVE IMAGES

Above his temple, the skin had snapped open to show a small chip of white—his skull. His eyes were so sunken and dark they looked like empty sockets.

"What else did I guess?"

He grinned at me, his ruined mouth split wide, and his jaw slipped onto his chest. He snapped it back into place and tested it out, opening his mouth and closing it, allowing me to see the bone and stretched tissues holding him together. I was distracted by his appearance, and I wasn't the only one. I caught a quick glance from Joshua, his eyes wide as he took in how much Dan's Negative had changed. The hijacker got down from the car, and I could just see Monica's face before she quickly turned away to avoid looking at Dan's NI.

"It was what you asked your friend," Dan's Negative continued. "Eduardo. I told you—I see everything. I know everything about you. I know how your little whoreish ass started sucking face with Joshua as soon as you realized he was awake."

A week ago, I would have shrunk with shame. But knowing about the affair had made me feel immune to these kinds of taunts.

"The last thing he emailed me. The—"

"Betrayal. Yes," Dan's Negative finished. "Everyone who has come back as a Negative Image has betrayed the person they're attached to in some way or been betrayed by that person. It's not a unique situation in the slightest."

It was like I'd been slapped in the face. Of course. I should have seen it before. It was a betrayal, but in some cases, it was hard to see. Sometimes, all I noticed at first was the hurt. Ainsley betrayed Joshua with her behavior, acting in a way that would jeopardize their relationship. Joshua had betrayed Ainsley by moving forward in their relationship despite his concerns. Eduardo's mother in Argentina betrayed him by killing herself and giving up the fight against her NI, even though that wasn't entirely her fault. Carrie's mother might have felt betrayed by her daughter putting her in a nursing home, or perhaps she had hurt Carrie through her difficult behavior. Destiny's father might have felt betrayed by her rejection of the regimented lifestyle she grew up with, or perhaps she felt betrayed by his judgment of her. The more I thought about it, the more I saw that this hurt could go both ways in many cases.

"If you're trying to figure out why *I'm* so strong, it's the degree. The degree of the betrayal matters. I mean, come on, think of what I've done to you. Think of how fucking long I was able to carry on with Monica right in front of your eyes, and you didn't fucking know!" He laughed, and the patch of bone on his skull grew; his eyebrow slipped as a flap of skin on his face detached.

"You're rotting."

"See how much work I've put in? I've literally been killing myself, torturing myself to get *you* to do the *same fucking thing*!"

The hijacker clapped his hands over his ears, and Monica ducked low to the ground. When she straightened up again, blood dripped from her ears and down her neck.

"Where is Dan? Where is the good part of him?" I asked.

"See, that's the part of you that I can't stand. The part of you that's making this so difficult. The other half is gone." He was in my face now, pointing a finger at me and threatening to nearly poke my eye out.

"I don't believe you. The other part is somewhere. I've seen him. I've heard him."

Greg Patisis was striding confidently towards us. I'd neglected to take in the news vans at the front of the building when we'd arrived, but

NEGATIVE IMAGES

several reporters followed Greg. I turned back to Dan's NI, but he was gone.

"Wrists," said the hijacker.

He grabbed mine, quickly snapping the plastic band with scissors and then did the same to Joshua. He got down and undid Monica's before he opened the back door for us. Once we'd all rubbed our wrists in relief, the hijacker spoke again.

"All right guys, this is how it goes down. You're going to walk in and surrender yourselves to the quarantine program. You're going to admit to these nice reporters that you were wrong, that after Joshua's near-death experience you realized you were in danger from yourselves. You'll admit that you've falsified recordings to better show your cause, but now you're ready to admit that it was a hoax, and you'd rather see everyone alive in quarantine than dead in their homes. If you don't do that, if you try to plead for help, make a run for it, or change your mind, then your friend Monica is going to die. We'll come up with you and stand very nicely next to you while you say all these wonderful things about the program. If it goes well, I'll have Monica drive me home, and she'll be free to go. If it doesn't go well, then Monica is going to die on the side of the highway somewhere."

Monica looked down, and I suspected she was trying not to cry. Joshua shook his head. We all knew it was a lie. Monica was in danger no matter what. She'd witnessed too much violence from the people working with Patisis. Out of the three of us, she would have been the safest in quarantine.

Camera flashes went off as the four of us walked forward to meet Patisis at the bottom of the steps.

He greeted us with a smile and gave the driver a quick nod of recognition. Patisis was confident and beaming, soaking up the glow of the camera flashes. My stomach flip-flopped as he reached forward to shake my hand. The hijacker nudged me forward when I tried to take a step back, and Patisis gripped my hand hard. A steely glint was in his eye, and I glared back at him, hoping my anger would be evident as the reporters took photos.

"Anita, Joshua, you've been some of the biggest dissenting voices in this quarantine program, yet you're here to surrender yourselves to it voluntarily. Why the change of heart?" Patisis spoke loudly, making sure every microphone would pick him up.

I raised a hand to my face to block the camera flashes. Would anyone wonder why I had a red mark circling my wrist?

Joshua and I hadn't answered, but with the hijacker on one side of us and Patisis on the other, it was clear we were supposed to give some sort of answer before heading inside.

"Well ... " I started, but my voice trailed off.

Dan's Negative appeared next to the reporter. He was different, but I couldn't figure out why at first—I'd gotten so used to him. He stepped towards me as the cameras moved backward to include him in the frame.

He looked exhausted, his blue eyes sunken. He gave me a sad, tight-lipped smile. The huge gash exposing his back teeth was gone.

My knees trembled, and I started shaking all over. I never thought I'd see him again. I had so many questions that I wanted to ask, yet I could hardly breathe. My heart felt like it was being ripped out of my chest.

It was Dan. He was whole, without the massive patches forming on his skull like the Negative.

And his eyes. He was looking right at me. Like he loved me.

NEGATIVE IMAGES

All I could see was him. No one else mattered as I made my way to him.

"*Dan?* How?"

"I don't have much time, Anita. I can't tell you what a struggle it's been to get here. But I had to do it. I had to get here to tell you to fight. You know he's not me, at least not all of me, right?"

I nodded. Tears flooded my eyes, making it hard to see.

"I'm so sorry. I'm sorry I cheated on you. I wanted to tell you, but—"

I held up my hands to stop him. I didn't want to waste this valuable time going over the wounds he'd caused. "What are you? Can you move on? Can you find some peace?"

Dan shook his head and shrugged. "I don't know what's waiting for me. I don't know how to get there. I just know that I needed to tell you how sorry I am."

I shook my head. "I thought our relationship was perfect. Even now, I still can't wrap my head around it. Why couldn't I be enough for you? Why didn't you want the same things that I did?"

He opened his mouth, then closed it. "I wish I had. It's just ... I knew you had this vision for what our lives should be. It was like you took this idea of creating over-the-top events for people, but you wanted that to be our whole lives. And Monica ... geez, I'm sorry. This is hard to talk about." He reached up and tucked a strand of hair behind my ear. I had to fight the tears from leaking out of my eyes. "Monica knew that life wasn't about being flawless, you know? She enjoyed the perfect moments, but she accepted the bad ones, too. And there was something freeing in that for me. But that's no excuse for hurting both of you the way I did. I just cared about you both, and after a while, I just couldn't untangle the mess I'd created. I wish I'd been more honest with you about what I was feeling. I wish I'd never put you or Monica in this situation."

My breath came out in a shuddering exhale. What he'd told me was worse than any of the insults that the NI had flung at me. I knew he'd betrayed me, but I'd been clinging to the hope that part of him hadn't wanted to. This assessment of our relationship, and the fact that it was far from perfect, came from what I'd thought of as the *real* Dan. It broke me on a deeper level to know that, no matter which version of Dan I spoke to, our relationship had never been what I'd thought it was. "I wish you hadn't done it. I'm still angry, Dan. And I want to forgive you. But I don't know how. I don't know if I can. I hate to admit it, but you were right. I did want everything to be perfect. I thought that was how things should be. And you're right when you say that that's not what life is."

"I'm so sorry. I'd give anything to make it up to you," Dan whispered. He wrapped his arms around me in an embrace, and he felt solid and real, exactly the way I remembered him. I wrapped my arms around his waist as he rested his chin on top of my head. I wanted to stretch out this moment. People gasped, jerking me back to where I stood outside Leavenworth.

At first, I thought it was because they were seeing me embrace what they thought was my Negative Image. They must have thought I was delusional. Or, they might have been confused to see Dan as a solid person. But both of these thoughts were wrong.

"Gun! He's got a gun!" I wheeled around to see Patisis, gun drawn, aimed at me. His face was sweaty and a mottled shade of purple. He didn't know what was happening, but we had abandoned his script.

Dan squeezed my shoulder. "You have a good life ahead of you, whether it's picture-perfect or not. And I think you might have someone

NEGATIVE IMAGES

to share it with, Anita." His eyes darted to Joshua before settling back on me. Then he turned towards Patisis. Somehow, as Dan walked towards him, I knew that I wouldn't see him again.

Patisis fired at him, probably expecting the bullet to go through him and hit me, but it struck Dan instead. The bullet hit his chest, but Dan kept walking as Patisis gaped at him. People stepped back as Dan moved in on Patisis. Finally, he was close enough to grab Patisis's wrist. He struggled for a moment before dropping the gun on the ground. Dan picked it up, and Patisis froze. The crowd was eerily still as they waited to see what Dan would do with it. I don't know what Dan had planned—the glassy-eyed expression on Patisis' face gave way to anger. He lunged at Dan, and without hesitating, Dan pulled the trigger. Patisis dropped to his knees and grabbed his arm. The crowd around me erupted in shouts and noise. Some people made a run for it while soldiers rushed in to aid Patisis. Dan locked eyes with me and gave me a sad smile. I was about to go towards him, but a soldier ran between us, blocking my view. When I could see again, Dan was gone.

Chapter Twenty-Six

For a wonderful moment, I thought it was over. But everyone was so concerned with Patisis or trying to get away that no one picked up the gun.

Then Dan's Negative appeared, his skull showing through his forehead, his mouth split so wide that the skin hung off in folds. He walked towards the gun, picked it up, and laughed.

The reporters burst into a mix of excited chatter and alarmed gasps and quickly reframed their shots to include the NI. I could tell they were confused, unsure of how this NI fit in and who it was attached to.

"Anita," Dan's NI said, his voice unyielding even though it sounded like he was choking on dirt. "You have to die so I can succeed. So I can finally have what I want. There's no more negotiation."

He aimed the gun at me and cocked it.

Everything around me slowed down. I took in the screams, the panic on Joshua's face, the determination on Monica's. This was it. Dan's NI was right, and he was going to win.

NEGATIVE IMAGES

Monica and Joshua rushed towards him. I focused my gaze on Patisis, knowing they wouldn't be fast enough to stop him. A gunshot rang out, and something shoved me, hitting me with so much force that I fell several feet away. But it hadn't been a bullet.

Monica lay on the ground where I'd been standing.

Dan's Negative twisted in agony. The skin flayed off his bones as though someone was ripping it off his body, and the shape of him continued to writhe as he disintegrated. The black orbs that had haunted me for so long were the last parts of him that I saw.

Then he was gone, not even leaving a pile of dust in his wake.

"Monica." I ran to her. She was shaking, a red stain expanding over her torso. "Hang on, Monica. Help is on the way."

No one moved.

"Someone help her! She doesn't have a Negative Image!"

One of the soldiers ran inside, hopefully to summon help.

I held onto Monica's hand.

"I'm so sorry." Her voice was low, weak.

"There's nothing to be sorry for. You've been here for me this whole time. I can't believe you took a bullet for me."

Monica gave a small smile and tried to laugh. "You're my best friend, Anita. I wish I could take it back. I wish I could take it all back."

She pulled her hand out of my grasp.

"What are you doing?"

Her breathing was labored. A part of me was aware that she was beyond help, but I didn't want her to die. I wasn't ready for it.

"Just in case." She struggled to get out each word. At first, I didn't take in her meaning, but then I realized that she was worried about coming back as a Negative Image.

I wanted to tell her what I'd learned; I wanted to hold on to her, to tell her she was wrong. But I didn't have time. I knew this was it.

Medics rushed by with a gurney and loaded her onto it. They ran her inside, but I think she was already gone. Her brown eyes were glassy and unfocused, her body unmoving.

They worked on her for thirty minutes before pronouncing her dead.

A few days later, Joshua and I sat in the near-empty office space of Legendary Events. Tricia was gone—I knew she'd betrayed me, but I was still glad I hadn't had to fire her. It made more sense to dissolve the company. Monica had been the real driving force behind it. She'd gotten the company to grow. Now, well, it seemed only right that the business should die, too.

"Are you sure you'll be okay planning so much of this?" Joshua asked.

"Monica had a lot of friends. It's actually almost planning itself. Once her death hit the news, people started contacting me, offering up services. When I told her parents, they asked me to help put it all together. There will be plenty of flowers, a limousine for the family, and a catered luncheon afterward."

Joshua took a seat across from me at the same conference table we'd sat at to plan his event. The office was too quiet, and it felt wrong to sit here without Monica in the space.

"Should we call Carrie? It's 12:30."

"Oh, yeah. Thanks for remembering."

Joshua dialed and Carrie answered on the first ring.

NEGATIVE IMAGES

"Hi, Carrie!"

We all exchanged too-exuberant greetings.

"Thanks for calling, guys. Listen, I wanted to talk to you about what you came to see me about in the first place. Figuring out what causes these things to happen. Getting more information to people."

"We never actually got a website up, Carrie," Joshua said apologetically.

"I know. But what I'm saying is that you should. Maybe we could. The three of us?"

Joshua looked as surprised as I felt.

"Now that I'm out—and I still can't thank you guys enough for that—"

"That really isn't even something we can take credit for, Carrie." I hated thinking back to those moments because, really, the reason everything fell apart was Dan's Negative shooting of Monica after Patisis opened fire. Without him, we probably would have been forced inside.

"We could argue over that all day. But I think you would both agree that people still need a resource where they can get guidance and information about, well, life with a Negative Image."

I cringed. Joshua looked down at the shiny tabletop. He still had Ainsley's Negative attached to him, as Carrie still had her mother. Dan's Negative hadn't reappeared. At least, not yet.

"Anita, I remember when I was still volunteering that just having that as some sort of outlet was so helpful to me. This is something I could really throw myself into. We all could. I heard you're closing up shop, right?"

"Yes."

Joshua was too quiet, his head bowed, so I couldn't guess what he was thinking. "It's not a bad idea, Carrie. And it does sound like it's something you want to pursue. You sound so ... energetic."

"I *feel* energetic. I feel like I have a chance to start over. And I don't want to waste my time on things that aren't meaningful to me."

"Wise words," I quipped. "I think this is something Joshua and I will need to talk about, but I'll let you know." I paused for a moment, unsure of how to word my next question. "I'm really glad you've got something that you think will give you purpose, but how about your NI? How are you handling her?"

Carrie sighed into the phone. "Well, I haven't gotten rid of her, and she's still driving a wedge between me and my family. But, you know ... I said in one of those clips that Patisis put up that it was important to me to have pictures of my family up to remind me of why I was in quarantine. And that was true. I know I'd mentioned that I needed to let them go when I was still in the hospital, but once I got there ... they were all I thought about. I need to be here for my boys. The only way for our family to be whole again is for me to try to keep my boys top of mind." Carrie gave a rueful laugh. "It's been tough. And it won't happen overnight. The boys are still scared of my NI, but as you proved, they can exhaust themselves. So, I guess I'm just counting on being able to outlast her. For now, it's enough."

"How is Aaron?"

She took a moment before she answered. "I'm not so sure. We have a lot to work through."

"I'm sorry to hear that. I hope you can."

"Thank you. He didn't fight for me the way I wish he had. But he wants one more chance. I've decided that I do, too."

"That I completely understand."

We said a quick goodbye. Afterward, Joshua still seemed withdrawn.

"What's up? You're unusually quiet." I bumped him.

"I just ... it seems like everyone is somehow moving on from this. Carrie sounds so driven now. You seem content in ending this chapter, and you haven't seen your Negative in four days. Even the country has somehow moved on. With Patisis going crazy, no one has been vocal about that quarantine program. Everyone left as soon as they were actually given the chance to. But I'm stuck. I don't know what needs to happen for Ainsley's Negative to loosen its hold on me. I just can't help but worry. She hasn't done any of the things your NI did. She's not disintegrating. How can I keep holding on?"

I reached across the table and took his hand. "Ainsley was a part of your life for a long time. Since high school, right?"

He nodded, eyes still focused on the table.

"She was your only family, essentially. Her NI always took a different approach with you than Dan's NI did with me. Maybe you just need more time."

He nodded, but he wouldn't look me in the eye.

"Joshua."

He finally looked at me.

"I am here. You're not going through this alone. I'm by your side until we figure this out."

"And after we figure it out?"

I tried and failed to hold back a smile. "I'll still be here."

Monica's funeral was well attended.

I orchestrated it perfectly, along with her parents. I even managed to keep my composure this time when I met with Leon Watts at the funeral home.

Monica got the most expensive casket. Mahogany, $10,000. I paid for it, hospital debts be damned, because I could not repay her for her sacrifice.

The planning process had given me something to focus on. The whole week had been devoted to funeral preparations, selling the office furniture, and getting out of the lease. It would take a little while to finish shutting down all the accounts, and Monica's parents had agreed to split the money from the business fifty-fifty.

I stood next to Joshua as the priest waved incense over the casket. Everything was over, and I had nothing planned. I was adrift, just like Joshua was the day we spoke to Carrie.

I wanted a chance to heal—I wished for one more conversation with Monica to understand how she had managed to conceal a secret of such magnitude from me for years when we spent up to 12 hours together in a day.

A wave of emotions rolled through me: regret, gratitude, emptiness, loss, all at the same time. Joshua stayed by my side, holding my hand as the pallbearers approached Monica's coffin. It was comforting to know that I didn't have to translate any of these feelings to him.

I think we may have been the only people at the funeral not bawling.

Ainsley's Negative sat on the other side of Joshua for the entire service, ensuring that the rest of our pew was empty. My parents had come to town, even though they hadn't known Monica very well, and they'd taken the pew behind us.

NEGATIVE IMAGES

I still hadn't seen Dan's Negative. I saw him in my thoughts—his skin hanging off his body, his jaw falling onto his chest.

It had been a week, and I tentatively thought—hoped—he might be gone for good. Perhaps after disintegrating, he didn't have the strength to return.

People online who saw the video from Leavenworth were even saying I'd been "cured."

I'd gotten hundreds of emails asking for advice from people wanting to replicate the process for themselves. But each case is unique; each person with a Negative Image has to find their own strength to stay and fight. It's such a personal problem that I doubt there will ever be a universal cure.

And as far as I knew, the only reason I'd won over mine was just sheer willpower—that and the other half of Dan who had shown up to fight for me. I still couldn't wrap my head around his appearance, and I didn't know if anyone else had experienced it.

"Do you want to go to the burial?" Joshua asked as we walked outside. A police officer was posted at the church doors, handing out funeral procession stickers to hang on the car windshields.

I wanted to go, but I knew Monica's mother held her death against me. When I approached her at the visitation, she'd turned away from me in tears, and I heard her tell one of her sons to keep me away from her. If I went, I might intrude on this last goodbye. On the other hand, not going felt even more disrespectful since Monica's last act saved my life.

I nodded, and Joshua took a sticker from the officer.

As we walked out to my car, I took his hand absently, and he squeezed mine. I'd been staying at his house for the last week—my own was too haunted, especially the garage. Ainsley's NI hadn't been thrilled by my presence. I glanced at her in the rearview mirror during the car ride. I was amazed that she was actually sitting quietly and giving us some space.

"Did you think any more about what Carrie suggested?" I asked.

Carrie had already given a few interviews during the week. She shared details I hadn't known. Besides taking away phones, they kept most prisoners in solitary confinement the entire time they were in quarantine. Some of those people will never be the same. And I can't say I was surprised to hear the worst of it: some people did die, and they were quietly buried in the prison yard. The families weren't even notified.

Joshua sighed. "Yeah. I mean, I can't just go back to my old job." He took his eyes off the road to give me a sideways glance. "I think I'm in. Are you?"

"Yeah. I needed a few days to make sure it was the right decision, but ... you're right. There's no going back to how life was before."

We arrived at the cemetery, walking slowly and staying at the edge of the crowd. It was hard to hear the blessing, but I was glad I'd come in case Monica, wherever she was, could see this.

I stood on tiptoe, craning my neck to see as Monica's mother placed a flower on the casket. For a second, I thought I saw a familiar head of tousled brown hair on a man next to the priest. Then I blinked, and he was gone.

Acknowledgements

Eight years went into this book, and it wouldn't be here without a lot of support. I am so grateful to Alex Brown for seeing the potential in this book and putting her energy behind it. Tina Beier has been masterful in her edits and really helped shape this story. Alyssa suggested several ways to make this book stronger, and Natasha Mackenzie created a wonderfully eerie cover. Taylor Hill, thanks for the thorough copyedit. Many thanks to the entire team at Rising Action Publishing, including Abby Sharp, Colleen Brown, and Angeleen Cruz.

Several people supported me through the early drafting stages of this book. Jessica Conoley, Natasha Hanova, Shelly Walston, Imari Barry, Lucy Berndt all gave great input. I'm very grateful to Jenny Schoeder, Louise Ross, and Brian Eastman for critiquing some early chapters and to Rachel Mans McKenny for years of support and writing advice.

Lastly, this book would not be possible without my family. Afam, thank you for always making my writing a priority, and for helping me realize that it *should* be a priority. Without your encouragement, love, and support, I wouldn't be here. My wonderful children Gabrielle, Michael, and Gwendolyn, I am so grateful for the inspiration and motivation you give me every day. James, Allie, Cece, and Eloise, thanks for being my biggest fans. Mom, Dad, and Stephen, I am so grateful for all that you've done—especially all the times you've babysat to give me time to write. I'm also incredibly grateful to my extended family, although I can't name everyone here.

Thank you for reading this book and coming along on this journey.

About the Author

Rebecca Schier-Akamelu is an American author who writes horror novels and non-fiction (which is usually much more positive). She loves the horror genre for all the dark thoughts it makes us confront and the way it changes people—for better or for worse. Her work has been published in the *Chicken Soup for the Soul* anthology and her short story "From One to the Next" was nominated for a Pushcart Prize. She is a member of the Horror Writers Association, and encourages her husband, three children, and dog to get excited every time spooky season comes around. *Negative Images* is her debut novel.

Looking for more Chills and Thrills? Check out Rising Action's other Horror and Thrillers on the next page!

And don't forget to follow us on our socials for cover reveals, giveaways, and announcements:
X: @RAPubCollective
Instagram: @risingactionpublishingco
TikTok: @risingactionpublishingco
Website: http://www.risingactionpublishingco.com

On a tiny, isolated island off the southern Alaskan coast, three girls have vanished without a trace, and Audra's close friend—the island's therapist—has been found murdered. A recent storm has severed all communication with the outside world, leaving Audra, the town's lead detective, trapped and at the head of a very personal case.

Her lead suspect, Valorie, the daughter of a notorious cult leader and the town's outcast, was discovered blood-covered and dazed at the crime scene. Valorie's memory is a gaping void, a dark well hiding traumatic secrets, including the truth about the teenage kidnappings that haunt the island.

As Audra digs deeper into the town's twisted history, it becomes clear other murders on the island, dating back decades, might be connected. The clock is ticking for the missing girls, and every clue leads Audra to question even those she's known her whole life.

Valorie must confront the horrors of her past while Audra's investigation becomes a descent into madness. On this cursed island, the line between neighbor and nightmare blurs, revealing that true horror often wears a familiar face.

World-famous paranormal investigator Eric Thompson's career took a nose-dive after a particularly gruesome case which left most of his camera crew dead. His partner and best friend also abandoned Eric, leaving him floundering.

He is soon approached by a mysterious woman who has purchased the supposedly haunted, but previously off-limits to paranormal sleuths, Morsley Manor. To drum up publicity about the house, she hires Eric to perform and host a paranormal investigation on the premises.

As he ventures over to England to uncover the darkness bleeding through the veins of Morsley, horrors begin to spring from every corner and Eric soon begins to realise that not all is as it seems...

In this haunting psychological horror, Willow's life has become a fever dream, her days lost in a twisted loop where time no longer flows as it should. Is she held captive by her husband Liam's iron rules—or by the insidious darkness of her own mind?

Her only connection to the world beyond her walls is a young girl named Sarah, whose unexpected visits to Willow's garden spark a glimmer of hope. But as cracks form in her carefully controlled existence, horrifying truths seep through, twisting the familiar into something sinister. The floral wallpaper peels back to reveal haunting messages carved into the walls, and the house itself pulses with malevolent life.

When Sarah suddenly vanishes, Willow is forced to confront the dark shadows of her past and the horrors lurking within her fractured psyche. The question remains: is Willow truly a prisoner of her home, or of her own mind?

Some doors, once opened, can never be closed. And some truths are better left buried in the garden.

Something is wrong in Bunker, Illinois.
Nora Grace Moon thought her toughest challenge this semester would be managing her OCD, but when her deceased roommate turns up as a reanimated corpse, her world starts to collapse.
When her uncle sends her a cryptic message, Nora realizes it must be a call for help. She reaches out to fellow gamer Wesley for advice, a US Marshal with real-life skills for tactical survival, not just in-game. They venture out into a world that is growing more and more deadly by the moment—not only are the undead spreading, but other humans are taking advantage of the societal breakdown. And unknown to Nora and Wesley, they have been targeted by an ancient archeological society who will stop at nothing until they have what Nora has: an artifact that will unleash a new world order of the undead.

IRL is a paranormal thriller about leaving the online world and dealing with things "In Real Life."